Murder at Ridley Hall – British Cozy Mystery Series Book 3

By Leena Clover

Copyright © Leena Clover, Author 2023

All rights reserved. No part of this publication may be reproduced, stored in a retrieval system, or transmitted, in any form, or by any means (electronic, mechanical, photocopying, recording or otherwise) without the prior written permission of the author.

This book is a work of fiction. Names, characters, places, organizations and incidents are either products of the author's imagination or used fictitiously. Any resemblance to actual events, places, organizations or persons, living or dead, is entirely coincidental.

First Published – November 30, 2023

CHAPTER 1

CHAPTER 2

CHAPTER 3

CHAPTER 4

CHAPTER 5

CHAPTER 6

CHAPTER 7

CHAPTER 8

CHAPTER 9

CHAPTER 10

CHAPTER 11

CHAPTER 12

CHAPTER 13

CHAPTER 14

CHAPTER 15

CHAPTER 16

CHAPTER 17

CHAPTER 18

CHAPTER 19

CHAPTER 20

CHAPTER 21

CHAPTER 22

CHAPTER 23

CHAPTER 24

CHAPTER 25

CHAPTER 26

CHAPTER 27

CHAPTER 28

CHAPTER 29

CHAPTER 30

CHAPTER 31

CHAPTER 32

CHAPTER 33

CHAPTER 34

CHAPTER 35

EPILOGUE

RECIPE – RAILWAY MUTTON CURRY

ACKNOWLEDGEMENTS

OTHER BOOKS BY LEENA CLOVER

NOTE: This book uses British spelling.

THE EARLS OF BUXLEY

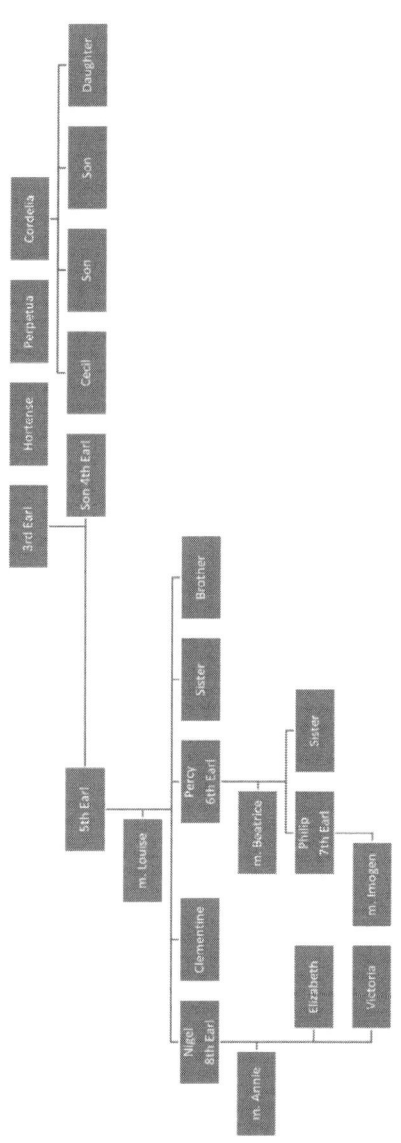

TEXT VERSION

Hortense

Perpetua

Cordelia

   Cecil

3rd Earl

   4th Earl

     5th Earl - married to Louise

       Clementine

       6th earl - Married to Beatrice

         Philip (7th Earl)

         Nigel (8th earl) - married to Annie

           Elizabeth

           Victoria

RESIDENTS OF BUXLEY

At Buxley Manor

Upstairs –

Nigel Gaskins – 8th Earl of Buxley, second son of the 5th earl

Clementine Barton – Nigel's widowed sister. She runs the manor with a firm hand, or tries to.

Hortense and Perpetua Gaskins – Nigel's great aunts

Imogen, Lady Buxley or Momo – Youngest Dowager Countess, widow of Nigel's nephew Philip, the previous Earl.

Gertrude Ridley or Bubbles – Imogen's unmarried sister, more or less a permanent resident of the manor.

Elizabeth Gaskins or Bess – Nigel's daughter

Downstairs –

Barnes – butler

Mrs. Jones – housekeeper

Mrs. Bird – cook

Wilson – lady's maid

Marci – scullery maid

At the Dower House

Louise, Lady Buxley – Nigel's mother, Dowager Countess

At Primrose Cottage

Beatrice, Lady Buxley – Nigel's brother's widow, Dowager Countess

At the Vicarage

Cordelia Chilton – Nigel's great aunt

Cecil Chilton – local vicar and Cordelia's son

AT RIDLEY HALL

Sir Dorian Ridley – Lord of the manor

Lady Ridley – Lady of the manor

Cedric Ridley – Sir Dorian's son

Chapter 1

Pale sunlight filtered through the diamond paned windows of the west wing of Buxley Manor, accompanied by a mild breeze. After an unseasonably hot October, the cooler weather was welcomed with sighs of relief by one and all.

A group of women sat sipping tea in the cosy parlour, nibbling on freshly baked biscuits. They couldn't be more different in garb and mannerisms but were united in one singular mission. Like their namesake, the Nightingales did not believe in letting their gender thwart them from doing what they wanted.

"November is well on its way." Louise, Dowager Countess of Buxley, began in a steely voice. The emerald brooch she wore matched the feathers in her sizable hat and complimented her stark black Victorian dress.

"Christmas will be upon us in the blink of an eye."

Lady Elizabeth Gaskins, fondly called Bess by friends and family, brightened at the mention of the festival.

"Mince pies!" She turned to her twin. "Mrs. Bird makes the most delicious mince pies, Vicky."

Their great aunt Hortense pressed a moist handkerchief soaked in lavender water to her forehead and agreed with Bess.

"And she makes the best Christmas pudding."

"Gluttons." The woman sitting beside Hortense gave a snort, pinning them with a stare. "Focus."

Bess laughed, not one to pout.

"Tell us why we are here, Great Aunt Perpetua. And we know how much you like your mince pies."

Louise gave a deep sigh.

"This is a good year for us." She darted a loving glance at Vicky. "The whole family is together under one roof."

"Dream come true," Perpetua seconded her, rubbing the prominent mole on her cheek. "Lady Luck has smiled on us at last."

Bess placed her arms behind her head and winced.

"I will tell you who hasn't been that lucky. Pudding, poor girl. That whole fiasco with One Eye Watkins has sucked the life out of her."

"Not as unlucky as poor Sir Lawrence," Vicky pointed out, frowning at her sister's use of the man's sobriquet. "He might have been a bit obnoxious …"

"Insufferable," Bess interrupted.

"Okay, that too." Vicky grumbled. "But he did not deserve to be killed."

The ladies were silent as they mulled over the shocking death of Sir Lawrence Watkins, a big game hunter who had been visiting the area, an esteemed guest at Ridley Hall. Famous for his brave conquests in Africa, Louise thought it was ironic that he had been shot dead in the woods.

"Was it deliberate?" Hortense mused, crumpling her handkerchief. "Or was he hit by a stray bullet? It's hunting season, after all."

Bess did not think so.

"It was murder alright. He was asking for it, in my opinion."

Vicky patted her arm but said nothing. She agreed with her twin but was more reticent about being critical of a dead man.

"Have you heard from DI Gardener?" she asked. "Surely the police must have made some progress?"

Louise chuckled and gave them a knowing

look.

"What do we care? Let them do their job for once."

Bess admitted DI Gardener had been tight lipped about the latest crime to rock their corner of the world. He had warned her to stay out of his way. Although she was tempted to disregard him, time was not her friend.

"Philip must be our priority," she declared solemnly. "We need to figure out what happed to him so we can all move on with our lives."

There was a moment of silence as the ladies mulled over her words. They knew she was thinking of her parents Nigel and Annie. Bess was afraid her mother would go back to America if her father continued to be accused of killing his nephew. The police had not found any evidence against him but he had been eviscerated by rumours and allegations for the past twenty years.

"We have made no progress, Grandma

Louise," Vicky sighed. "How does it matter that he hated French food?"

"And loved his horse?" Bess pitched in. "Or loved coffee?" She sprang up and began pacing around the room. "It's all too silly for words."

"Don't forget that custom saddle," Vicky chirped. "Everyone agrees he rode hard but the only reason he got thrown off his horse must be foul play. He was that good a rider."

Ever since they had ramped up their efforts to investigate Philip's death, they had been going around in circles. Bess and Vicky had talked to plenty of people and unearthed many trivial facts that had turned out to be useless.

"What about your theory that Sir Lawrence had a hand in Philip's death?" Perpetua asked.

"That would be convenient," Hortense objected. "The poor man is not here to defend himself."

"Or to confess to the heinous crime," Louise

added. "No, girls. Pinning the blame on a dead man will not help exonerate Nigel."

They agreed the villagers would not be convinced unless the police got a confession.

"I don't know if Sir Lawrence killed Philip or not, Grandma." Bess bit her lip. "But he riled people up and said bad things about Papa."

Vicky wanted to know how long they planned to continue looking into Philip's death.

"We must be realistic, Grandma. Nothing has come to light in twenty years and all our efforts this year have produced nothing so far."

Hortense and Perpetua shared a glance and nodded, waiting to hear what Louise had to say.

"Quitting so soon, my dear?" Her eyes sparkled with barely suppressed anger. "I thought you were made of sterner stuff."

Bess knew her grandmother's bark was worse

than her bite.

"Nobody is talking about giving up. All Vicky means is we must assign a finite amount of time to this investigation. I think that is prudent."

They went back and forth over the suggestion until Louise admitted Vicky was right.

"End of the year, then." Her lips pursed with new resolve. "That gives us barely two months, ladies. We will have to buck up."

Hortense proposed a different approach.

"I think we know enough about Philip the earl, thanks to Vicky and Bess. But almost nothing about the day of the hunt."

Bess reminded her they had tried questioning the villagers about that fateful day but none of them had been forthcoming.

"Try again!" Louise ordered. "Ask them what they were doing that day. People tend to remember that."

"Wear them down," Perpetua added. "Wear them down, girls."

Bess and Vicky were thinking the same thing. They would have to think of a different approach to tackle the locals.

"Agreed!" Bess assured the ladies. "We will keep you posted, Grandmother. Shall we take a break now? I could use some fresh air."

Louise told her they were not done.

"Not so fast, young lady. There is one more item that we have not discussed."

Bess knew what was coming and she had no wish to talk about it. Vicky stepped in for her.

"Mom and Pops are spending a lot of time together, Grandma. That's good, right?"

"Not if she runs back to America on a whim, like last time," Bess burst out. "Papa will be devastated."

Louise wanted to know what her son and his estranged wife had been up to. Bess claimed she had no idea but Vicky was eager to reveal everything.

"They have been visiting the neighbours, of course. Rosehill, Oakview, Ridley Hall … everyone is very happy to meet Mom after so many years."

Nigel and Annie had taken a trip to London to watch a show at the Strand and have lunch at the Savoy. They frequently went on long walks on Buxley land, taking a picnic lunch along with them. Wary at first, the tenants were gradually beginning to get used to Annie's presence. It was high time there was a countess at Buxley, they said.

"Your mother is a kind soul," Hortense smiled. "She wins hearts wherever she goes. No wonder Nigel fell for her all those years ago."

Bess lay down on a sofa and gave a wide yawn.

"Where are your manners?" Louise berated her. "Forgiveness is a virtue, Bess."

Hortense exclaimed the tea was cold and rang for the butler.

"What are we having for lunch, do you know?" she tried to diffuse the tension.

Vicky took the cue and began talking about food in America.

"I love everything our cook makes but sometimes I really crave a hot dog or a hamburger. When we go to America, I will take you all to Nathan's on Coney Island."

"Not on your life!" Perpetua gave a shudder.

Vicky started explaining it was made of beef. Hortense told her they were too old to attempt the transatlantic voyage.

"Speak for yourself," Louise scoffed. "Annie has invited me to visit her in New York and I plan to take her up on it."

Bess swung her feet to the ground and sat up, her mouth settling in a smirk.

"Aha! So she is going back!"

"No, child. We are all going there on a holiday next summer. Your father is talking to the White Star line to book our passage." She glared at Bess. "It was supposed to be a surprise for you girls, so be kind enough to act a bit when he tells you about it. He is very excited about the trip."

Bess felt like a heel. Her anger deflated and her shoulders slumped at the thought of disappointing her father. She knew how he had suffered over the years. Her mother's arrival had brought a smile to his face. Nigel Gaskins, Earl of Buxley, was a man reborn. His wife's sudden arrival had been like a ray of sunshine. He had been carrying the weight of the world on his shoulders and suddenly found himself without the burden.

"I want him to be happy too, Grandmother." Her conflict was splashed across her face. "But …"

"Leap of faith." Perpetua did not mince words.

There was a knock on the door and the butler Barnes arrived, followed by two maids holding trays loaded with pots of tea and coffee.

"You rang, my lady?" he bowed. "I presumed it was time for some refreshments. Mrs. Bird just baked a fresh batch of scones."

Hortense fanned herself with her handkerchief and thanked him. Louise gave a nod of approval.

"Lady Clementine wished to remind you that lunch will be served in an hour," Barnes intoned.

"Yes, yes." Louise waved him off. "Tell her we know what time lunch is served at Buxley Manor. No need to crack the whip."

Barnes cleared his throat and darted a look at the maids, silently ordering them to leave the room. He followed after making sure they did not need anything else.

Bess was quiet as she slathered clotted cream on half a scone and topped it with strawberry jam. The great aunts and her grandmother had finally struck a chord. She had to give her mother a chance.

"I have been in a tight spot or two," she began, nodding at her twin. "The wish to flee is uppermost, isn't it, old girl?" She was thinking of the time she had spent as an ambulance driver in France during the war. Vicky had been a nurse and they had both lived through excruciating circumstances.

Bess took a sip of her favourite Darjeeling, sensing all eyes in the room were on her.

"Annie was alone in a foreign country and she must have been frightened. I suppose she deserves a second chance."

Vicky wrapped her in an embrace and the great aunts beamed with approval. Louise snorted in disgust but there was a twinkle in her eye.

"What a terrible palaver! Now stop grinning like a fool and pass those biscuits, Bess."

Chapter 2

Bess drank her tea, barely listening to the conversation around her. Her declaration had made everyone happy, especially Vicky. She just hoped she would be able to keep her word.

A sharp rap on the door made them all set up.

"That must be Clementine," Louise muttered. "Come to chastise us for eating too much cake."

Barnes entered, wearing a solemn expression.

"What is it?" Bess asked, trying to ignore a sense of foreboding.

"You are wanted in the parlour, my lady." He bowed. "You and Lady Vicky."

Louise read the worry on their faces and

hastened to reassure them.

"I am sure Nigel is fine, Bess. Isn't that so, Barnes?"

The butler nodded. "Lord and Lady Buxley are in the library. There is a caller who wishes to meet Lady Bess at once."

There was a stunned silence when Barnes revealed the identity of their guest.

"Sir Dorian Ridley?" Bess burst out. "That fusspot? What on earth does he want with me? Are you sure he did not ask for Momo, Barnes?"

The butler assured her he had not made a mistake.

"There is only one way to find out, my dear." Louise gave a shrug. "It is not polite to keep a guest waiting, one as esteemed as Sir Dorian. Why, he's practically family."

"Manners!" Perpetua chided.

Bess flung her arms in the air, wondering why she had to be polite to a man who took every opportunity to belittle her.

"Enough of this drama. Behave yourself, Bess."

Vicky laughed at their banter and left the room, pulling Bess along with her. They crossed the west wing and entered a hall that led to a morning room their aunt used when she had a spare moment. Barnes stood outside, his hands folded in front of him.

He opened the door and announced them. "Lady Elizabeth and Lady Victoria, Sir Dorian."

A stocky man with bushy red hair peppered with grey stood at a sash window with feet planted apart, hands clasped behind his back. He whirled around and glared at them.

"About time."

Bess knew Sir Dorian had a short fuse. He

thought Bess was a spoilt brat who was a disgrace to her family and never held back his poor opinion of her.

"What brings you here, Sir Dorian?" she asked, staring at the mutton chop whiskers that spanned most of his face.

Vicky sensed her sister was going to be contrary. She ushered the older man to a wingback chair by the fireplace and took a seat facing him.

"Sit down, Bess." She patted a spot on the sofa.

Barnes poured a snifter of brandy and handed it to Sir Dorian. He clutched it like a lifeline and thanked him.

"Good man."

"Will that be all, my lady?" Barnes asked Bess.

She dismissed him with a nod and a smile.

Sir Dorian drained half his glass in one gulp and stared at the floor. Bess was getting impatient.

"I haven't seen Momo today. Or Bubbles. Are you here to take them home, Sir Dorian?"

He drank the rest of his brandy and dissolved into a coughing fit. Bess considered thumping him on the back. Reading her mind as usual, Vicky suppressed a giggle.

"About Lawrence, poor chap. The police have been very tight lipped." Sir Dorian burst out. "Especially that Detective Inspector Nigel cannot stop singing praises of."

"DI Gardener?" Vicky prompted.

Sir Dorian waved a hand in the air. "Yates is loyal. He came by to warn me."

Yates was the police constable serving the village of Ridley. Bess was finally curious. She sat back to let Sir Dorian finish.

"They are going to make an arrest soon, the police." His eyes grew wide.

Vicky glanced at Bess and asked the question they were both thinking of.

"Have they figured out who killed One Eye Watkins?" She bit her lip. "I mean, Sir Lawrence?"

Normally, Sir Dorian would have called the girls out for their impudence. But he didn't even bat an eyelid. Bess realized he was not himself.

"Cedric. My poor boy!" He gave them a helpless look.

Bess leaned forward in her seat, astonished.

"Wait a minute, Sir Dorian. Do you mean to say Cedric killed Sir Lawrence Watkins?"

"Of course he did not." He denied, miserable. "According to Yates, they might arrest him anytime."

"That's terrible!" Bess exclaimed, well acquainted with the Ridley heir. "What on earth are they thinking?"

Although several years older than Bess, Cedric Ridley was a fun loving youth who believed in living each day to its fullest. He spent a lot of time in London and was known to party hard with other like minded wastrels.

Sir Dorian took out a handkerchief from his coat pocket and blew his nose. Bess had never seen him so dispirited. His expression was penitent as he stared at the girls.

"My dear, I need your help."

It was the last thing Bess expected to hear.

"If anyone can prove my boy is innocent, it's you. Clive Morse cannot stop singing your praises, the way you caught that bounder who murdered his head groom. And you figured out who killed poor Miles Carrington." He paused to take a breath. "Even Lawrence was impressed by your pluck. Said you had the mettle to survive in the jungle."

Bess couldn't believe what she was hearing. Her chest puffed up with pride. She had gone from being an impudent miss to a much sought after sleuth in a matter of months. But Sir Dorian had censured and berated her since she was a child. She was not about to forget all that just because he needed her help.

"We are here for Cedric," Vicky spoke up, reminding her who actually needed them. "But we cannot promise anything."

"Yes." Bess seconded her. "What if he is guilty, Sir Dorian? Do you expect us to lie to the police?"

His nostrils flared at the suggestion. Sir Dorian banged a fist on the chair's arm, turning red as a tomato. "If Cedric harmed Lawrence, I will shoot him myself."

Bess felt a new respect for the man.

"You have our word, Sir Dorian. We will do

everything we can to find out what happened. It will help if Cedric is forthcoming and answers our questions. He should hold nothing back."

"I will talk to the boy," Sir Dorian promised.

The girls stood up to take their leave. Vicky rang for Barnes, sensing Sir Dorian could use another glass of brandy. They left the room and rushed back to the west wing, eager to tell the Nightingales about their latest assignment.

Louise and the aunts were astonished when they heard about the reason for Sir Dorian's visit. None of them had a good thing to say about Cedric Ridley.

"He's a pampered, entitled brat!" she exclaimed.

"No sense of duty," Perpetua sneered.

Hortense backed her up, dipping her hand kerchief in a basin of lavender water. "Should have been married by now. I hear he is fond of his drink."

"Parties, women, debauchery," Perpetua spat.

Bess laughed. "So he likes to have a good time," she dismissed. "That does not make him a murderer."

Louise agreed with her.

"We will have to keep an open mind if we are to get to the bottom of this."

A clock chimed, signalling it was time for lunch. Bess and Vicky trooped down to the dining room after the older women, wondering what their Aunt Clementine had ordered for lunch, their mouth watering at the delicious aromas that wafted around them as they drew closer.

Nigel and Annie were already at the table, eating roast chicken and potatoes. Momo and Bubbles sat at the other end, discussing some dress patterns. They seemed unaware of their father's visit.

"Your mother and I are going for a walk after lunch," Nigel told the girls. "Why don't you join us?"

Bess noted the smile lurking on Annie's face.

"Nigel is going to teach me how to fish."

"But you hate fishing, Mom!" Vicky was surprised.

The footmen cleared the plates and served the pudding, spotted dick with warm custard.

"Are you coming or not?" Nigel frowned.

Bess gave a shrug. She had nothing better to do so she might as well get some fresh air. Vicky was more enthusiastic about the prospect.

"Don't be late for tea," Clementine warned, always concerned about her schedules.

Two footmen followed the group, lugging fishing equipment, as they set off toward the south end of the property to Nigel's favourite fishing spot. Bess and Vicky walked a few paces behind, letting their parents take the lead. The hues of autumn were fading, signalling that winter was around the corner.

"She does make him laugh," Bess grumbled as Nigel guffawed at something Annie said.

Bess had never seen him so full of life. He was like a man reborn since Annie had come back. What would happen if she abandoned them again and rushed off to America?

"You agreed to give her a chance," Vicky nudged. "Don't you backtrack now."

Bess thought her sister almost looked wistful. She felt they were watching glimpses of a childhood that had been rudely snatched from them. But it was never too late to build new memories. She broke into a run and reached her father, taking his arm, pulling him toward the flowing stream.

"How about a swim, pater?"

Nigel's eyes shone with mirth. "I dare you, Bessie. The water's too cold, even for you. It's November, my dear."

Annie was up for the challenge and so was Vicky. They waded into the water and sprang back as the cold hit them, giggling like little girls. The afternoon passed in merriment and they even managed to catch some trout. Finally, it was time to head back to the manor.

The day was pleasant and warm enough to have tea under the big oak in the garden. Barnes could be seen leading a procession of men to set up the elaborate tea. Bess proposed a break as they neared the folly.

"Aunt Clem expects us to be late, Papa. We don't want to disappoint her."

"No need to be unkind, sweetie," Annie chided. "Your aunt means well."

Bess bristled at the censure but held back from saying anything. Was that how a mother behaved, she wondered.

Momo was pouring tea by the time they reached the oak. She handed a cup of Darjeeling to Bess. Bubbles picked up a cucumber sandwich and asked about their afternoon.

"You don't have time for me now," she pouted, darting a glance at Annie. "When are we going to London? I need to hire staff for my flat."

Vicky accepted a cup of coffee from a footman and sat back to see how Bess handled the situation. Bubbles rarely thought of anyone but herself.

"Has Grandma gone back to the Dower House?" Bess asked Clementine.

"Mama was feeling a bit under the weather," she replied. "And the great aunts wanted tea sent up. I doubt any of them will turn up for dinner."

Bess was pensive as she went up to her room after tea. The day had been a blur of activity but she was not sure if they had made any progress in their mission. She forced herself to summarize what she had learnt about Philip. He rode hard to the point of being rash but there was a general consensus that he could never lose control of his horse. The horse itself was a magnificent thoroughbred Philip was very fond of. Overall, like many of his peers, he was obsessed with everything about the horse, even going so far as to hire an artisan to come and live at Buxley to create a custom saddle.

Philip hated French food but loved coffee. His marriage with Momo had been arranged by their parents but he loved her enough to cancel a most coveted hunting trip to Africa. And of course, he was very serious about his responsibilities of being the earl.

Philip had a definite personality but nothing they learned about him had pointed to a motive to kill him. The villagers idolized him but could he really have been that perfect?

Bess felt all their efforts were futile until they found a chink in his armour, something that proved he was not infallible.

Chapter 3

The formal gardens at Buxley Manor wore a cloak of dense fog the next morning. Bess shivered in the cold wind blowing in through the window, staring at the perfect symmetry of the various flower beds and topiaries an army of gardeners worked hard to maintain. Her mother hated the topiaries. When Bess was a child, she had often played truant by purloining a pair of shears from the gardening shed and snipping at them. Aunt Clem had sent her to bed without pudding many a time to atone for it.

Vicky sat on the bed, stifling a yawn.

"You don't suppose I can skip going down for breakfast? Back in New York, I often had breakfast in my room."

Bess pretended to be shocked, placing her

hands on her cheeks and shaking her head.

"Only married ladies have breakfast in bed, my dear. The likes of us have to trudge down to the breakfast room to get our due."

Vicky asked about their plans for the day as she dressed. Bess was in a desultory mood and explained they could not do much until the fog lifted.

"We might go for a ride later, old bean."

Breakfast was in full swing downstairs. The sideboard was loaded with the usual buffet of eggs, bacon, kidneys and kedgeree. Annie, Momo and Bubbles were planning a shopping trip to Paris while Nigel looked on in approval.

"We are going to have a grand Christmas this year," Bubbles declared. "The whole village should know that Lady Buxley is back and here to stay. We will get you a red silk dress, Annie, and maybe a fur coat. You look ravishing in red."

Annie thought she was too old to wear red.

"It's time for us to take a step back, Bubbles. Let the girls shine. Perhaps they will catch the eye of some deserving young man and fall in love."

"Ridiculous!" Bubbles dismissed her with a wave of her hand. "Our sort don't fall in love, Annie. Ask Momo. Marriages of the aristocracy are arranged in solicitor's offices."

Bess was at the buffet, loading her plate with kedgeree. She paused to see how her mother would respond. Annie laughed, refusing to take umbrage.

"You can be so cynical, Bubbles. Everyone knows Nigel and I married for love."

Nigel was looking flustered at this exchange. He picked up his poodle and began stroking him, always eager to avoid conflict.

"I say, er, Bubbles. What? What, what, what … Annie is right, of course."

Momo's eyes were moist. Clementine poured her a fresh cup of tea and fussed.

"Try this raspberry jam, dear. Your mother sent it for you."

Bess knew Momo still grieved for Philip and had obviously been in love with him. She ate a forkful of kedgeree and wondered how she might distract her.

"Fancy going for a drive? We can go to Cheltenham or Broadway and do some early Christmas shopping."

Momo gave a tremulous smile and began slathering jam on her toast. She started talking about the weather and everyone breathed a sigh of relief.

Bess was working on a second helping of kedgeree when Barnes came and positioned himself behind her chair.

"What is it, Barnie?" she turned around.

"You are wanted on the telephone, my lady. The Dowager, your grandmother."

Bess put her fork down and hurried down the hall, wondering what Louise wanted that early in the day.

"Good morning. Everything fine? You are not sick or anything, are you, Grandmother?"

Louise wasted no time in letting her know she was in top shape.

"What have you found out so far?"

"About?"

"Cedric Ridley, of course. Have you forgotten you agreed to help Sir Dorian?"

Bess assured her she had not. She had just not found the opportunity to do anything about it.

"Are you going to make him beg? Look, my dear, I know he hasn't always been kind to you. But you can be the better person."

"Kind?" Bess burst out. "You mean he has taken every opportunity to belittle me and insult Papa about how he has brought me up. What's more, he has the same opinion about Vicky."

Louise asked her what she meant. Had she decided she did not want to investigate the hunter's murder?

"When did I say that?" Bess chuckled. "It will keep the Nightingales on their toes. I believe you and the aunts will not let us rest."

"Get on with it, then," Louise barked. "I expect some kind of report by dinner."

Bess was thinking ahead as she listened to her grandmother.

"I wonder why Momo or Bubbles have said nothing about this," she mused. "Surely they must have met their father yesterday?"

They agreed she should talk to them first. Although Bubbles spent most of her time at

Buxley Manor, Ridley Hall was her official home. Bess thought she must know Cedric better than Momo.

"You know how Bubbles is, Grandmother. I will have to coax her into answering my questions."

Louise snorted before hanging up.

Bess was thoughtful on her way back to the dining room. Vicky sat nibbling on a piece of toast, listening to Bubbles ranting about how she needed to be in London. The rest of the party had left the room.

A footman placed a fresh pot of tea before Bess.

"Let's do it, Bubbles." Bess stirred sugar in her tea. "We can take the 10:35 express from Chipping Woodbury. The chauffer will drive us there."

"You mean today?" Bubbles sat up in her seat, her eyes shining. "Right now?"

"No time like the present." Bess gave a shrug. "You can telephone ahead and inform whoever needs to know."

Vicky made her excuses. She did not feel up to the train ride and a jaunt in London.

"I say, old girl." Bess frowned. "What's wrong? Tell Barnes to call Dr. Evans."

"I just need a day in bed," Vicky told her. "You need to hurry if you want to catch that train."

Fifteen minutes later, Bess and Bubbles were on their way to Chipping Woodbury. Barnes had handed her a shopping list.

"Mrs. Bird has requested you to get some of these items from Harrods, my lady."

"I say, Barnes!" Bubbles was impatient. "Don't we have servants for this kind of thing?"

Bess ignored her and patted Barnes on the arm.

"It's for her mince pies, I suppose. Tell Cook I

will get everything she needs."

The Rolls Royce offered a comfortable ride as it sped along the country lanes. Bubbles took Bess to task.

"You are not a little girl anymore. It is high time you stopped mingling with the servants."

"Oh Bubbles!" Bess laughed. "You are such a snob."

"You are an earl's daughter and need to be on guard, now that you are of age. People will try to take advantage."

They reached the station, saving Bess from having to respond. The train was steaming in when they got the tickets and made their way across the crowded platform to the first class compartment. Even though the train did not make a lot of stops, it would take over an hour to reach London.

Bess sat by the window, staring at a big clock in the distance. A whistle blew and the guard gave the signal for the train to move. She closed her eyes, preparing herself to take a long nap. Bubbles had already buried her head in a book. The train picked up speed and the rhythmic motion soon lulled Bess to sleep. A sudden lurch woke her up some time later. The browns and oranges of the countryside had become sparse and London was visible in the distance.

"I hope Vicky's not sick." She yawned.

Bubbles was admiring herself in a pocket mirror, applying a fresh coat of lipstick, preparing to disembark.

"She's a big girl, Bess. You worry too much."

"Vicky's my twin. We already spent most of our life apart."

Bubbles smoothed her hair and gave Bess a meaningful glance.

"That's right. What do you really know about her? I would watch my back if I were you."

Bess was bewildered but she just nodded her head in agreement. Bubbles said the most outlandish things sometimes and then forgot all about them. It was best to just agree with her.

The train lumbered into the station and they stepped down and got carried along with the crowd. It was almost noon and people were rushing to the railway canteen to grab a bite before catching a train or heading out in the city. Bess longed for a cup of tea but Bubbles had a solid plan. They flagged a taxi outside the station and were soon on their way.

"We can discuss my needs with the staffing agency and then go to the Savoy for lunch. That should fortify us to do some shopping."

"I thought we came here to interview candidates." Bess quirked an eyebrow.

"Don't be silly." Bubbles shot her down. "You don't expect me to hire my own maid? The butler will do that, after I appoint one."

They reached a grey tower block and took a lift

up to the seventh floor, walking down a dark corridor to reach the office at the end.

The woman at the staffing agency reminded Bess of her history teacher at school, dressed neatly in a white blouse and dark skirt, with a perfect chignon on top of her head. She stared at them over her horn rimmed glasses.

"Miss Ridley, I do not have an appointment for you in my calendar."

Bubbles was flippant.

"Oh really? Well, since I am here, why don't we discuss my needs?"

The woman's displeasure was clear. She took a deep breath and asked for details, pulling out a stack of files from a drawer in her desk.

"We can do away with a housekeeper," Bubbles commanded. "But I do need a butler with impeccable references, someone who has worked in a good family. A cook, a maid, a chauffeur … that will do for now. I will bring my own lady's maid, of course."

They discussed some profiles. Bubbles discarded half a dozen applications and declared it was getting late.

"Why don't you mail me the rest?" She scraped her chair back and stood up, prompting Bess to do the same. "We are meeting the Marquess of Turnbridge in twenty minutes. Can't be late, you know."

Bess wasn't aware they were meeting anyone so she assumed Bubbles was bluffing.

"What a ghastly woman!" Bubbles grumbled as they sat in another taxi and headed to the Savoy.

"Are we really meeting Curtis?" Bess asked.

Bubbles thought he would turn up sooner or later if he was in town.

The maitre'd at the opulent Savoy Grill greeted them and made sure they had a good table in the centre of the room. Champagne and oysters were ordered, along with a roast, and Bubbles finally smiled.

"This is the life, eh?" She sipped the bubbly and looked around, nodding at one or two faces she recognized.

Bess wasn't sure they smiled back but Bubbles was oblivious.

"I say, did you meet Sir Dorian yesterday?"

Bubbles gave a shrug. It was no secret that she did not get along with her father.

"Quite a rum business at Ridley, what?" Bess continued. "I mean, Cedric never hurt a fly."

Bubbles agreed that her brother was a milktoast.

"At least that's the impression he likes to give."

Bess treated herself to an oyster on the shell and frowned.

"Are you saying he is dishonest? Forgive me if I don't agree with you, old bean."

Bubbles had always indulged Bess, being the outrageous, fun loving aunt rather than a virago.

"Cedric is biding his time until he comes into his inheritance. Won't be long now."

Bess assumed Bubbles was pulling her leg. It was evident she had no idea of the calamity that was about to fall on her family.

"Do you know Cedric is the top suspect in Sir Lawrence's murder?" She took a gulp of champagne. "You don't think he actually did it, do you? That's preposterous."

Bubbles stuck her fork in an oyster and finally grew sober.

"No, Bessie. Cedric is irresponsible and a bit vacuous. But he would never hurt anyone." She drank some champagne and signalled a waiter to refill her glass.

"There is one thing, though. He is an excellent shot."

Chapter 4

Dark clouds lined the horizon as Bess and Vicky drove to Ridley. Clementine had made sure they bundled up and were protected from the bitter wind. Breakfast had been a bit rushed although Bess made sure she had her fill of kedgeree. She hoped Lady Ridley would offer them tea.

Bess had given a brief update of her trip to the Nightingales the previous night. Clementine had spotted them huddled in a corner of the drawing room after dinner and asked what they were up to. The group broke up after agreeing that the girls needed to visit Ridley Hall.

Louise had arrived at the manor just as the girls were setting off that morning.

"Remember your manners, Bess." She wagged a finger at the girls. "You are going there to help them."

Both the girls promised to ignore any slurs Sir Dorian directed at them.

"So Bubbles thinks Cedric is waiting for his father to die so he can inherit Ridley Hall?" Vicky asked. Bess had provided more details of their trip before the girls went to bed. "That's awful."

Bess yanked the wheel to avoid a pothole and raised her voice so she could be heard over the howling wind.

"Bubbles does that. She makes shocking statements and makes fun of people's reactions."

Bess explained Bubbles did not believe Cedric would hurt his chances of living a good life. He had been brought up in the lap of luxury and was too used to being cosseted.

"She says he has a temper but I have never seen him angry. He must hide it well."

Vicky wondered what possible motive Cedric might have had to kill a guest in his home. The police would not narrow him down as a suspect unless they had found something against him.

The butler Hawk received them at Ridley Hall and led them to a parlour where Sir Dorian and Lady Ridley were having tea.

"How is everyone at Buxley Manor?" Lady Ridley inquired, always eager to learn how her girls fared, especially Momo.

"You can meet them at dinner tonight," Vicky smiled. "Aunt Clem will telephone any minute with an invitation."

Sir Dorian was subdued, exhibiting none of his usual ire. He asked how he might assist them. Bess told him they wanted to question the servants.

"Say no more." He clasped his hands behind his back and bellowed. "Hawk!"

The door opened and the butler came in. Nobody was surprised at his prompt arrival.

"Ask the servants to line up in the hall," Sir Dorian ordered. "I need to address them."

Ten minutes later, they followed Sir Dorian and Lady Ridley to the cavernous hall at the base of the main staircase. Bess was familiar with the housekeeper and a footman or two but many of the rest were not known to her.

"Lady Bess and Lady Vicky are going to ask you some questions. Anyone who does not cooperate can look for another position."

Bess noted the fear on some of the faces and hoped Sir Dorian's warning would encourage them to tell the truth. Lady Ridley tried to soften the situation by thanking the servants, earning a glare from her husband. She suggested they use a small, rarely used room near the back staircase.

Vicky thought they should interview the butler first and Bess agreed. They followed him to the room and assured him they did not need any refreshment.

"Can you give me a list of all the servants who work here?" Bess began. "Don't leave anyone out, Hawk."

They began talking about Sir Lawrence Watkins, the illustrious guest who had been shot dead in the woods surrounding Ridley Hall.

"Tell us about him, Hawk," Bess cajoled. "What kind of guest was he? Did he have too many special requests? Was he kind to the servants?" She leaned forward, as if to include him in a confidence. "Bit overripe, wasn't he? Liked to blow his own horn."

The butler's eyes widened. He seemed to grow taller before their eyes.

"It is not my place to comment on a guest, my lady." Hawk was stern. "Sir Lawrence was an esteemed guest and I was sorry to learn of his demise. The entire staff grieves for him."

Bess wished he would stop being pompous.

"Tell us about his routine. Did he go for a walk every day?"

Hawk had a ready answer for that. Sir Lawrence was particular about his exercise. He took his dog out at least twice every day, often spending a couple of hours on a long hike.

"And do you know the time he went out?" Bess prodded. "Was it the same time every morning and evening?"

Hawk thought for a moment.

"More or less, my lady. Unless he went out somewhere with Sir Dorian. As you know, he spent a lot of time at Buxley Manor and Castle Morse. And he liked to visit the local pubs."

Vicky asked if there was a particular trail or route he favoured. Hawk denied knowing anything about that.

"Does all the staff live here at the hall?" Bess

asked. "Or do you have people coming in from the village?"

"I live here, of course, along with Cook and the housekeeper. Four maids and three footmen also have quarters here. The gardener has a cottage on the property and the stable master …"

Bess tried to speed him along. Hawk pulled himself together and admitted that one or two of the newer maids lived on the outskirts of the village. There were many other people who worked on the estate but did not live at Ridley Hall.

"Would any of these know about the route Sir Lawrence took?" she pressed. "Try to recollect, Hawk. Has any of the servants mentioned coming across him in the course of their day?"

The butler looked crestfallen. He apologized for not being much help. Bess assured him they would give a good report to Sir Dorian. She made another request.

"When you make that list of people who work here, Hawk, can you please specify who lives at the hall? That might help us identify who comes in from outside and might have run into Sir Lawrence."

Vicky forced Bess to think about the people living at the hall.

"How can you say that none of these went for a walk? They might go out for some fresh air or have the day off."

Hawk cleared his throat. His staff worked hard from dawn to dusk and rarely had any free time.

"A person who walks to the hall every day had a higher chance of seeing Sir Lawrence," Bess argued. "Anyway, knowing where they live will give us a fair idea of their schedule and help us spot any aberrations."

Vicky conceded she had a point.

Hawk needed a day or two to put the list

together so the girls decided to postpone questioning the servants.

"Don't take too long," Bess warned. "We have already lost a lot of time. I would rather question the servants before the police come to arrest Cedric."

Lady Ridley invited them to stay for lunch but Bess politely declined.

"Aunt Clem is expecting us. Say, do you think we might have a word with Cedric?"

Sir Dorian had just entered the room. He uttered a string of expletives berating his son. Lady Ridley told them he was in London taking care of some business.

"Gambling away my hard earned money, more like," Sir Dorian thundered. "Or drowning in a vat of whisky. Maybe I should let the police take him away. Teach him a lesson."

"Now, Dorian," Lady Ridley pleaded. "You promised."

"So I did, my dear. But that nincompoop is doing no favour to himself, spending money like it grows on trees. What's the matter with this new generation, I wonder."

Vicky's eyebrows had shot up. Bess felt the same. Did Sir Dorian really believe in Cedric's innocence? They said their goodbyes and Lady Ridley confirmed they would come to Buxley for dinner.

Clementine had promised mutton curry for lunch and Bess drove back with a heavy foot on the accelerator. Vicky clutched the door, periodically urging her to slow down.

"That was a total waste," she complained. "We should have checked if Cedric was home."

Bess had assumed he would be, judging by the dire picture Sir Dorian had painted.

"At least this will pacify Grandma. We have done our duty."

"Do you mean we are not going to investigate

further? What about the lists you asked that butler to get for us?"

Bess was having second thoughts. She thought they should focus on solving the mystery around Philip's death.

"Haven't we been doing that all year?" Vicky argued. "The two things are parallel, sis. Do this for Momo if not for Sir Dorian."

Bess agreed Vicky had a point. Momo doted on her younger brother and would be devastated if he had to undergo any hardship. She marvelled at how Vicky was always two steps ahead, thinking of the bigger picture.

"Mom taught me that." Vicky explained. "Her compassion and empathy have helped her build a reputation in a male dominated business. Hundreds of people work for our railway company, you know."

Bess wanted to know how her mother planned to run the business from Buxley Manor. Did that mean she would go back to New York?

Vicky was thinking about the fateful day twenty years ago when Philip Gaskins had met his death. Something stirred in her mind and she patted Bess on the arm to get her attention. They had just entered the gates of Buxley Manor and were going up the drive.

"Asking Hawk for that list has given me an idea. Let's write down the names of all the people who were present here on the day of the hunt."

Bess told her they already knew that.

"Haven't we talked about it ad nauseum?"

"But seeing them all in one place on a piece of paper might make a difference," Vicky insisted. "Between guests, servants, people at the manor and anyone else, it is quite a number."

Bess caved. It was the first thing they would tackle after lunch.

Barnes met them at the door and led them to the dining room. Clementine exhaled when she saw them.

"You are back in time, I see. Cecil was here to speak to Nigel. He stayed for the curry."

Bess and Vicky greeted the vicar, darting a curious glance at a young man who sat next to him. His brown hair was streaked with blond and his arms were sinewed. He looked like someone who worked outdoors and used his muscles. What was such a man doing with Cecil?

Clementine was keeping a close eye on him. She bit her lip when he fumbled once, knocking over a water glass. A footman sprang forward to remove the offensive piece and replace it with another.

"What was Cecil thinking? Bringing some country boy to my table?" she railed when the vicar had left with his guest. "Nigel should not have allowed this."

Annie was smiling as she took a sip of her coffee.

"Did you notice that mark on his face, Clem? Quite peculiar, don't you think?"

Bess caught on immediately. She had come across a few unsavoury aspects of the vicar's life earlier that summer. Her jaw dropped as she connected the dots.

"I say, Annie!" she stared at her mother. "You don't think …"

Chapter 5

Dinner that night was hectic with a bevy of guests including the Ridleys and Cordelia Chilton, with her son Cecil the vicar and the young man who had appeared at lunch. Bess wore a sleeveless dress barely skimming her knees that would normally have earned Sir Dorian's ire. His mouth twisted in disapproval but Lady Ridley gave him a slight nudge with her elbow and he said nothing.

Annie was seated near the young man whose name turned out to be Robert. Louise, Hortense and Perpetua scrutinized him and peppered him with a few questions that he answered in a polite manner.

"Robert is a fine craftsman." Cecil's voice held a note of pride. "People pay big money to commission one of his pieces."

Clementine muttered and shook her head when the young man used the wrong fork. She pounced on Cordelia when the women left the gentlemen and tea was brought in.

"What is Cecil thinking, bringing a lout like that to my table?"

Before Bess could defend her great aunt, her sisters rushed to support her.

"You better get used to it, Clementine," Hortense tittered. "You will be seeing a lot of him."

Louise beamed in approval.

"I am so glad Cecil is not a snob like you, Clementine. He is setting a fine example."

Bess took pity on her aunt and explained what they had all guessed. Robert was Cecil's estranged son. Clementine uttered a small cry and fainted. Pandemonium erupted and the doctor had to be called.

The Ridleys left early, Lady Ridley promising Bess she would let her know as soon as her son Cedric returned from the city.

Bess found herself at a loose end the next day. Vicky was spending the day in the library, catching up on her reading. She had received communication from London and Edinburgh regarding her interest in becoming a doctor. Expecting to be quizzed on her knowledge, she wanted to be prepared.

The early morning mist cleared by eleven and the sun came out. Bess bundled up and walked into the village. She spotted a tall figure step into the Buxley Arms and picked up her pace.

Detective Inspector James Gardener sat at the bar, eating apple pie. She climbed up on the stool next to him.

"Cedric Ridley? A lazy, pampered aristocrat who cannot be bothered to do an honest day's work?"

DI Gardener smiled but said nothing.

Harvey, the proprietor, came out and started cleaning some glasses.

"Will you have lunch with us, my lady?"

She asked for a cup of tea.

"Are you preparing to meddle in police business again, Lady Bess?" DI Gardener quirked an eyebrow. "I might warn you to stay away but what would be the point?"

Bess told him how Sir Dorian had beseeched her to help. She had no choice. The Inspector gave a deep groan and asked after Vicky.

"It can't be Cedric," she burst out, then realized she wasn't sure.

The Inspector left soon without disclosing any details about his case. Bess returned to the manor and thought of going for a long walk after lunch.

Lady Ridley telephoned the next morning. Cedric was back from London. Bess and Vicky promised to drive over after breakfast.

"Will you be back in time for lunch?" Clementine asked.

"Mama will feed us," Bubbles told her, announcing she was going to Ridley Hall with the twins. "I think I will stay there for a day or two."

Bess took her time savouring her kedgeree and poured a second cup of tea. Bubbles told her to hurry up.

"What's this?" Bess was curious. "Are you actually eager to go to Ridley Hall?"

Momo asked her the same but Bubbles just gave a shrug and stood up, announcing she would wait outside in the car.

"Toodles, my dear." She planted a kiss on her sister's cheek.

The drive to Ridley Hall was uneventful. Vicky was quiet while Bubbles would not stop chattering. The butler led them to the parlour.

Lady Ridley welcomed them and ordered tea.

"Dorian is working on some correspondence in his study."

Bess saw Vicky fold her arms and knew what she was wondering. Where was Cedric? They had come there to meet the fellow, after all.

Tea arrived with spiced cake and biscuits. Bubbles picked up the tea pot and poured, easily assuming the role of hostess. They talked about the weather and discussed the local gossip. Finally, Bess could not hold herself back.

"I say, Lady Ridley, where is Cedric?"

The poor woman looked embarrassed. Bubbles glanced at a clock on the wall and told them it was too early for her brother. He rarely made an appearance before noon. Bess thought they were wasting time.

Sir Dorian appeared for lunch. They had just finished the soup, a hearty ham and split pea, when Cedric sauntered in. He was freshly shaved and in the pink of health.

"What ho!" He sat down next to Bess. "We had a crazy time at this new jazz bar in town, young Bess." He whispered in her ear. "You were missed."

Sir Dorian cleared his throat and glared at the scion of the family.

"You are out of touch with reality, my boy."

Cedric ignored him and declared he was starving. There were chops with roasted potatoes, a partridge pie, and bread and butter pudding with raspberry jam. An excellent Stilton followed. Bess admitted Sir Dorian kept a good table.

"You are in hot water, Cedric." Bess tackled him as Lady Ridley poured tea in the parlour.

He brushed off her concern and stretched his

legs, placing his arms behind his head.

"No need to worry, old bean. The police will never find a shred of evidence against me."

Bess felt alarmed. Vicky sat at the edge of the sofa, keeping a close eye on Cedric. Did he mean he had committed the dastardly act and disposed of the evidence? She felt her ears grow warm and tried to calm down.

Cedric spotted her blush and burst into laughter.

"You think I killed that old goat, don't you?" His bonhomie was replaced by anger. "Et tu, Brute?"

He cast a malevolent look at Bubbles. Bess shrank back when he suddenly leapt up and pointed a finger in her face.

"You are all just waiting for the police to come and take me away. Papa would gladly pin this murder on me so Bubbles can inherit the Hall and reign supreme."

He stalked out without another word. Lady Ridley was mortified. Bubbles was speechless for a change. Bess had never seen Cedric pull this kind of stunt.

Lady Ridley recovered and made excuses for her son.

"He is not himself, my poor boy. Tries to maintain a stiff upper lip but he is terrified. You see why he needs your help, don't you, my dears?"

Bess hastened to assure her they would do their best.

"Mom will be waiting for us." Vicky spoke. "Aunt Cordelia has invited us to tea at the vicarage."

They took their leave and couldn't get into the car fast enough.

"That was terrible!" Bess cried as Ridley Hall went out of sight. "Cedric is an idiot."

Vicky wanted to know if he had always been irascible.

"If a fly comes and sits on his nose, Cedric can't be bothered to swat it." Bess narrowed her eyes. "No, no. Whatever happened there was not normal. I don't know why Cedric behaved like that. As far as I know, the Hall is entailed so it will come to him, anyway. No question of Bubbles inheriting anything."

Vicky was tired. She had been on tenterhooks lest Sir Dorian find fault with her behaviour. They decided to forget about the Ridleys for the rest of the day.

Tea at the vicarage was a jolly affair. Cordelia, who Bess thought was a cold fish, was like a new person. She beamed when she showed off a writing desk Robert had given her as a present. The vicarage was dowdy at best, filled with generations of castoffs from the manor and the glossy new item stood out.

Annie put Robert at ease and Bess and Vicky followed.

"We are cousins of sorts, I guess." Vicky surprised him with a tight hug. "You can be the older brother we never had."

Barnes had a message for them when they returned to the manor.

"Your grandmother telephoned, my lady. She has requested your presence in the west wing tomorrow morning at 10 AM."

Bess thanked him and placed a call to Louise, assuring her she and Vicky would be there.

Dinner was quieter than usual with no guests. Vicky planned to spend a few hours studying so Bess took a long bath and rifled through some fashion magazines before going to bed.

The next morning saw the twins heading to the west wing, fortified with toast and kedgeree. Louise wore a hat festooned with what looked like dry twigs and a russet dress, both a nod to the autumn wind raging outside. Hortense was fanning herself with a handkerchief while Perpetua sat like a stone, staring at the clock on the wall.

"Tell us everything," Louise commanded.

Bess and Vicky took turns talking about their meeting with Cedric. Louise rang for Barnes and summoned Momo.

"She might know a different side of him."

Momo arrived, looking perturbed.

"What is it, Grandmother?" she wrung her hands. "Are you feeling ill?"

Louise assured her she was in the pink of health. Bess explained what they wanted to talk about. Momo grew ashen when she learned about Cedric being a suspect in the hunter's death.

"But why has no one mentioned this to me?" she cried. "Papa said nothing when he was here two days ago." Her eyes filled up. "Poor Cedric! Mama has always pampered him, you know? Him being so much younger than us girls. That poor boy."

Bess stroked her back and urged her to calm down.

"The police have not taken any action against him yet so we have time. Maybe Constable Yates was confused. I met the Inspector the other day and he said nothing about Cedric."

A ray of hope appeared in Momo's eyes.

"You talked to DI Gardener? Promise me you won't annoy him, Bess. He might take it out on Cedric."

Bess felt a surge of anger. DI Gardener might be standoffish but he was not unfair. He did everything by the book.

"Can we ask you a few questions, Momo?" Vicky took the lead. "We are trying to understand Cedric's personality."

Louise told them to stop beating around the bush. Momo needed to toughen up.

"You can't say boo to a goose and that's a fact, Momo. We think you are more sheltered than your brother."

Vicky rushed forward with the most important question of the day.

"What possible motive could Cedric have for killing Sir Lawrence?"

Momo told them Sir Lawrence thought Cedric was a libertine and good for nothing. "You know how vocal he could be!"

The ladies nodded as one. They were all aware of what an obnoxious loudmouth Sir Lawrence Watkins had been.

"That is not enough to take his life, surely?" Bess frowned.

Momo explained how Sir Lawrence had talked her father into forcing Cedric to do an honest day's work. It started with cutting off his allowance.

"I bet that did not go down well," Louise marked, knowing the expensive tastes of young men. "But Lawrence was a fool with no children of his own. Dorian should have known better before taking such a drastic step."

Bess asked for Momo's opinion.

"Cedric is in his mid thirties but I doubt he has ever made an effort to meet the tenants or peruse the accounts. He runs a mile from responsibility."

Momo lamented he was nothing like Philip who had taken the role of earl very seriously.

"Yes, yes." Bess was impatient. "But is he capable of murder?"

Momo denied it vehemently. Cedric was docile with not a shred of interest in worldly matters.

The picture she painted did not match the show of temper they had seen from Cedric the previous day. Bess felt inclined to believe

Momo but could not brush off a premonition.

Was Cedric a wolf in sheep's clothing?

Chapter 6

Bess had never seen her father so excited. Nigel had taken her into confidence that morning. He was planning a special dinner for Annie and Vicky. The butler, housekeeper and cook had been roped in and everyone was enthusiastic about the project.

"Let's go on a drive and take our tea at a pub."

Nigel proposed having a picnic and Bess agreed immediately. They would come back in time for an early dinner.

"But what about Aunt Clem? Will she approve?"

"It can be just us, Bessie." Nigel beamed. "You girls and your mother."

Bess could not curb her excitement through

lunch. She and Nigel glanced at each other often and giggled. Annie asked what they were up to.

"Nothing, my dear." Nigel waited while a footman cleared the soup and placed a fresh plate before him. "We are thinking of our picnic. It's a pleasant day for a nice jaunt, what?"

Clementine complained father and daughter had been tight lipped.

"What do you know about this, Barnes?" she prodded. "Nothing happens at the manor without your blessing."

Barnes maintained an impassive expression but his eyes twinkled with humour.

"I have no idea, my lady," he replied smoothly.

Clementine gave a shrug and told them that Mrs. Bird was preparing a generous basket for their tea.

"Have a good time, then."

Nigel had to take care of some paperwork so he retreated to his library after the pudding. Bess decided to visit Momo in the east wing. She was suffering from a cold and spending the day in bed on the doctor's orders.

They set off at three. A few fluffy clouds dotted the clear blue sky and a stiff breeze carried the scent of apples in the orchards. Workers in the fields stopped and waved as the Rolls passed them. Annie shook hands with some of them and got out of the car to talk to an old woman she recognized.

"We will never get off our land at this rate," Bess warned.

Annie told her the woman was a midwife. She had come to live at the manor when the twins were going to be born.

"Mrs. Green brought you into this world, girls." Annie laughed. "We owe her a lot."

Vicky embraced the woman and thanked her and Bess nodded grudgingly. She had to admit Annie had a magnetic personality. People were attracted to her wherever she went and they were all happy to bask in the glow of her attention.

After Annie promised to visit Mrs. Green at her cottage, they set off again. Bess took them to one of her favourite spots. They had to climb up a small hill but the view at the top was spectacular. The picnic was decimated. Mrs. Bird had packed sandwiches and two kinds of cake, along with ginger biscuits and thermoses filled with tea and coffee. Soon, it was time to go back.

Annie and Nigel sat in the back. Bess could not hold back a smile when she saw Nigel slide closer to her mother and put his arm around her. Overall, it was a magical day but Bess was waiting for the bubble to burst.

A slight haze hung in the garden when they got back to the manor. Vicky tipped her nose up in the air and sniffed.

"If I didn't know better, Mom, I would swear I smell barbecue."

Annie laughed at her but her face changed when she took in a deep breath. She whirled around and looked into Nigel's eyes.

"You wonderful man, what have you done?"

He gave Bess a knowing look and smiled mischievously.

"I know you and Vicky are homesick, my darling. So Bessie and I arranged a special dinner."

"An American dinner, Vicky!" Bess cried, forgetting her worries in the excitement. "Hamburgers and baked beans and maize grilled over an open fire."

"Corn on the cob!" Annie exclaimed.

Mrs. Bird had unearthed an old recipe book

Annie had brought with her when she first got married. The beans had been simmering on the cooking range for twenty four hours. One of the footmen had been given the task of flipping the burgers on a makeshift grill.

The whole family cheered when Nigel, Annie and the twins reached the clearing in the garden where dinner had been set up. Bubbles was back and was already sampling a burger. Clementine sipped a glass of sherry and looked relaxed. Louise and the aunts looked on in approval.

Bess was exhausted by the time they had eaten every bite of the ice cream and could not stop yawning as she began ascending the staircase to her room. Vicky was right behind her.

Barnes waylaid them, holding a silver tray with an envelope on it.

"A message from Hawk at Ridley Hall, my lady."

Bess grabbed the missive and thanked him,

tearing it open on the way up.

"Is it the list?" Vicky wanted to know.

Bess nodded, all the lassitude she had felt disappearing in an instant. The sisters huddled together on the big four poster bed and poured over the list.

"There are five people who come in from the village," Vicky summed up. "Two maids, a footman, an under footman and the boot boy."

Bess pointed at the number of people who lived in the big house. They also made up a considerable number.

"It will take us ages to talk to all of them, Vicky."

"We will have to assume that the people who live in the house had no reason to go out during the day. Think about it, Bess. Sir Lawrence went out after breakfast. That must be the busiest time for the servants. I doubt any butler or housekeeper would let them go for a walk at such a time."

Bess realized she was right.

"So let's focus on these five people now. I think we can eliminate the boot boy. I vaguely remember him as a snot faced urchin with hardly any meat on him. Where would he have access to a gun or learn to shoot?"

Vicky was busy running her finger down the list.

"This isn't much use to us," she grumbled. "There is no mention of the time these people come to the hall, or when they leave."

"Giving us no way to determine when they might have been in the woods."

Bess got up to telephone Hawk about the missing information. Vicky held her back.

"I think it's better if we ask them outright."

"Don't give them a chance to prevaricate, you

mean," Bess approved. "That means another trip to Ridley Hall."

Vicky brought up the Christmas shopping.

"I was thinking of going to Chipping Woodbury to that jewellery shop to order something nice for Mom." She gave Bess a knowing look. "We could get matching pendants, all three of us."

"Why not?" Bess was nonchalant. "Whatever makes you happy, dearest."

They made plans to leave after an early breakfast. They would question the servants at Ridley Hall, then go to Chipping Woodbury and have lunch at The Laughing Mongrel. The afternoon would be devoted to shopping.

"You are barely listening." Vicky nudged Bess who was staring out of the window. "I thought you would be hankering for those sausages you like."

Bess assured her that lunch at The Laughing

Mongrel was a great idea.

"Sir Lawrence wasn't from around here, Vicky. In fact, he has not visited the region since Philip's accident."

"What are you getting at?" Vicky hugged a pillow and frowned.

"I doubt he knows anyone other than the families, like the Ridleys, the Morses, the Carringtons … us. He did not seem like the type to hobnob with servants."

Vicky did not think Sir Lawrence had been stuck up. He had been used to mingling with natives, having lived in Africa for so many years.

"But there is no reason why he would be familiar with the servants at Ridley Hall," Bess emphasized. "Likewise, they scarcely knew him."

Vicky understood Bess. The servants at Ridley Hall had no motive to kill Sir Lawrence.

"That leaves Sir Dorian, Lady Ridley and Cedric."

Had Sir Dorian nursed a grudge against the dead man?

"That's it though. Are they the only people living there? They might have had guests at the time Sir Lawrence was killed. Or someone might have been visiting for the day, to take tea or lunch."

Vicky thought it was too late to place a call to Ridley Hall. Bess shook her head. Every delay meant the real killer was getting away from them.

"No time like the present."

They went down to the hall and telephoned the Hall. Cedric picked up and launched into some ridiculous tale of his recent exploits. Bess asked him to call the butler.

"I say, old girl, does this sound a bit upside down?"

Finally, Hawk came on the line and asked how he might be of service. Bess posed her question right away. The butler did not disappoint. Bess listened for a few minutes before placing the receiver in its cradle.

Barnes came across them and inquired if they needed anything. Vicky admitted she could use a cup of cocoa.

"You might have rung, my lady." Barnes bowed and promised to send the hot drink.

Bess didn't say a word until they were back in their room.

"I can't stand the suspense," Vicky cried. "What did Hawk say?"

There were two illustrious guests at Ridley Hall. Both of them had been there to meet Sir Lawrence.

"One of them is Simon Watkins," Bess began. "He is the hunter's nephew."

The other man was from Africa and also a hunter like Sir Lawrence.

"His name is Edwin Brindley. Or Grindley. I am not sure which. He is a friend."

Vicky asked if she was sure these two men were living at Ridley Hall. Why had they not encountered them before?

"Where else would they stay?" Bess asked. "There is plenty of room and Sir Dorian is a generous host. Look how many months One Eye Watkins spent at Ridley Hall."

Vicky thought they were getting somewhere. The nephew and the friend surely had some history with the dead man.

"Sir Lawrence has no children, remember?" Bess mused. "Unless I am mistaken, this nephew is his heir."

"You mean he will inherit everything Sir Lawrence owned?" Vicky quizzed. "Any idea what he was worth?"

They had heard about his estate in Kent. And he had always bragged about the big prize money he won every time he killed a lion or an elephant. A man who had reportedly killed a hundred lions would have accumulated quite a fortune.

A maid arrived with two steaming cups of cocoa. Two slices of cake rested on a plate, along with ginger biscuits.

Bess took a sip of the hot, sweet drink and grinned at Vicky.

"I think Cedric might stand a chance after all."

Chapter 7

Louise took the girls to task the next morning. Bess was just savouring the perfect bite of kedgeree, followed by a sip of freshly brewed Darjeeling. The Gaskins family acquired their tea straight from the source, from a tea plantation owned by one of their friends.

"Have you established that boy's innocence?" Louise asked.

Nigel and Annie had their heads together, making plans for how to spend the day. His head jerked up at the mention of the crime.

"What's that, Mama?"

"Cedric Ridley is going to be arrested for the murder of Sir Lawrence," Louise stated, pinning her son with an accusatory glance. "Get your head out of the clouds for a moment, Nigel." She almost smiled, telling Bess she was just having some fun. "You might be better informed, know what's happening at your doorstep."

It took very little to fluster Nigel. He stared at his offspring, his eyes bulging.

"I say, Bess. What's this new palaver? What …"

Annie squeezed his hand, silently helping him to calm down. Nigel cleared his throat, getting ready to say his piece.

"What happened at Ridley Hall has nothing to do with us."

"I thought Sir Lawrence was your friend, Pops," Vicky teased. "And he seemed so taken with Mom." She winked at Annie.

The whole family knew Sir Lawrence Watkins had been casting aspersions on Nigel's character that summer, stirring old memories, riling up the locals. He had even hinted at

Annie having illicit relations with the dead Miles Carrington.

"That is beside the point." Nigel slammed a fist on the table, surprising them with this uncharacteristic action. "You will not put yourself in harm's way again. I am going to call Ned at Scotland Yard as soon as I finish breakfast. Let the police do their job."

Bess told him DI Gardener was already working on the case.

"Well then," Nigel smiled. "No need for you girls to meddle, right? Your mother is planning a trip to Paris. Why don't you join her?"

Bubbles had been crumbling some toast on her plate, looking bored. She plunged into the conversation at the mention of their trip to France.

"Yes, Bessie. Let's do that. I need a nice dress for the New Year ball, something that will dazzle all of London."

Bubbles had been decorating her flat in the city for the past few months and was making plans to throw a lavish party to announce her arrival. Vicky sported a look of disbelief at this callous comment. Bess felt sorry for the Ridleys. It seemed like Cedric was on his own and needed all the help she could provide.

Louise shocked them by agreeing with Bubbles.

"We can all go. I will convince Hortense and Perpetua. Nigel, call your man at Cook's and make reservations for us."

Momo, Annie and Bubbles headed out to discuss the impending trip. Nigel set off on his morning constitutional.

"Finally!" Louise smirked. "Now tell me what you are up to, my dears."

Bess told her they intended to go to Ridley Hall again to find out more about the household. Apparently, there had been some guests at the hall at the time Sir Lawrence was murdered.

"We want to know their current whereabouts, Grandmother. One is apparently a nephew of Sir Lawrence and another man comes all the way from Africa."

Lousie told them the men were still at the hall. She could be confident of her information.

"Where else are they going to be? I have never met them, though." Her eyes narrowed. "There is an easy way to remedy that, girls. Invite them for dinner. That will give us an opportunity to observe them closely."

"Spy on them, you mean?" Vicky laughed. "If they have anything to hide, Grandma, I'm sure you'll spot it a mile away. You and Aunt Hortense and Aunt Perpetua. You're the bee's knees!"

"The cat's pyjamas," Bess cackled, agreeing with her sister. "As you wish, Grandmother. I will notify the kitchen."

Barnes cleared his throat. He had been standing a few feet behind Louise, taking in the conversation.

"It's alright," Bess assured him. "I can have a small chat with Mrs. Bird."

The kitchen had been a haven for Bess all her life. Being the only child in a manor full of older people, she had not lacked attention. But none of the family could match the warmth she found in the ample bosom of the cook. So the kitchen was where Bess went when she needed to be coddled or kissed.

Mrs. Bird greeted her with open arms, her eyes alight with genuine pleasure.

"You will be careful this time?" She patted Bess on the back. "Things are just coming together."

Bess assured her she had no wish to confront any cold blooded killer. At the same time, she could not disappoint Sir Dorian. They chatted for a few minutes, Vicky listening with an indulgent smile, leaning against a counter. When Mrs. Bird learned they were going to

Ridley Hall, she promised to have a footman put some refreshments in the car. Bess thanked her and went upstairs with Vicky, eager to get going.

The misty morning had given way to pale sunlight but it was cold outside. Bess wove a woollen muffler around her head and slammed on her goggles, suddenly impatient. The car was halfway across the Buxley grounds when they saw Nigel in the distance. He waved at them and Bess slowed, preparing herself to receive another barrage of warnings.

"You can expect a nice leg of lamb for dinner tonight, Papa. We are inviting the Ridleys and their guests. Grandmother's orders."

Nigel gave a shrug. Dinner guests were the norm rather than exception at Buxley Manor. He was a generous host who believed in sharing the bounty life and fortune had bestowed on him.

Vicky asked him if he had heard of Sir Lawrence's nephew. Nigel picked up his poodle Polo who was yapping for attention.

"Simon Watkins? He's about my age. Lawrence has talked about him."

Bess asked if they had been close.

Nigel let Polo escape from his arms and head off to chase a rabbit.

"Lawrence had a skill. Being a professional hunter must not have been a walk in the park. Don't know how he managed to survive in the wilds of Africa for so many years." He chuckled. "But it wasn't for the fairer sex." He held up a hand before Bess could say anything. "Times were different when we were young."

Nigel told them Lawrence had wanted a wife and a family like any other man but he could never find a girl who would accept his lifestyle. Victorian misses of their class did not fancy pitching a tent in the jungle or being on tenterhooks each day, uncertain if their husband would be mauled by a lion. So there was no marriage or children and no heir.

"He spent a lot of time at his estate in Kent this year," Nigel told them. "I think he and Simon built up a good rapport during that time. Lawrence believed Simon was a worthy heir."

Earlier that summer, Sir Lawrence had talked of marrying a woman of child bearing age but he must have known the idea was farfetched.

"So is Simon Watkins his legal heir, Papa?"

Nigel pleaded ignorance. A stiff breeze had picked up and he was beginning to shiver. He told them to be on their way so they could come back in time for lunch.

"And now girls, I'm going in for a nice hot cuppa. Sure you don't want to join me?"

The girls promised to be back soon and set off.

"I say," Bess groaned. "Papa's got me thinking of tea. What's in that basket Mrs. Bird packed for us?"

They nibbled on biscuits and enjoyed the

bracing weather, making good time. Hawk gave them a stiff smile and led them to the parlour. Lady Ridley sat with an open book on her lap, looking pale and worried. Sir Dorian paced the room, mumbling and sputtering under his breath.

"What's wrong?" Bess cried, sensing the tension in the room.

Lady Ridley sunk deeper into the sofa, expelling a deep breath. Sir Dorian rushed toward the girls and grabbed Bess by the arm, giving a nervous laugh. He seemed to be struck speechless. Vicky led him to an armchair and gently nudged him to sit. She coaxed the truth out of the anxious couple while Bess rang the bell, summoning the butler.

"That Inspector is here, questioning Cedric in my study." Sir Dorian finally revealed. "I fear they have come to arrest him, my dear."

Bess rushed out of the room and stomped to Sir Dorian's study, only to be thwarted at the entrance by Yates, the local constable. He was almost apologetic but he told Bess he could not let her in.

"My job's on the line, my lady. The DI said no interruptions."

Bess returned to the parlour, her shoulders slumped in defeat. Sir Dorian was nursing a balloon of brandy and Lady Ridley sipped tea.

"Everything's fine." Bess balked at the thought of giving them false hope. "I am going to talk to DI Gardener the moment he comes out of that room."

She accepted a cup of tea from Lady Ridley and took a quick sip, gathering her thoughts. If push came to shove, she would point the finger toward the dead man's nephew. It would buy them some time. The police had to question him at any rate.

DI James Gardener breezed in twenty minutes later with Cedric in tow. His expression gave nothing away. Bess jumped up and demanded to speak to him.

"I say, this is all balderdash! What evidence do you have against Cedric? You need to focus on the other suspects."

James flashed a disarming smile and looked at the teapot. Vicky took the hint and poured him a cup. Bess was having none of it.

"You have some nerve! Swilling tea while planning to destroy the family." She was undaunted by the flash of anger she saw in the Inspector's eyes. "We demand an explanation."

Calmly, in a voice barely above a whisper, James Gardener told her he did not owe her any. He was just doing his duty and was not obliged to keep anyone apprised of his movements. Then he proceeded to lean against the fireplace and drink his tea. Cedric had collapsed on a sofa and was staring at a suit of armour languishing in a corner.

Vicky began talking about the weather and the tempers in the room finally cooled. The Inspector told them he could give them five minutes. The girls trooped to the study after him, surprised he had caved.

"I have known Cedric all my life." Bess folded her arms and glared at the Inspector. "He does not have the mental capacity to plan a murder."

Vicky tried a different approach.

"I don't know him, at all. All I can tell you is another person could have done it. You should at least explore other options."

James Gardener agreed with them. Neither girl could have guessed what he said next.

"Why don't we join forces?" He quirked an eyebrow and smiled. "I agree you are more familiar with these people. And the servants are wary of the police."

He urged the girls to share anything they might have learned.

"Every little bit helps," he winked.

Bess refused to be taken in.

"Of course. And there are some bits of information only the police have access to. Like the exact spot where Sir Lawrence was gunned down. Can you pinpoint the location on a map?"

James threw back his head and laughed, his eyes glowing with admiration.

"I can do better, my lady. Why don't I take you to the scene of the crime?"

Chapter 8

James Gardener set a brisk pace but Bess was determined to keep up with him. The grounds of Ridley Hall were not very familiar to Bess, unlike those of her home Buxley Manor or that of Castle Morse, her friend's. Sir Dorian was not known to be affable and he rarely had time for a precocious child. So although Ridley Hall was home to Bubbles and Momo, it was rarely visited.

Vicky had no qualms asking the Inspector to slow down. Bess felt her hesitate and saw her shudder as a nasty gust of wind buffeted them. The day had grown more inclement.

"Would you rather keep Lady Ridley company?" Her concern was genuine. "I am sure the Inspector will protect me from any unsavoury elements."

James made some wisecrack about her reputation.

"I am a working class man, my lady," he quipped. "Don't you need a chaperone to be around me?"

Bess blew a raspberry in his face.

"What is this lady business? Haven't I asked you to call me Bess?"

They left the manicured gardens adjoining the Hall and took a shrub lined path that led them to an orchard at the back of the rambling edifice. A long avenue of trees stretched before them, laden with the season's late apples. Bess surmised most of the fruit had already been picked. She couldn't resist plucking a fruit off a tree, biting into the crisp juicy flesh.

The Inspector led them on to a well trodden path strewn with fallen leaves. Autumn was making its presence known, creating a beautiful palette of russet, yellow and brown in the foliage around them.

"Where does this path go?" Vicky asked, wrapping her arms tightly around herself.

"Winds through the woods for a few miles and curves back here," the Inspector answered. "There's a hill over yonder with a bird's eye view of the area. It's a nice bracing walk for a robust person."

Bess remarked that would not have deterred a man like Sir Lawrence.

Vicky wanted to know how many people used the path.

"We found some of the servants live in the village. Would they have to take this path to reach the Hall?"

James scratched the stubble on his chin, admitting he was not sure. Bess was quick to point out his error.

"You must find out if this is the only way they can get to the manor. If that is the case, all of them would have been here on that fateful day."

Vicky thought most servants would begin work very early in the morning. Sir Lawrence had not headed out until after breakfast.

"All good points," James lauded, surprising Bess with the sincere compliment.

He suddenly veered to his left and stepped off the trail. The girls followed, intrigued. Bess felt her pulse quicken, anticipating what they would see next. They walked through a thick cover of trees until they came to a circular area marked with rope. The Inspector pointed at a clear patch. A mound of dry leaves at the side suggested the area had been swept clean.

"Does the rope help?" Vicky wanted to know. "There is no guard here. What's going to stop anyone from ducking under it and walking through?"

James gave a shrug. The villagers had been warned to stay away from the area.

"A constable was posted here for a week or so. We have conducted a thorough search of the area, looking for evidence. I doubt we missed anything." His eyes were sharp as they scanned the area. "I think most people think twice before directly disobeying the police." He darted an amused glance at Bess. "We cannot control the wild ones, though."

"Sir Lawrence was shot, wasn't he?" she probed.

James gave an affirmative nod.

"And the mighty police must have found the weapon?"

"Yes, Lady Bess. We have the weapon in our custody." He gave her a warning look. "Constable Yates has been duly warned. I hope you will not try to hoodwink him."

Vicky intervened before Bess could respond.

"That should make your job easy, once you check for fingerprints. Did you find any?"

James gave a deep sigh. He told them the gun was being tested for exactly the same reason. But analysing fingerprints took time. There was a process to be followed and he wanted to be sure everything was done by the book.

Bess asked after the type of gun. Had it been a rifle, the kind used by hunters? James shook his head and revealed the murder weapon was a pistol. He held up his hand to ward off any more questions.

"We should leave now."

While they were talking, the sky had grown darker and the watery sunlight filtering through the tree tops was almost gone. The weather was steadily growing worse and the cold was unbearable. Bess could hardly feel her toes so she did not raise any objection. They began the slow trek back to the Hall.

Bess asked the question that had been at the back of her mind since Sir Dorian sought her help.

"Why do you suspect Cedric, Inspector? Did someone see him near this spot that morning?"

Vicky supported her. "Yes. Why not the butler or Sir Dorian himself. What does Cedric Ridley gain from Sir Lawrence's death?"

A drop or two of rain fell and James urged them to pick up the pace.

"Not directly, no." He threw a worried glance at Vicky and offered her his coat.

Bess noticed her sister's cheeks were red. Tears streamed down Vicky's eyes and she sneezed twice in quick succession.

"I say, old bean, are you alright?"

Vicky could barely nod.

James offered her his arm for support and she leaned on him readily. Bess was alarmed, eager to drive back to the warmth of Buxley Manor.

"And indirectly?" She asked James. "Cedric?"

"They had a big showdown at the pub. Needless to say, most of the villagers witnessed it."

Bess told him how Sir Lawrence had influenced Sir Dorian to curtail Cedric's allowance. He would be cut off without a penny unless he mended his ways and straightened up.

"That sums it up," James replied. "Cedric warned the old man to stop meddling and go home."

The dead man had stood his ground and tried to talk sense into Cedric. It had not ended well. Threats were made and dire warnings were given.

"Cedric has never taken any initiative," Bess told him. "Frankly, he is too lazy to follow up on any threat he may have made."

Sir Lawrence was more likely to shoot someone in a fit of anger. He had, after all, killed a hundred lions in Africa. And once he had killed a lion and an elephant in a single day.

They walked through the orchard and neared the main house. James reminded her Sir Lawrence was the victim.

"You do promise to be careful?" He waited until they both nodded. "I hope you will let me know the moment you unearth any new information. Don't venture into the unknown. Please, at least think of your poor parents."

Bess bit back a retort. She was twenty one, old enough to make her own decisions.

"What are you doing for dinner tonight, Inspector?" Vicky nudged her sister. "It would be great if you can come to Buxley Manor. Consider this a formal invite but I will try and get Aunt Clem to give you a call."

James thanked her and grinned.

"It would be my pleasure. May I ask if this is in honour of a special occasion?"

Vicky explained the Ridleys were coming and were bringing their guests along. The Inspector would be able to observe them in a relaxed environment without interrogating them. Who knew, one of them might make a casual remark that would help the investigation.

James approved of the idea and promised to see them that evening.

"I am loving this collaboration."

He laughed at the furious expression Bess wore and took their leave. The girls debated getting into their car without going back into the house.

"I need to warm up a bit, Bess." Vicky implored.

A small door at the side of the hall opened and Hawk peeped out. The girls rushed inside and ran down a dark passage until they reached the main hall. Hawk offered to notify Sir Dorian.

Bess was loathe to bother him.

"Actually, we would like to talk to you, Hawk.

Can we, perhaps, go to your office?"

Lady Ridley came out of the parlour and took in their appearance.

"Tell Cook to send a tea tray, Hawk," she ordered. "Quick, before these poor dears catch a cold."

She shooed the girls into the parlour and insisted they sit by the fireplace. Neither of them protested. Vicky rubbed her hands, trying to get her circulation going. Bess thought her eyes were bright and vowed to call Dr. Evans as soon as they got home.

"Clementine will give me an earful if anything happens to you," Lady Ridley fretted. "She called to invite all of us to dinner. We accepted, of course. Simon and that Mr. Brindley will also come with us."

Bess realized he was the man from Africa.

Hawk entered, followed by a maid lugging a tray loaded with tea and coffee. Lady Ridley dismissed them and began to pour. Vicky's hand shook as she took a sip of the coffee.

"Try the spiced cake," Lady Ridley urged. "Cook only makes it this time of the year."

Bess asked after Cedric, half expecting to hear he had gone back to London.

"He is coming to dinner?" she asked. "Momo will be happy to see all of you."

Lady Ridley told them Cedric had no choice. The Inspector had warned him to stay in the area.

"The poor boy doesn't like being tied down," she lamented. "He has always been a free spirit." She wrung her hands in despair. "Our children have been unfortunate. My dear Momo, widowed in her youth. Bubbles, an old maid. And Cedric shows no sign of settling down even in his thirties."

Bess tried to console her.

"They are happy though, Lady Ridley. Isn't that what matters most?"

The older woman looked uncertain.

"Bubbles is looking forward to living at her new flat in London. She is an inspiration for the rest of us. I have never heard her complain about being single."

"Girls want different things these days, I suppose," Lady Ridley mumbled. "It's very different from the world I was brought up in."

Vicky was looking a lot better after scarfing down the cake and coffee.

"Change is inevitable, Lady Ridley. Mom always taught me that."

"Sometimes I forget Bubbles and Annie belong to the same generation," Bess laughed. "I am so used to thinking of her as a big sister."

Lady Ridley asked if she knew any young women who would be interested in meeting

Cedric. Bess promised to let her know.

"Don't worry, Lady Ridley. This whole murder business might be a boon in disguise if it motivates Cedric to give up his bachelor life and settle down."

Chapter 9

Lady Ridley finally calmed down after repeated assurances from Bess and Vicky. The girls bid her a good day, eager to be on their way. Hawk followed them out to the front door.

"Say, Hawk." Bess halted mid step. "Can you spare us a few minutes?"

He obliged and led them to the small room near the door leading downstairs. Although cramped, it had a fireplace with a mantel decorated with photographs of the Ridley children at various ages. It was obvious Hawk doted on them. Bess was not surprised, since their butler Barnes had a similar affection for her.

A short young woman knelt by the fireplace, engrossed in her task. Strands of gleaming coppery hair had escaped from her cap, shielding the side of her face. Hawk seemed displeased, asking her to hurry up.

"How can I help you, my lady?" He invited them to take a seat.

Bess urged Vicky to sit in the lone chair facing the butler and leaned against the table herself. She put Hawk at ease, assuring them they only had some basic questions about the whereabouts of the staff.

"Was anyone out sick that day? Or did not come to work for some reason?"

Vicky followed up with her own question.

"Do you keep a record of the staff's movements, Hawk? When they come and go, for instance? At my Mom's home in the Hamptons, the staff is required to note the time and sign in a register when they come in. They do the same when they leave for the day."

Hawk opened his mouth to respond but paused when Bess spoke again.

"Is there a specific time when they have to begin work?"

"I run a tight ship." Hawk answered proudly. "The servants begin work at a certain time, of course. Any deviation from routine is recorded. Those coming from the village note their time in a register."

Bess leaned forward, eager to learn more.

"So, tell us, was any of the servants late on the day of the murder?"

There was a loud crash followed by a squeal. A pail of dirty water none of the girls had noticed before lay overturned, spreading across the floor. The maid stared at it in dismay, her hands covering her mouth which was hanging open. Bess noticed her stricken expression and was sorry for her.

"Get a mop and clean it up, girl." Hawk ordered, his tone stiff but his expression as inscrutable as ever.

"Yes, Mr. Hawk." The girl mumbled and rushed out, her cheeks red and eyes full of tears.

"I say, what a clumsy maid," Bess clucked. "Was listening in, I suppose."

Vicky rushed to the girl's defence.

"It was an accident, Bess. Don't be unkind."

Hawk cleared his throat, looking uncomfortable. He apologized on behalf of the maid.

"Empty headed, these young girls." He shook his head. "Please give me a few minutes, my lady." He stood up and leaned toward a shelf on the wall, pulling down a big register. "Allow me to check back to the day."

Bess fiddled with a pen on the desk while Hawk shuffled through the pages, dabbing his finger when he reached a certain entry. He screwed his eyes together to read what was written on the page.

"One of the maids coming in from the village was late," he announced, agitated. "Clumsy and tardy."

The twins shared a glance, taking in his meaning at once.

"Was that the same girl who was here a minute ago?" Vicky spoke. "She certainly looks like a greenhorn."

Bess wanted to know her name.

"Wilma McLeod," Hawk replied. "She is new. Not from around here, my lady."

Vicky asked why the girl was late. Hawk told them the housekeeper would know that.

"Mrs. Macdonald must have taken the girl to task, no doubt. Shall I send for her?"

Bess told him he could talk to her when he got a chance and report back to them.

"You can telephone us at Buxley Manor,

Hawk. If Lady Ridley asks, tell her it is for Cedric. She won't mind."

Vicky thought they were spending too much time on the maid.

"What if any of the servants went out for a stroll after they began work?"

Hawk looked pained.

"Servants at Ridley Hall do not play hooky, my lady. They have their work cut out and there is hardly any time for leisure." He hesitated. "Some of them sneak in a smoke after meals but they rarely venture far from the main house."

Bess asked about the inhabitants. Surely some of them took a walk during the day?

"Lady Ridley inspects the gardens every morning," Hawk admitted. "But she does not leave our grounds." He pursed his mouth. "Sir Dorian takes a morning constitutional once in a while."

"Can you be more specific?" Vicky pressed. "How many times per week? Is it certain days of the week only?"

Hawk could not be sure. It all depended on his mood.

"It is not my place to question him." He clasped his hands together. "Sir Dorian suffers from dyspepsia. The doctor has ordered him to walk for at least an hour to aid the process of digestion." He turned toward Bess. "I think Sir Dorian tends to overindulge when he eats at Buxley Manor. On such occasions, he definitely goes for a long walk the next morning."

Vicky sneezed, startling them. She blew her nose in her handkerchief, unable to hide her irritation.

"That's neither here nor there. Next you will start on his gout."

Bess gave a loud snort while Hawk looked peeved.

"How do you know Sir Dorian is afflicted with gout, my lady?"

Vicky sneezed again. She gave Bess a helpless look.

"What we mean is, do you know for sure if Sir Dorian went for a walk on the day Sir Lawrence was killed? That is what we need to know, Hawk."

The poor butler was beginning to look a bit worse for wear. He shook his head. Bess asked him about Cedric, although she could anticipate the answer.

"And what about Cedric? Does he ever go for a walk?"

Hawk grew distressed.

"Can I order some tea for you, my lady?" he asked Bess. "Or perhaps you will stay for lunch?"

Bess ordered him to stop beating around the

bush.

"I have an idea about Cedric's lifestyle. Nothing you say will shock me, Hawk. Although I don't think he brings any of his floozies here."

The butler's eyebrows shot up.

"Master Cedric is a favourite below stairs, my lady. He's a bit on the wild side, like any gentleman of his class, but he would never …" He flushed. "He is not that sort."

Bess knew there were some things Sir Dorian would frown upon and forbid.

"Define wild."

Hawk told her Cedric came and went as he pleased, spending a lot of time in London at his bachelor pad. When he was home, he kept odd hours, sleeping long past noon, expecting trays sent to his room.

"He is rarely awake at breakfast."

"Fat chance he went for a walk that morning then," Bess murmured. "Did you explain Cedric's lifestyle to the police?"

Hawk looked scandalized.

"I would never say a word against the family."

Vicky decided to stop talking about the Ridleys and move on. Maybe Hawk would have some gossip on the guests.

"What about Sir Lawrence's nephew? Or that man from Africa?"

Hawk glanced at a clock on the wall and asked them to excuse him.

"Can we continue this some other time? It is time to inspect the dining room and get ready to serve lunch. Sir Dorian is very particular about his meals."

Bess told him it was fine. They had just wanted to invite the two guests to dinner at Buxley Manor. Hawk told them Lady Ridley had already asked him to relay the message to his guests. He had no doubt they were looking forward to the evening.

The girls thanked him and headed out. The rain had stopped but the temperature had dropped even more.

"Annie won't be pleased if you fall sick, Vicky."

Bess felt the cold seep through her gloves, turning her fingers numb as she maneuvered the car around the winding lanes. Silvery mist hung on the trees and swirled around them, disappearing in an instant. They both heaved a sigh of relief when they reached Buxley Manor. The door swung open and Barnes appeared, his stoic expression changing to concern when he took one look at Vicky.

"Lunch is in progress, ladies." He took their coats and mufflers and warned them. "Lady Clementine telephoned Ridley Hall to ask if you were coming."

The family was gathered around the table, about to embark on their meal. Annie had talked Clementine into delaying it.

"Sorry we are late, Aunt Clem," Bess apologized as she slid into her seat. "Had to drive slow because of the mist."

Clementine appeared mollified.

"Better safe than sorry, my dear," she quipped. "I am not the ogre you make me out to be."

They tucked into thick and creamy potato and leek soup. Bess was hungry and glad to be inside in the warmth. There was mousse of salmon followed by pork cutlets and a trifle with pears and apples.

"We got a brace of pheasants from Ridley Hall," Bess told them. "Courtesy Sir Dorian. I suppose the old boy expects to have them at dinner tonight."

Vicky sneezed thrice in rapid succession. All eyes in the room flew toward her.

"You are going to bed right now, young lady," Clementine ordered before Annie could say anything.

Nigel looked anxious and insisted on sending for Dr. Evans.

"Relax, Pops," Vicky groaned. "It's just a cold."

Momo and Annie sided with Clementine and dispatched Bess to accompany Vicky upstairs, promising to send their maid with a hot toddy. Vicky laughed at their concern but did not resist much.

Bess followed Vicky to her room and tucked her in bed, feeling her forehead.

"I say, old girl, you're burning up."

Vicky told her she was not worried. There were plenty of people to take care of her. They sobered as they thought about the less than perfect conditions in wartime when they had served at the front. Both had ignored their own distress many a time to get the job done.

"Let them pamper you," Bess coaxed. "Mrs. Bird will ply you with willow bark tea and broth. And her chicken soup is not to be missed."

The door opened and their maid Wilson came in, bearing a tray.

"Mrs. Bird sent this, my lady. You are to drink it hot."

Both girls dissolved into giggles.

"What mischief are you up to now, Lady Bess?" Wilson grimaced. "You make sure your sister takes care."

She left after both girls promised to follow her instructions.

"She thinks I am still seven," Bess groaned. "Say, what about that maid at Ridley Hall? She never came back."

Vicky mentioned her fiery curls.

"Must be high spirited. Wonder if she is related to the housekeeper."

Bess had thought the same because they both had Scottish names.

"She cracked her knuckles. Twice."

Vicky had noticed the same.

"That does not make her a killer, Bess. Nor does that extra finger on her left hand."

There was a knock on the door again and Dr. Evans arrived, accompanied by Annie and Clementine. He started to examine Vicky, declaring she exhibited all the symptoms of a nasty cold.

"Could be contagious," he warned. "Better stay away from your twin for a while, Lady Bess."

Chapter 10

The weather grew worse that afternoon. Rain pelted the window panes in a steady deluge, reducing the visibility to barely a few feet. Bess was at a loose end, being banished from Vicky's room. She roamed the hallways, debated telephoning her friend Pudding and finally found herself outside the library.

Polo, Nigel's brown poodle, rushed toward her as soon as she went in. She picked him up and scratched his ears, steeling herself for what she might find. Nigel and Annie sat on the sofa, side by side, holding hands.

"Are you feeling well?" he asked. "Maybe we should cancel tonight's dinner party."

Bess assured him she was hale and hearty.

"You were quite irritable as an infant." Annie

glanced at Nigel, silently waiting for him to comment. "Vicky followed your cue. She would burst into tears the moment you cried out and both would start bawling within seconds."

Bess admitted it was nice hearing something about the first year of her life. She listened to a few more anecdotes and left her parents, pleading fatigue.

"I better get a nap in before the evening."

She tossed and turned in her bed and gave up trying to sleep after an hour, deciding to check on Vicky.

"You shouldn't be here," Vicky warned her with a smile. "Sit in that chair near the window."

Bess rolled her eyes and complied.

"I wish you could be there for dinner but I don't think that is possible."

"Have you thought about what you will say to them?" Vicky sneezed. "Try to be subtle. We don't want them thinking we suspect them."

Bess admitted it would be tricky but she would manage.

"I can act like an empty headed debutante when needed."

They both laughed at the jest. Vicky advised her to just be herself.

It was almost four and they rang for tea. Vicky picked at the food, nibbling on a cucumber sandwich which she did not finish. Bess saw her stifle a yawn or two and ordered her to rest, promising to look in on her after dinner.

Drinks were being served when Bess went down at seven, dressed in her favourite black frock, aiming at looking demure. Bubbles was pretending to listen to an imposing man with sun bleached hair and eyes the colour of cornflowers. He towered over her, drinking deeply from a glass of whiskey.

"Come and visit us in the Happy Valley," he boomed. "I own one third of it, my dear. My wife and I are famous. We have hosted some members of the royal family, let me tell you. Our hospitality is second to none."

Bubbles sipped her champagne, nodding at intervals. Bess was familiar with the animated look on her face. Bubbles was bored and was looking for an excuse to get away.

"Bess, darling!" she crooned. "Come and meet Edwin from Kenya. He has such nice stories to tell."

The blue eyed man shifted his attention and gave Bess a onceover.

"I say, what a breath of fresh air."

Barnes announced dinner was served. The group began a slow exodus, Nigel and Annie taking the lead. Bess had scarcely had a chance to greet all the guests. Sir Dorian and Lady Ridley had arrived with their two guests but Cedric was missing. No doubt he had found a livelier way to spend his evening.

Bess was seated between Momo and a grey haired man about Nigel's age. She was surprised when he introduced himself as Simon Watkins. She had assumed he would be more youthful. Scruffy in appearance, he had luxuriant moustaches that reminded her of Sir Lawrence. His tawny eyes were kind, belying his relation to the pompous, fearless hunter.

"Please accept my condolences." Bess was sincere. "Nobody deserves to be killed in cold blood."

She had not liked the dead man and had been counting the days until he left the area but she kept these facts to herself.

"He was one of a kind, Uncle Lawrence." Simon Watkins shook his head. "Still cannot believe he's gone. I feel his voice ringing in my ears, you know."

Lady Ridley was deep in conversation with Annie. Clementine was paying full attention to

Edwin Brindley, all agog. Sir Dorian and Nigel were talking about cricket. Bubbles looked cross, sans a willing ear for her future plans.

Simon Watkins took a sip of the mulligatawny soup and gave an approving nod.

"Uncle Lawrence was very fond of Buxley."

Bess ate her soup, planning her next question.

"Are you fond of Africa too?"

Simon dabbed his mouth with a napkin and laughed.

"Oh no, no. I have never been out of this country. A bit timid for Uncle Lawrence, of course. Polar opposites, actually. Simon, my boy, he used to say. You need to get out and see the world. But I am a farmer at heart, happy to be around home and hearth."

He had grown up on the family estate in Kent and married the girl his parents liked. They had two boys and three girls. He had been groomed to manage the estate since Sir Lawrence had always been out of the country.

"Everyone assumed I was the heir since Uncle never married," he shared, spearing a piece of roast pheasant. "But I never allowed myself to hope. Part of me wondered if he had a native wife somewhere in Africa. Not out of the realm of possibility, you know."

With a start, Bess realized they had never considered that scenario.

A few more courses arrived and were duly appreciated. Simon kept up a steady monologue, inadvertently revealing most of the things Bess wanted to know.

"He was a generous man, generous to a fault." Simon's eyes watered. "I am glad I got to spend so much time with him."

"Did he really come to England after twenty years?"

Simon told her the family had given up all hope

of laying eyes on him again. They had been pleasantly surprised when he declared he was coming for a visit.

"I was a young chap the last time he was here and we scarcely saw each other. But I used to follow him around when I was a boy, eager to learn about all his adventures."

They had resumed that after Simon came to Ridley Hall, going on long walks on the estate, talking about future plans.

"I blame myself, Lady Bess." Simon accepted some buttered potatoes from a footman. "He should not have been alone that morning. If I had been with him, I might have helped in some way. Raised the alarm or got help." He paused, deep in thought. "Or it is possible the killer might have been discouraged by my presence."

A determined one would have sought other opportunities to get at Sir Lawrence but she agreed he might have escaped getting hurt that particular morning.

"Were you engaged otherwise that morning?" Bess cleared her throat.

Simon Watkins hung his head in shame.

"I was fast asleep! We stayed up late the previous night, savouring some of Sir Dorian's excellent whiskey. Uncle Lawrence drank on a grand scale, like everything else he did in life. He egged me on."

Simon could not match him but he had imbibed more than usual, resulting in his sleeping late the next morning. By the time he shaved and went down, Sir Lawrence was already dead.

The pudding was served, an apple charlotte with warm custard.

"You must be eager to go back to Kent. How does it feel, being a man of means?"

Simon flushed. "Times are hard, what with the aftermath of war, but we get by."

Bess did not care if she was indelicate.

"Sir Lawrence left all his wealth to you. That should make a difference. What is the first big thing you will buy? A new wardrobe for your wife and daughters, perhaps?"

Clementine caught the last bit and frowned at Bess.

"Don't be vulgar, child. I taught you better than that."

"Lady Bess is not wrong," Simon gushed. "But my wife and daughters will have to wait in line."

Bess opened her mouth to ask him to elaborate but a glare from Clementine forced her to clam up. Did Simon mean he did not have access to his inheritance? Or did he have debts that needed to be paid first? The Inspector could find out. She vowed to talk to him about it, ask him to inquire into Simon's background. He would have to give her credit for volunteering information and being upfront. Her face broke into a smile at the thought.

Annie stood up and the ladies retired to the parlour. Bubbles asked Bess to play some records but someone suggested cards. The men came in and there was a lively debate about going shooting later that week. Sir Dorian thought it would be in poor taste. Edwin Brindley's voice was louder than most.

"I am not used to sitting around twiddling my thumbs, chaps. Life goes on. How do you think we survive in the bush?"

He reminded Bess of Sir Lawrence. Had they really been friends?

She tapped on his arm and proposed a game of chess.

"Do you find that terribly boring? Must be tame for a robust man like you."

He took up the challenge.

"You need both brains and brawns to survive

in the jungle, my dear."

Bess kept a low profile, intending to let the man win. He did not disappoint, ending the game in five short moves.

"Are you sure you know the game, old girl?" he crowed.

"Oh Mr. Brindley, you are marvellous! Sir Lawrence told us you were the life of any party."

He had said no such thing but Bess believed she was not far off the mark. There was a twinkle in his eye and he was dressed in a well cut jacket, unlike Sir Lawrence who had favoured safari suits. Edwin Brindley stroked his goatee and beamed, pleased.

"My wife and I like to entertain, Lady Bess. No one throws a better party in the valley. Come and stay with us for a few months."

Bess thanked him for the invite and asked what brought him to England.

"Lawrence and I always went head to head over everything," he began. "Although now that the poor chap's not with us, I will admit he was better than me."

Bess widened her eyes, asking if he also hunted lions and elephants.

"Of course!" Edwin Brindley boasted. "And zebras, rhinos and a lot more. There is no greater sport."

A new game had begun and he took his time making his first move.

"There is a big hunting tournament coming up. It only happens once in ten years and it's a test of many faculties, endurance being the most important."

He had come to Ridley Hall to make sure Sir Lawrence intended to compete.

"There is a big prize money and a revolving trophy the winner keeps. Lawrence and I have been looking forward to competing in it for years."

Bess dropped the pretence of being ignorant at chess and killed off his knight, eliciting a loud guffaw.

"Oh ho, just as I thought. I like a good challenge, my lady. That is exactly why I was here, to coax Lawrence to go back home with me. A win means nothing without a worthy adversary."

Or he had come to Ridley Hall to dispose of the said adversary. Used to killing animals for sport, was he the kind of man who would kill a human just to win a silly tournament?

"Even though you would not have won if Sir Lawrence was alive?"

Edwin Brindley answered with a shrug, advancing his bishop to kill off a pawn.

He could have written to Sir Lawrence, Bess mused. Why had he come to Ridley Hall in person, just to extend an invitation?

Chapter 11

Bess found she had time to kill the next morning. Fortified with a substantial amount of kedgeree, she decided to visit some old friends in the neighbourhood. The day was clear but cold and the drive to Rosehill put her in a good mood. She spent the morning catching up with Mabel Carrington, talking about the Marquess who was infatuated with her. He was a far cry from the previous man she had shown an interest in.

Bess didn't need much encouragement to stay for lunch. The sky was overshadowed with a thin layer of clouds on the drive back. Fat drops of rain started pelting the ground as Bess entered the village of Buxley. She sought refuge in the Buxley Arms.

"A pot of tea please, Harvey." She greeted the proprietor and asked after his family.

"We are in for some rough weather, Lady Bess." He rubbed his elbow. "Me joints creak, you know."

Bess sat at a table by the window, tapping her foot in rhythm with the rain that beat against the panes. A Hispano Suiza screeched to a stop outside and the familiar person of DI James Gardener jumped out, making a dash for the door.

He flicked the droplets of water off his clothes as he came in and looked around, making a beeline for her.

"The place is almost empty." Bess protested, secretly happy to see him. "Aren't you on duty?"

James told her he was allowed to take a break.

Harvey arrived with the tea and spoke to the Inspector.

"The missus has saved a slice of pie for you. It will be out in a minute."

Bess poured the tea, added milk and sugar and stirred it with a vengeance.

"Woke up on the wrong side of bed?" James teased. "Where is Vicky?"

Bess nibbled at a jam biscuit and gave a shrug, avoiding a direct answer.

Harvey arrived with a steaming plate of steak pie, served with roasted carrots and rich gravy. James thanked him and dug in.

"I hope you have moved on from Cedric and found other suspects." Bess observed him over the rim of her cup. "There are at least two, in my opinion."

The Inspector encouraged her to enlighten him.

"Simon Watkins, of course!" Bess cried. "He is the heir. Gets everything now that Sir Lawrence is dead. The estate in Kent, money and who knows what in Africa."

"He seems like a hard worker." James countered. "Watkins is a solid family man with hardly any vice. You do know he has been slaving for Sir Lawrence all these years? Got a pittance for a salary, barely allowing him to clothe his family. No fripperies for them, he said."

Bess slammed her hand on the table.

"And he grew tired of playing second fiddle. The only reason he must have gone along with this arrangement was because he thought he was the heir. I bet the family assumed Sir Lawrence would be mauled by some wild animal one of these days, making life easy for them."

"Wasn't he mauled by a lion?" James inquired, pushing his empty plate away and picking up the napkin.

With a frown, Bess told him that was old news. Sir Lawrence had survived the attack, although he had lost an eye in the process, gaining fame as One Eye Watkins. But that was not relevant.

"Don't you see? Sir Lawrence had not come to England for twenty years. Then he suddenly turns up and talks of getting a bride, one who can bear him a child. That would shake up Simon Watkins."

"His future became uncertain," James acknowledged. "But that does not mean he killed his uncle."

Bess argued it gave him a strong motive.

"Many people have motives, Bess. That does not mean they act on them."

He asked if she had discovered anything about Cedric's movements that morning. So far, his answers had been vague, making them suspect him more. He was hoping the man would share the truth with Bess.

"He just laughed!" Bess fumed. "You must understand, he is a pampered, entitled brat who has never been denied anything. I don't think he realizes how serious a charge of murder is."

She thought of how Cedric's temper had flared and decided the Inspector did not need to know that. Although Bubbles was sure he would not do anything to compromise his cushy life, she did not stress he was innocent.

"Do the Ridleys back him up?"

"We don't know where he was, Bess." James admitted Cedric's whereabouts had not been established.

Bess told him there was no reason why any of the family or servants would keep a watch on Cedric all night. She remembered what Simon had said about spending time with Sir Lawrence the previous night.

"They were drinking heavily. Isn't it possible Cedric was also with them? He might have slept in too. The butler said Cedric rarely wakes up before noon anyway."

"Oh yes!" James rolled his eyes. "The lifestyle of the privileged few."

The rain had stopped and little puddles of muddy water had formed across the yard outside. Children came out of their homes and started a game, screaming with glee as they jumped in and out of the water.

A gun fired somewhere in the distance and Bess realized what she had wanted to tell the Inspector.

"Simon Watkins was emphatic Sir Lawrence never carried any guns or weapons with him on his walk."

Although James had not confirmed it, she had a hunch that Sir Lawrence had been killed by his own pistol. Vicky was sceptical, thinking the idea was a bit fantastic. So she was prepared to be brushed aside but James lapsed into silence.

"That means someone purloined his pistol beforehand."

"Aha!" Bess pounced. "That means Sir Lawrence was killed by his own pistol."

James held up his hand in defeat. It was not supposed to be public information.

"Can I trust you to keep this to yourself? I am sure you will tell Vicky but please do not let it go any further."

Bess nodded. The Nightingales would have to be told, but the Inspector did not have to know that.

"Only someone living at Ridley Hall would have access to the murder weapon." Bess frowned. "You have known that all along. That is why you suspect Cedric."

James said nothing.

"But what about the other people in the house?" Bess pushed. "Simon Watkins, that hunter fellow and the servants? Any of them could have gone to Sir Lawrence's room to steal that pistol."

She sat up as she realized something else.

"And Simon Watkins knew Sir Lawrence would be unarmed. He admitted that himself."

James sat back with his arms folded, a slow grin spreading across his face.

"Have you listened to a word I said?" Bess felt her temper rise. "This collaboration will not work if you ridicule every idea I put forth."

He placed his hand on hers and squeezed. It was the last thing she had expected.

"Scotland Yard could use a detective like you."

Bess refused to be mollified, growing more exasperated.

"I say …"

"When all this is over, will you …"

Harvey arrived with a fresh pot of tea.

"Looks like the rain's let up for a bit, Lady Bess. You better get back to the manor before it starts coming down again."

Bess had been thinking the same. She pulled her hand away from the Inspector's, feeling a bit ruffled. If he had set out to unsettle her, he had succeeded. Had Harvey noticed? She felt her cheeks flame and hoped her face would not give anything away.

Harvey saw that the sugar pot was empty and went back to get some more.

"One more thing," Bess told James. "Sir Lawrence was an excellent shot. Only a fool would confront him when he was armed."

"You have made your point."

"Well then," Bess stood up. "You can infer what you may. I am going home."

She resisted the urge to look over her shoulder and stepped out into the cold. A low drizzle began after she had entered the manor grounds. The car drove itself to the back of the manor. Bess jumped out and walked into the kitchen, looking around for Mrs. Bird.

"Wipe your feet on the mat." A familiar voice rang out. "I just cleaned that floor."

She felt herself engulfed into a tight embrace and relaxed, breathing in the comforting scent of butter and vanilla mixed with cloves. Ever since she was a child, Bess had found solace in the kitchen. The cook recognized the child was lonely and provided the warmth that was lacking in the rest of the family. They loved her, no doubt, but were not demonstrative. Starved for affection, Bess was used to heading downstairs to the kitchen whenever she was upset about something.

The kettle whistled and Mrs. Bird told her to sit while the tea steeped.

"I just had some at the Buxley Arms," Bess confessed. "But I could use one more cup. It's freezing out there."

Knowing her way around the kitchen, Bess measured some flour and began working butter into it. Making scones was her tried and tested way to cool down.

"When will it be time for mince pies?" she asked Mrs. Bird.

The cook pulled the cloth off a tray and beamed.

"I thought I would make a test batch, my lady. Try some."

Bess didn't need an invitation. She bit into one eagerly and chewed, letting the complex flavours of the dried fruit and multitude of spices roll over her tongue.

"Delicious!" she pronounced.

"Your mother loves them," Mrs. Bird told her. "This is going to be a happy Christmas, my dear. I have ordered double of everything, seeing as we might entertain more people. Lady Clem and your mother are making a guest list for the grand Christmas dinner."

Bess added some milk to the dough and kneaded it just enough, rolling it out until Mrs. Bird gave an approving nod.

"How is Vicky, do you know?"

"Dr. Evans was here. Two more days in bed and she will be fit as a fiddle." Mrs. Bird shivered as the door opened and a scullery maid entered, bringing in a freezing draft. "Frost is coming," she warned. "You stop gallivanting in that car of yours and stay in too."

Bess told her she needed to be at Ridley Hall.

"Sir Dorian actually spoke to me," she laughed.

The Buxley household was well acquainted with the cantankerous Sir Dorian. None of the servants liked the way he criticized Bess or talked down to her.

"How the mighty fall!" Mrs. Bird shook her head. "You let that be a lesson, imp." She pulled a cake out of the oven and started whisking butter. "All these recent deaths …" she paused. "Had their head in the clouds, didn't they? Even silly young Joe Cooper."

Bess used a ring to cut the scones, agreeing with Mrs. Bird.

"Sir Lawrence was especially full of himself. Never lost an opportunity to brag about his exploits."

She began brushing some butter on the rounds, thinking of Edwin Brindley.

"Are you saying that's what got him killed?"

Mrs. Bird had begun slathering the icing on the cake.

"You figure out who he offended with that pride and you will have your murderer."

Chapter 12

Bess woke up to a roaring fire the next morning. It had snowed through the night and a freeze had set in. She dragged herself to the window and took in the white vista outside. Mist swirled around the topiaries that dark morning and snow covered every inch of the grounds. There was not a soul in sight and she assumed the groundsmen were billeted at home in their cottages, unwilling to brave the chill.

She went next door to check on Vicky.

"Good morning!" She was sitting up in bed, sipping a cup of chocolate. "It's beautiful outside, isn't it?"

"You are looking a lot better."

"I'm fine. Mom likes to fuss. She insists I stay in bed for a couple more days."

Bess realized Annie had already visited Vicky that morning. She felt a stab of jealousy she tried hard to ignore.

"Mom and Pops were both here. They peeped into your room too."

Bess declared she was hungry and asked Vicky if she wanted to accompany her to the dining room, rightly guessing she would say no.

Everyone except the great aunts was seated around the table, in various stages of breakfast. The talk revolved around the snow.

"What an absolute bore!" Bubbles appeared disgruntled. "Do you think this will impede the trains?"

Bess ate her kedgeree, waiting for an uproar.

Clementine spoke first, telling Bubbles she wasn't leaving the manor.

"Must you be so disruptive? I forbid you to step out of the house, Bubbles."

"She's right," Momo endorsed. "Be a dear and stop being difficult. Let's go to the attic and look at old pictures."

Bubbles flung her napkin on the table, sprang up and declared she couldn't wait to go live in her London flat.

"I say!" Nigel cried after she left the room. "That's not cricket. What's wrong with her, Momo?"

Bess munched on a piece of toast while Annie and Clementine tried to pacify Momo who was in tears. The trio finally moved to the parlour, leaving her to drink her tea in peace.

She spent the morning curled up in the library with a book, playing fetch with Polo. Dense fog sprang up that afternoon and most of the inmates retired to their rooms after lunch. Bess gave in and took a long nap before heading to meet Vicky for tea.

Mrs. Bird kept up a constant supply of delicious soups, roasts, pies and curry for the next two days. Bess enjoyed her favourite Railway Mutton Curry, surprised to see Annie devour it. Vicky was up and about and rearing to go out.

"We are going for a drive," Bess announced at breakfast on the third morning. "Do you want to come with us?" she asked Momo and Bubbles.

Momo agreed readily when she learnt they planned to visit Ridley Hall.

"Mama sounded glum on the telephone. She needs cheering up."

A pale sun had peeped through the clouds, melting some of the snow. Bess was careful as she drove through the slush and mud. The trip took longer than usual but they finally drove through the twin posts at the entrance and started on the curvy road leading to the hall. Smoke rose through the chimney pots, a sign of life in the otherwise bleak landscape.

Hawk met them at the door, pleased to see

Momo. Lady Ridley was beside herself.

"What a nice surprise, my dear." She peered around her eldest daughter. "Your sister didn't come?"

Momo asked after Cedric.

"Your brother sticks to his habits. Will you talk to him? Your father's not getting any younger. It is high time Cedric took an interest in running the estate."

Lady Ridley called for tea.

"Vicky and I will be back shortly," Bess announced and left the room before she had to face any questions.

Vicky followed her, curious. They walked down the hall and exited into a walled garden. Bess opened a tiny gate that led outside. Snow covered every surface and it was difficult to make out a path.

"We are going for a walk, old girl."

Bess headed for the woods, trying to step around puddles of slush. Tiny streams of muddy water ran everywhere, creating a random pattern across the grounds.

Digging their hands in their coat pockets, they set a good pace, keeping their mouths closed to preserve body heat. Apart from a set of footprints coming from the opposite direction, there was not a single person in sight. The skies darkened and the woods seemed to close in on them.

Bess moved closer to Vicky and the two girls clasped hands.

"We have been through worse, sweetie." Vicky consoled.

The eerie atmosphere gave them goosebumps but they plodded on, refusing to give up.

"Whoever murdered Sir Lawrence must have taken the same route."

Vicky wasn't so sure. They would hardly notice

if they strayed from the path. She asked Bess where they were going.

"To the crime scene, of course."

"And what do you expect we will see there? Just look around, Bess. We are the only ones foolish enough to be here."

The path widened and Bess led them through a few turns to stop in a clearing.

"This is the spot, I think."

The rope marking the spot was gone.

"How can you be sure?" Vicky argued, beginning to lose her temper. "I say, Bess, this is ridiculous. We need to go back now! Right now!"

Bess admitted she did not have any firm plan in mind when they set off for the spot.

"They say the killer always returns to the scene of the crime."

Vicky told her to take a good look around them. Bess was smiling.

"I have the most marvellous idea!"

Expecting something outlandish, Vicky's eyes grew wide as she heard what Bess had in mind. The idea had merit but it was a two edged sword.

"Are you sure?" Her jaw quivered. "There is no saying how the killer will react."

"We need to shake the tree. As it is, we are not getting anywhere."

They hurried back to the house, picking up the pace, eager to leave the eerie surroundings. Lady Ridley and Momo sat in the parlour with Sir Dorian.

"Oh good, you're back." Momo sounded relieved. "Shall I ring for tea?"

Bess and Vicky stood by the fire, warming their hands and toes. Sir Dorian was grave.

"I say, girls, I know I asked for your help but you will be careful? Nigel will have my head if anything happens to you."

The tea arrived, with coffee for Vicky, sandwiches and a lemon cake. The Ridleys were talking about the special dinner they had planned in memory of Sir Lawrence. Bess thought it would be the perfect occasion to carry out their plan.

"Why don't you invite DI Gardener?" she suggested. "Cedric will be there and we can show the Inspector we are all grieving for poor Sir Lawrence."

Lady Ridley nodded. One more at the table would not make a difference.

"I think I will stay here for a day or two, Bess," Momo told them. "Will you tell Bubbles?"

"Capital, my dear. You should do it more often." Sir Dorian was pleased.

Bess knew he doted on Momo.

"Can we have a moment, Sir Dorian?" she asked. "It won't take long. We have to get back home before lunch."

They followed him to his study, encountering Cedric on the way. He was lumbering down the stairs, wearing a crumpled suit, unshaven.

"What ho, Bess darling!"

Sir Dorian quickened his step and the girls rushed after him, giving Cedric an apologetic look.

"Do you have any leads?" Sir Dorian went behind his desk and invited them to be seated.

Bess heard the hope in his voice and was sorry to disappoint.

"Actually, this is regarding a different matter, Sir Dorian. We hoped you might be of help."

He guessed they wanted to talk about Philip.

"I never suspected your father. Why do you

think I let Momo live at Buxley Manor all these years? If I had the slightest doubt about Nigel, I would have brought her back to Ridley Hall."

Bess could not hide her relief. Had they overlooked an important ally? Vicky plunged ahead with their question.

"We have been trying to construct a timeline of what happened that day. It hasn't been easy because most people don't remember. And some don't want to get involved."

"Maybe you are not asking the right questions, my dear." Sir Dorian was gentle. "That day is etched in my memory. How can I forget the day my poor young daughter became a widow?"

Bess felt encouraged. She felt a new respect for Sir Dorian. Had she been prejudiced about him all these years or was he turning over a new leaf?

"Buxley Manor was filled to the rafters for the hunt," she began. "There were plenty of houseguests and then more arrived in the morning. We are making a list of all the people that were present."

Sir Dorian agreed that would be a daunting task but the servants could help.

"Our housekeeper keeps records of these things. Have you asked Mrs. Jones if she does the same?"

"I say!" Bess admitted. "We never thought of that. What a marvellous idea, Sir Dorian."

Vicky told him they wanted to know something else.

"After a while, we realized that everyone did not go on the hunt. We need your help in determining who stayed back at the manor."

Sir Dorian began calling out one name after another.

"I did not go," he began. "There was a big dinner the previous night with all the rich, spicy dishes Buxley Manor is known for. I had a bout of dyspepsia and did not fancy a day out in the cold." He paused to think for a moment. "Nigel went, of course. With Miles and Trips Carrington, Sir Lawrence, Clive Morse and Philip."

"And who stayed back?" Vicky prodded.

"Your mother Annie, of course. And a very disgruntled Momo. She was in a delicate condition and had been advised to rest. There was a row that morning between her and Philip. She really wanted to go."

Bess checked off other names. Most of the other ladies had stayed back as usual.

"Grandma Louise and the aunts, Lady Morse, Lady Ridley, Aunt Clem …"

"Clementine did not live at Buxley Manor in those days," Sir Dorian corrected. "Beatrice, Philip's mother, was there."

A late lunch had been planned to welcome the

men back. The household was in turmoil as the servants scurried around, making sure everything was perfect.

Had they hired extra help from the village, Bess wondered. She would have to ask Barnes. She thanked Sir Dorian for his assistance.

"Frankly, my dear, I am not sure how that helps."

Vicky told him they were optimistic. It was like trying to piece together a jigsaw puzzle.

"We are determined." Bess stood up. "I am going to put an end to all those nasty rumours. They do irreparable harm."

Sir Dorian agreed with her. That is why he wanted to find out who had killed Sir Lawrence.

"If it is Cedric, so be it. The law will punish him. But I do not want a cloud of suspicion hanging over us. I have seen how it can destroy a family."

Bess almost blurted out their plan.

"I don't want to be unkind, Sir Dorian, but I don't think Cedric would exert himself enough to plan such a crime."

Sir Dorian laughed.

"For once, I am glad my son is a lazy so and so."

Chapter 13

A deep fog persisted the next two days, restricting movement. But the sun came out after that and a thaw set in, melting the snow, turning the roads into ice. Bubbles had gone to stay at Ridley Hall at Momo's urging. Clementine took to her bed with a cold so Bess and Vicky had the run of the place. They spent some time with the Nightingales one morning, bringing them up to date with what had happened in the past few days.

Annie was more talkative at meal times, regaling them with anecdotes of life in America. Bess was interested to know how she had managed as a young mother with a baby. Her admiration for her mother grew as she learned of her struggles and she had to accept Annie had a spine of steel.

The twins were happy to see Nigel and Annie

spend more and more time with each other. It was clear they were trying hard to forget the painful past and build a new life together.

Bess and Vicky were sprawled in the parlour with their feet up when Barnes came in one afternoon.

"You are wanted on the telephone, my lady," he told Bess. "Detective Inspector Gardener."

Bess rushed to her feet, scoffed at Vicky's knowing smile and went to the hall at a more sedate pace.

"Inspector! Has something happened?"

She got an earful.

"Why am I invited to this dinner at Ridley Hall?" James demanded. "I wager you had something to do with it."

"I thought you could use a good meal."

James was not convinced. "Whatever mischief

you have planned, think twice before doing it." His irritation travelled across the wires. "I am warning you, Bess. I have never met a girl with such a cavalier attitude toward her own life."

Bess simpered and asked him how many girls he had met.

Letting out an angry retort, he disconnected the line.

"But you will come?" Bess knew he wasn't at the other end.

Vicky questioned if they needed to take a step back. They could not predict the repercussions of their plan. Bess was confident it was the way to go.

Tea was more elaborate than usual on the day of the Ridley Hall dinner. Always uncertain of how they would be fed somewhere else, Mrs. Bird produced a variety of hearty sandwiches and a large sponge cake liberally layered with cream and jam. Every one other than Clementine was going, even the great aunts and

Louise.

"Will you take Cecil and Aunt Cordelia with you?" Nigel requested the girls. "Even with two motors, it is going to be a tight fit."

Bess wore a demure cream frock that was most unlike her. She did not want to get off on the wrong foot by drawing attention to her clothes. The sun had already set when they left for Ridley Hall, the orange glow at the horizon fast fading into the night. Hawk welcomed them and escorted them inside.

More than a dozen people were having drinks, noshing from trays of appetizers on a side table. Lady Ridley was apologetic.

"I am afraid you will have to make do with whatever Cook rustled up."

The London caterers the Ridleys had hired cancelled at the last moment.

"Apparently, the fog in town is terrible," she explained. "And the trains are not running on schedule."

Momo consoled her mother and Annie backed her up. The purpose of the gathering was to remember Sir Lawrence.

A few neighbours had been invited, people who had known and admired the dead man. Sir Dorian was going to buy a round of drinks for everyone in the village at the local pub in memory of his friend.

DI Gardener stood by himself, away from the clusters of guests, observing them while sipping a whiskey and soda. He tipped his head to acknowledge Bess. She excused herself and went over to greet him.

"Do you think he is in this room?"

"Cedric Ridley?" James looked around. "No, he has not made an appearance yet."

"Why can't you keep an open mind?" Bess complained. "Isn't that your job?"

Hawk entered the room and announced that dinner was served.

Bess had requested to be seated near the middle of the table so she could observe everyone. Vicky was right next to her. Momo and Bubbles were opposite. Nigel, Annie and the ladies from Buxley Manor were near the head of the table. The vicar Cecil was at the other end, close to the Inspector.

Soup was served and Bess noticed some new faces. Lady Ridley had mentioned hiring temporary staff from the village. Sir Dorian raised a toast to the dead man and the meal commenced, interspersed with toast after toast as the guests shared reminisces of Sir Lawrence Watkins. Edwin Brindley was most vocal while Simon Watkins sported a sober expression.

They ate fish and pheasant, all excellently prepared and started on the joint of beef. Bubbles whined about being stuck at the Hall. Vicky asked why she was so restless to go to London.

"You try rusticating in a little village all your life, darling! Nothing could be more terrible."

Bess knew Vicky believed Bubbles was ungrateful and she agreed. Cosseted all her life, a permanent guest at Buxley Manor, her every whim catered to, she grumbled when things did not go her way.

"I say, Bubbles, nobody was holding a gun to your head. You might have joined the land army or learned to drive."

This was the first time Bess had ever criticized Bubbles. She saw her eyes harden and wondered if she had gone too far.

Two footmen brought out a magnificent jelly, along with blackberry jam roly poly, Sir Lawrence's favourite. A maid followed with warm custard.

Bess waited until everyone at the table was served. She picked up her wine glass and tapped it with a spoon to get their attention. Out of the corner of her eye, she saw Vicky give her a reluctant nod. The Inspector swallowed a bite and gave her a warning glare.

"As you know, we are all gathered here to give Sir Lawrence a proper sendoff. He is the most fearless man I have ever come across and he always inspired me to be the same." She looked around the room, making sure she had their attention. "Vicky and I have been trying to figure out who killed One Eye Watkins." A gasp travelled across the table. "And I want you to know that we have the killer in sight."

Pandemonium erupted.

"Who is it, Bess?" Cedric asked. "Can you please tell the Inspector so the police can stop harassing me?"

Bess told them she had found some definitive evidence in the woods. She would be turning it over to the police the next day.

"By noon tomorrow, we will declare who murdered Sir Lawrence."

This was the cue for Vicky to speak up.

"She's right. We have irrefutable proof."

There were no second servings of pudding that night. Lady Ridley stood up and escorted the women to the parlour. Bess and Vicky brought up the rear. She felt a heavy hand on her arm and was pulled aside.

"What in the blazes was that, Bess?" James thundered. "I warned you."

He thought the childish prank could be dangerous. Once again, Bess had betrayed his trust and gone rogue.

"We'll be careful," Vicky promised him. "Don't you see, we had to do something to bring the killer out in the open."

"I thought you were the sensible one!" James fumed. "And what exactly is supposed to happen now?"

The twins outlined their plan. They would go

to the woods early the next morning to the spot where Sir Lawrence had been shot.

"We can hide there, lie in wait," Bess explained. "The murderer is bound to come there and the police will catch him red handed."

Vicky told him they would be safe with the Inspector and his constables to protect them. They arranged to meet at Ridley Hall after breakfast the next morning.

"You think this murderer will wait until you have eaten your kedgeree?" James ridiculed.

"I say, you don't expect me to drive in the dark on an empty stomach? 8:30 is the earliest we can manage."

The men began trickling into the parlour, eager to join the ladies. Most of them were eager to leave. Bess realized they suddenly wanted to be as far away from Ridley Hall as possible.

"At least something is happening," she whispered to Vicky.

Nigel came to round them up.

"You are not a child, Bessie. Actions have consequences. I hope you don't live to regret them."

Suitably chastised, Bess was quiet on the ride home.

"Was I foolish, Grandmother?" she asked Louise.

"We shall know soon enough." The Dowager would not say more.

Back at Buxley Manor, Bess told Barnes she wanted to be woken at seven. She also requested he pack some food so they could eat on the way to the Hall.

"That was a very brave thing you did, my lady." Barnes was already aware of what had taken place at Ridley Hall.

"The Inspector called me reckless."

She followed Vicky up the stairs and wished her goodnight. Two hours later, she was wide awake, wishing she had accepted the glass of warm milk Barnes had offered to send up. The tiny sliver of doubt in her mind would not let her rest. What if the Inspector was right and she had stirred the pot too much? She paced around the room, stopping to glance at the dark skies outside. Finally, she climbed up in the window seat and sat there, waiting for a sign of dawn.

The maid shook her awake.

"Time to rise and shine, Lady Bess." Wilson placed a mug of chocolate in her hands and began pulling clothes out of the wardrobe. "Lady Vicky woke long ago."

Rubbing her eyes, Bess hastened to get ready. Barnes stood at the bottom of the stairs, holding a basket of food. Vicky leaned against the banister, her coat buttoned up to her neck, gloves and muffler providing further protection.

"Thank Mrs. Bird for us, please." Bess slid into her coat and said goodbye.

Nigel had insisted they let the chauffer drive them to Ridley Hall that morning. The twins ignored the cold and settled into the back seat, encouraged by the clear skies and bright light, and proceeded to have a leisurely meal. Mrs. Bird had packed boiled eggs and tiny squares of buttered toast slathered with marmalade, along with slices of cake.

They barely noticed when the Rolls entered the grounds of Ridley Hall. A red Hispano Suiza was parked outside the hall, next to another official police vehicle. The Inspector stepped out when he saw them and pulled out his pocket watch.

"You are late."

Bess squared her shoulders and asked him to lead the way, longing for a cup of Darjeeling. A cold wind followed them into the woods, bringing thoughts of warm fires and hot drinks. James led the way and the constables brought up the rear.

"I did not expect you to turn up," he admitted. "It's freezing out here."

"We have been through worse," Bess quipped, always ready to remind him that she had spent the war on the front lines unlike him. "Remember that time in Lille, Vicky?"

The Inspector advised her to be quiet.

"You don't want to spook the murderer. We are here to catch him red handed, remember?"

Bess demanded if he planned to mock her for the rest of the day, drawing a laugh out of him. Vicky turned around to smile at their antics, scarcely noticing James had been leading them to the clearing where Sir Lawrence had been shot. The witty comeback she had planned froze on her lips as Bess let out a piercing scream. Vicky whirled around to see the source of her sister's terror.

The constables swept past her to assist James

who was already cradling the body hanging from the branch of a tree.

"She's gone, Sir." Constable Yates murmured. "We are too late."

Stunned and speechless, Bess and Vicky held on to each other as they stared at the wisps of red hair that had escaped from the maid's cap.

Chapter 14

Detective Inspector James Gardener sprung into action, barking orders at the constables. Bess felt a buzzing in her ears as she tried to assimilate what was going on. Everything around her seemed to happen in slow motion.

Vicky moved forward to check on the poor girl but the Inspector ordered her to stay where she was.

"I am a trained nurse," she reminded him. "Let me check her pulse or try to revive her."

His face fell.

"She's gone, Vicky. Stone cold dead. There is nothing you can do for her now."

His eyes were peeled to the ground as he walked the perimeter of the tree. A constable had been dispatched to get the doctor.

"Don't touch anything," he warned, glancing up in the trees around them, standing with his hands on his hips. "Until we know more, I am treating this as a suspicious death."

His shoulders were slumped in defeat and Bess could sense the anger simmering under the surface. This was not a man she was willing to cross. His gaze landed on her, inscrutable.

"Go back to Ridley Hall and stay there."

He ordered the other constable to escort them back to the house. Bess did not dare to protest. She let Vicky take her arm and began the trek back to the hall. Neither girl said a word, each trying to process the gruesome sight in their own minds.

Hawk took their coats at the door, commenting on their early return. Bess realized the people in the house were oblivious to the tragedy that had befallen their young maid. There was a steady hum of conversation from the parlour, interspersed with an occasional laugh or two.

Lady Ridley sat on a sofa, looking more animated than usual. The reason was clear. Momo sat next to her.

Bubbles reclined on a chaise a few feet away.

"You're back! So you finally saw some sense. What possessed you to come out in this bitter cold, Bess?"

Momo, always tuned to people's emotions, rushed to embrace Bess.

"What is it, my darling? You look like you saw a ghost."

Bess opened her mouth but not a word would emerge. Vicky spoke up, delivering the news in a toneless voice.

"There has been a death in the woods."

Lady Ridley turned white and swung a helpless gaze around the room. Vicky realized her mistake.

"It's not Sir Dorian or Cedric."

Momo was chafing her mother's wrists, telling her the family was alright.

"But it is someone from this house," Vicky sighed. "A young maid. I am not sure what her name is."

Bess found her voice.

"Something Scottish. She's the one with the red hair."

Hawk stumbled in, his eyes wide.

"My lady …" he took in the scene in the room, and went straight to a cabinet under a window.

Bess noticed there was a drinks tray with glasses. Hawk picked up a crystal decanter full of amber fluid and poured two fingers in a glass, hurrying back to offer it to Momo.

"Brandy, my lady."

Momo thanked him and held the glass to her mother's lips, murmuring soothing words to her. Hawk had returned to the table and filled more glasses. He began handing them out, starting with Bess. She accepted the drink and threw it down in one gulp, snapping awake from her daze as it burned down her throat. She had not felt a single thing since she had seen the maid hanging from the tree.

"What's happening with the tea, Hawk?" Bubbles played with a strand of her hair. "It's past eleven and I am parched. Are you planning to starve us today?"

Hawk apologized.

"We just got the news downstairs, my lady. As you can imagine, the whole place is in disarray. Two of the maids fainted and the housekeeper will not stop crying. Young Wilma was a relation, you see."

"Just do what you can." Bubbles dismissed. "Isn't it your job to whip the servants in shape? Maybe it is time you retired."

A line of sweat had appeared on Hawk's brow. Unable to hide his alarm, he apologized again and started to leave.

"That's harsh, even for you, Bubbles." Momo's eyes flashed fire. "Don't you have an ounce of compassion for a fellow human being?"

Bess sought Vicky. She wanted to get as far away from Ridley Hall as possible.

The door flung open again and Sir Dorian swept in with Cedric right behind him. For once, he was dressed in a well pressed suit and clean shaven. Bess remembered hearing about an early meeting they had with the estate manager.

"My dear!" Sir Dorian rushed to his wife, his eyes filled with worry. "How absolutely shocking! You must be distressed."

They had been closeted in his study with the manager, discussing estate business. Hawk had notified them of the incident.

"It was Wilma McLeod," Lady Ridley sobbed. "That Scottish girl with the red hair, Dorian."

"That spitfire!" Cedric exclaimed. "I say! Are they going to pin this one on me too?"

Bubbles roared with laughter, causing Sir Dorian to splutter with rage.

"The noose is tightening around your neck, little brother," she crooned. "Beware."

Bess thought it was the last straw.

"For heaven's sake, Bubbles!" she erupted. "Have you no soul?"

"What have I done?" Bubbles gave a shrug, bewildered. "Whether he has committed one murder or two, Cedric will hang."

Sir Dorian let out another string of expletives.

"When do you go to your flat in London?" he asked. "You may be my daughter, but you are not welcome here."

Finally, Bubbles sat up, placing her feet on the ground. Her eyes bore into her father's, full of loathing.

"Please, Father. All this for a mere maid."

Momo had teared up, her distress evident. Sir Dorian placed a hand on her shoulder.

"I am so glad she did not change you with her malice, my dear. Nigel is a saint and so is Clementine." He turned to Bess and Vicky. "I owe a big debt to the Gaskins family. Everyone at Buxley Manor has borne a lot because of my wayward daughter."

"But what have I said?" Bubbles cried.

Vicky explained they had found the dead girl swinging from a tree.

"How on earth am I supposed to know that?" Bubbles shrieked.

"You mean you saw that horrendous sight?" Cedric's eyes popped out of their sockets.

"Hawk didn't say anything about that."

Sir Dorian wanted to call the doctor. Vicky assured him they were fine. She gave them a brief account of how they had come across the dead body, skimming over the grisly details.

"But why would the poor girl take her own life?" Lady Ridley whimpered. "Do you think life was hard for her below stairs?"

Bess was not sure the girl's death was suicide.

Cedric had a convenient theory. The maid had murdered Sir Lawrence for some reason and had been unable to live with her guilt. She had taken the easy way out.

"Even if you are correct," Vicky spoke. "Why would the girl go back to the same spot to hang herself? She could have done it anywhere."

Bubbles declared she was trying to get attention, even in death. Everyone ignored her.

There was a knock on the door and Hawk

came in, followed by a maid pushing a tea trolley. Her face was blotchy and her eyes were red. Bess saw her hands were shaking and moved forward to help her.

Momo started to pour the tea while Bess cut slices of cake and handed them around. Cedric perched on the sofa next to his mother and expounded another theory.

"What if it was revenge?"

Bess asked him to elaborate, surprised he was volunteering anything. On most days, he was too preoccupied to participate in any conversation.

"Let us assume the girl did shoot old Sir Lawrence." He held up a hand. "Don't ask me why, just hear me out."

He had a captive audience.

"Someone saw her or figured out it was her and decided to avenge the old boy."

Bess thought the theory was outlandish enough to be true.

"But why do it there, in the woods?" Vicky questioned.

"Poetic justice!" Cedric beamed. "He killed her at the exact spot where she had shot Sir Lawrence. It all adds up."

Bess could not believe anyone had that kind of affection for Sir Lawrence Watkins. Whoever this person was, he had not only taken another life, he was willing to die himself if he was caught.

Sir Dorian had another theory.

"It is more likely she saw something she shouldn't have."

The maid was inquisitive, spotted in places she was not supposed to be. The housekeeper had reprimanded her many times, lamenting she did not know her place.

"Young Wilma figured out who shot Lawrence." He nodded, as if trying to convince himself. "She must have confronted this person."

"And she became a liability?" Momo asked in a low voice.

The murderer had silenced her before she could say anything.

Bess and Vicky both thought this theory had merit. Not to be outdone, Cedric began to imagine how it had happened.

"You set the cat among the pigeons last night, Bessie, when you declared you had identified the killer."

They had hinted about finding evidence in the woods. What's more, they had even declared their intention of going there the next morning. Inquisitive by nature, the maid Wilma had gone to the spot to look around, hoping to steal a march on them.

"You think she might have hoped for a reward?" Momo asked.

Sir Dorian thought it was possible. The maid was the kind who would do anything to gain favour.

Cedric bobbed his head vigorously, continuing with his story.

"She must have stumbled onto the killer who had also gone there, only to get rid of the evidence."

There was a confrontation, resulting in the maid's demise.

Bess thought there were a lot of holes in the theory but at least part of it must be true. They were no nearer to solving Sir Lawrence's murder. The situation had just become even more complicated.

Vicky cleared her throat, giving her a silent signal. It was time they went home.

Bess assumed Momo would want to stay on at Ridley Hall to be with her mother. But she was not surprised when Bubbles declared she was going with them.

"What's for lunch today, Bess, do you know?" she stifled a yawn and followed them down the hall and out to the waiting car.

Vicky sported a stiff expression and Bess knew the last thing her sister wanted was to spend the next hour in a closed vehicle with Bubbles.

She was about to step into the car, longing to get back to Buxley Manor when she heard a shout.

Chapter 15

James bore down on her, his face puce, his eyes drilling holes into her. He jabbed a finger at her chest as he came near.

"You! You are the one who killed her, Bess. I hope you are happy."

He turned around and stomped off without giving her a chance to say anything. Bess felt her knees turn to jelly. Her heart thudded at an alarming rate as she stared after the Inspector, trying to comprehend his words. She scarcely noticed when Bubbles tugged at her hand from inside the car and told her to get in.

The car rolled down the drive and picked up speed, leaving Ridley Hall behind.

"He's got some nerve," Bubbles spat. "That Inspector does not know his place. How dare he talk to you like that?"

Vicky was quiet in the front seat but Bess could sense her dismay. Had they caused the maid's death? What on earth had made her come up with the foolhardy plan? Scenes from the previous night's dinner flashed before her eyes. Bess felt like a spectator looking in on the scene. How great she had felt, making that outlandish statement. She had been arrogant, thinking she could singlehandedly trap the murderer. Her actions had caused a death. It did not matter if the Inspector forgave her. Bess could never forgive herself.

"Don't be too hard on yourself, my dear."

Bubbles took her hand and squeezed it, offering silent support. Her eyes were dull as she stared out of the window at the bleak landscape.

"Oh no!" Vicky turned around in the front seat, her eyes flashing fire. "We should forget about this and throw a party. Maybe we should drive straight to London and go dancing in a jazz club."

Bubbles turned ashen.

"That's not fair."

"I have never met a more self-absorbed person than you," Vicky cried. "A poor, innocent girl died and all you could think about was cake."

Bubbles opened her mouth to explain.

"That's just my way, Vicky. We have only just met. You don't really know me."

Vicky told her the little bit she knew was bad enough.

Bess stirred from her stupor.

"I say, Vicky, old thing, that's harsh. You are just lashing out at poor Bubbles." She wasn't done. "But she's not entirely wrong, Bubbles. You have been more flippant than usual lately. What's gotten into you?"

Bubbles gave a deep sigh. Bess was surprised to

see her eyes were moist.

"Darling, you know this is my way of dealing with life. Stiff upper lip and all, huh?" She saw Bess wasn't convinced. "Watching you grow up was one of the deepest pleasures of my life, Bessie. That's the reason I stayed at Buxley, to keep Momo company and make sure you had someone to spoil you, make you laugh."

"And you did," Bess affirmed.

"The war changed everything, of course." Bubbles carried on. "You came back strong and independent, just the kind of young woman I had dreamed you would become, Bessie. Then she came along." She tipped her head at Vicky. "And now Annie's back too."

Bess frowned, not sure what Bubbles was getting at.

"Aren't you happy for me?"

"Oh I am, my dear. Of course I am. But you don't need me anymore. Neither does Momo. I fear she will never blossom as long as I am around. Who knows, she might finally notice the vicar and let him court her."

Bess could not believe what she was hearing.

"Are you feeling unwanted? Nothing could be farther from the truth."

Bubbles insisted it was time she went away and built a new life for herself.

"I am not as brave as you are though. That is why I am pretending more than usual."

Vicky was not convinced.

"You mean all your nasty behaviour is just a front for your insecurity?"

Bess saw Bubbles clench her fists but her face relaxed in a smile.

"That's just it, Vicky. So will you cut me some slack, my dear girl?"

Bess felt sorry for Bubbles. She thought Sir

Dorian had gone a bit far when he rebuked her. If she was hurting, she was doing a good job of hiding it.

"I say, you are getting too maudlin, Bubbles. You don't have to go to London. Buxley Manor is your home."

They were so engrossed in the conversation, they barely noticed as the car entered the village of Buxley and drove through the manor gates. Soon, the chauffer was pulling up at the front entrance. The door opened and Barnes came out, his face a picture of concern.

Bubbles strode past him and went down the hall to the parlour. Bess waited to reassure the butler that she was fine.

"I won't ask how your morning was, my lady. We just heard the distressing news."

Vicky thanked him for taking care of them.

"Oh Barnes, it was awful!" Bess moaned. "I think I am going to have nightmares for weeks."

"The Dowager Countess is waiting for you in the west wing," he informed them. "Shall I send some tea there or would you rather have lunch?"

Bess wasn't sure.

"Better not keep Grandmother waiting."

She followed Vicky down the hall, eager to talk to the Nightingales.

"We must explain," she panted. "What if …"

Vicky didn't need her to complete the sentence.

"Can you change the past, Bess? If we are culpable, the least we can do is own up to it."

Louise sat in her favourite chair by the fireplace, dressed in dark grey, wearing a burgundy hat that matched the rubies flashing in her brooch. Hortense sat before her, dabbing her face with a lavender soaked handkerchief while her sister Perpetua stared out of the window.

"Grandmother!" Bess cried, flinging herself on a sofa. "We have just been accused of murder!"

Louise told her to dispense with the drama.

"You spend too much time with Bubbles. Start acting your age, Bess, and tell us what you mean by this vulgar display."

Vicky sat down and rephrased what Bess had said.

"She means the Inspector holds us responsible for the maid's death."

Apparently, Barnes had not informed the ladies of the latest crime at Ridley Hall. Bess and Vicky took turns narrating the tale.

A pall fell across the room.

"Every life is precious, my dear, even a servant's." Louise pinned them with her gaze.

"I was afraid something like this would happen."

The twins were aghast. Why had she not warned them before?

"You had already made your scandalous statement," Louise explained. "A bullet once fired cannot be retracted, my dears. The same it is with words."

Hortense took pity on them.

"It may have nothing to do with what you said. The girl might have died anyway."

"Spilled milk." Perpetua was concise. "Let this be a lesson."

Louise agreed with her.

"Think twice, thrice, before you make explosive statements."

Vicky asked them if they believed the girl had taken her own life.

"One of the theories is that she shot Sir Lawrence and could not live with the guilt. So she committed suicide."

All three ladies dismissed the idea.

"That would be very convenient." Louise asked if Cedric had suggested it.

Barnes came in, looking concerned, followed by a maid.

"Tea, my ladies. Lunch has been set back by thirty minutes." His eyes softened as he turned to Bess. "Mrs. Bird decided to make mutton curry at the last minute."

"Capital!" she blurted. "Would you thank her for me, please?"

Barnes and Mrs. Bird might be servants but they were also family. Bess could not imagine life without them. She wondered if anyone would grieve for the dead girl. Sir Dorian had mentioned some connection with the housekeeper.

Vicky walked to the window with her coffee, nibbling on a ginger biscuit. Bess found she was hungry and ate the ham sandwiches Barnes had supplied with the tea.

"We have to treat this like any murder, girls," Louise announced. "Start by finding out more about her background. Who was she friendly with? Who hated her and so on."

Bess reminded them there would be no help from the police.

"After today, I won't be surprised if DI Gardener gives me the cut direct."

The ladies exchanged smiles but said nothing.

"Whatever has happened to 303?" Bess asked suddenly. "He followed Sir Lawrence around like a shadow."

Vicky asked what had made her think of the dog.

"Lady Ridley told me one of their footmen is

looking after him. But he will need a home soon."

Bess assumed her friend Pudding would adopt the poor dog. She had developed a close bond with him earlier that summer.

Louise told them to stop blithering and address the matter at hand.

"Did you ascertain any facts about the girl's death?" she asked Vicky.

"No, Grandma! I barely got a minute to examine her."

"I think I am coming down with something." Louise announced with a twinkle in her eye. "Send for Dr. Evans after lunch."

Bess wanted to telephone him right away.

"Certainly not, my dear," Louise rasped. "Not until I enjoy the mutton curry."

Vicky understood her grandmother's

intentions.

"Does he know the doctor in Ridley?"

Louise gave her a knowing smile.

"There is none at present. The older one retired and his replacement did not turn up."

Bess widened her eyes as she understood what Louise was saying.

"So Dr. Evans will conduct the post mortem."

Chapter 16

Nigel went ballistic when he heard about the latest death at Ridley Hall.

"You're not going there again and that's final. I won't have anything happen to you. This is a rum business, girls. I am calling Ned at Scotland Yard. Obviously, that boy he sent is not working out."

Bess told him the Inspector would never give up.

"They call him Bulldog Gardener for a reason. I am sure he knows more about this business than he's letting on."

Bess chafed at the bit as she said this. She was longing to drive to Ridley Hall to investigate the maid's death. But Vicky asked her to see reason.

"Give him a day or two. Pops will calm down. And we need a break too. We are too close to the whole business. I fear we are being short sighted."

Bess agreed with that theory.

"Do you think the solution is obvious but we are not seeing it?"

Annie wanted to spend more time with them so she suggested a visit to the nearby town of Chipping Woodbury.

"Let me buy something for you," she urged Bess.

"I have more than I need." Bess did not want her mother's money. She had been starved of affection and a mother's love all her life and Annie could not return that. But at least she was trying. Vicky's stare reminded her she was going to make an effort and be nice so she relented. "But I suppose we can look around."

They had a leisurely breakfast, just the four of

them. Bubbles had gone back to Ridley Hall and Clementine was off doing something in the attics. Barnes came and stood before Bess, his arms folded.

"What's the matter?" she asked.

"Mrs. Bird has requested your presence in the kitchen." He cleared his throat and turned to Nigel. "You too, my lord. It is time to stir the Christmas pudding."

Bess realized she had almost forgotten the tradition.

"But it's not Sunday!" she cried.

"Nevertheless …" Barnes sighed. "Mrs. Bird says better late than never. She insists she will not proceed until you stir the pudding, my lady."

Annie squealed with excitement.

"I remember doing this when I married your father. Isn't this fun? I love traditions."

They trooped down to the kitchen behind Barnes. Bess felt a bit surreal but she realized she was happy. Mrs. Bird was beside herself when they entered the kitchen. She wiped her hands on her apron, her rosy cheeks beaming with pleasure.

"My Lord, Lady Annie …" she gave a small curtsy. "I am making thrice the number of puddings. It's going to be just like old times."

After they had each stirred the pudding and sampled the mince pies cooling on the kitchen table, Annie thanked the cook and declared they needed to get going.

"Does this mean we will have mince pies for tea every day now?" Bess asked Mrs. Bird, receiving a slap on the arm in return.

She folded the plump, homely woman in an embrace, promising to go visit her soon, rushing upstairs to catch up with the others. Nigel braved the cold and stepped out to see them off. The chauffer had brought the Rolls around and held the door open for Annie.

"Have fun, girls." Nigel waved them off. "Stay out of trouble."

It was a clear, bitterly cold day. The bright sunlight had melted any residual snow and the countryside was bleak, bare branches of trees stark against the blue sky. Annie told Vicky about a letter she had received from America.

"Your cousin plans to come here in the New Year. I think she dreams of nabbing a title for herself."

"Just like you did," Bess quipped.

Annie corrected her with a smile.

"Your father did not have a title when I fell in love with him. We planned a life in America. But fate had something else in mind."

Bess thought fate did not come into the picture but she said nothing.

"Do you remember that day? The day of the hunt?"

"In excruciating detail." Annie's face clouded. "How could I ever forget?"

The town of Chipping Woodbury wore a festive look. Red bows adorned the doors of the tiny shops and the lamp posts were wrapped in tinsel. It was a big change from the austerity of the war years. They shopped with abandon, buying gifts for different members of the family and the servants.

"I am glad we are doing this together," Bess mused, selecting a pair of leather gloves for Barnes while Vicky chose a cashmere muffler. "We can make sure we don't all buy the same thing."

An hour later, they entered the Laughing Mongrel for lunch. The proprietor Jones rushed forward to greet them, staring at Annie with awe.

"My lady, welcome! Welcome to my humble pub."

He begged them to relax and enjoy the meal.

Mugs of ale arrived, accompanied by roasted chestnuts.

Bess debated bringing up the past. She had never heard Annie's version of what happened at the hunt. Vicky guessed what she was thinking and gave her a silent nod, taking the lead.

"Do you mind if we talk about that day twenty years ago, Mom?"

Annie squared her shoulders and told them to go ahead.

"Your grandmother told me what you have set out to do. Be careful, girls. Whoever killed Philip is a threat. Your father and I want you to be safe. We are very clear about that."

"Don't you think Papa's suffered enough?" Bess forged ahead. "We have been talking to the servants and some of the guests. It seems you stayed back at the manor that morning. Was that because you were a woman?"

Annie shook her head.

"Our family has prided itself on being ahead of the times. Louise never imposed any silly restrictions on me, neither did your father." She tasted her ale and pronounced it was good. "I expected the place to be a bit behind the times, you know. But I never had any reason to complain."

Bess asked her to tell them about the day.

"You and Vicky were babes, had barely begun to stand up. I wasn't up to riding to the hounds. Nigel and I went down for breakfast. All the guests were there, of course. It was quite a big crowd. The women waved the men off for the hunt."

"Not a single woman went?" Vicky asked.

"Momo wanted to go. She and Philip had quite a spirited discussion around it but he was adamant. Momo was expecting their child and the doctor had advised rest. Riding was out of the question."

They had heard the same thing from Sir Dorian. Bess asked her to continue.

Annie told them all the women had dispersed, falling into groups according to their ages. She had accompanied Momo to her parlour in the east wing and stayed there till noon, going back later to check on the twins.

"You had a nurse, of course, but I liked to spend as much time with you as possible. Your Aunt Beatrice called it uncouth."

"I say, was she nasty to you too?" Bess exclaimed. "She had no reason to be bitter while Philip was alive."

Annie laughed. "Beatrice was always high handed."

Jones arrived with a maid carrying their food, huge platters of sausages resting on buttery potato mash, doused in rich onion gravy. He waited until Annie tasted the food, blushing when she pronounced it was the best thing she had tasted since coming back to Buxley.

Bess poured more gravy on her sausages and cut into them, eager for Annie to continue. Vicky asked the question she had been wondering about.

"What about Bubbles, Mom?"

"Right beside Momo, of course. She followed her around like a shadow in those days."

"Still does," Bess replied. "They have always been awfully close."

Annie reasoned that was the way of sisters. She had always longed for one.

Vicky asked why Bubbles had not gone on the hunt. She was an excellent rider and had many anecdotes about hunts she had been on.

"She stayed back to support Momo."

Everyone, especially Sir Dorian, was surprised because Bubbles had been excited about the hunt. She commissioned a new riding habit for the occasion and flew off the handle when

Philip forbade Momo from going.

"She can be obstinate, especially when she wants something. The two sisters are polar opposites."

"Just like us." Bess smiled at Vicky. "She looks before she leaps while I jump off a cliff without sparing a thought for the outcome."

Annie's eyes grew moist. She shook her head and told Bess she was wrong. They were two peas in a pod.

"Beautiful inside out, selfless and courageous." She dabbed her eyes with the napkin. "I am so proud of you."

Bess felt a strange feeling roll across her body, hot and cold at once. Then she realized she had goosebumps. For the first time since Annie had arrived at Buxley Manor, she felt an affinity toward her. Maybe there was hope for them.

Jones arrived with apple crumble and warm custard. They declared they were too full for pudding but ate some to appease him.

"Storm's coming up, my lady," he warned. "I hope you are going straight back to the manor."

Bess glanced out of the window and thought she saw a familiar back. The sky had darkened and the atmosphere was hazy. They said goodbye to Jones and rushed out, gasping for breath as a cold wind hit them.

Annie napped on the way back and Bess tried not to giggle.

"Our mother snores?" She laughed with Vicky. "You never told me that, old bean."

"So do you." Vicky pointed a finger at her.

"I say, I do not!"

They talked in whispers until they reached the manor, barely making it up the stairs before fat raindrops began to fall. Barnes stood at the door with an umbrella.

"Thank you, Barnes." Annie followed the girls down the hall. "You are a gem."

They made a beeline for the library where they found Nigel dozing on the sofa, Polo in his lap. The poodle jumped down when he saw them and ran around, yipping in excitement.

Nigel woke with a start, his face breaking into a wide smile as his eyes settled on them.

"My three favourite ladies! I hope you had a good time, my dears."

"The very best, Papa!" Bess plopped down on the sofa next to him. "Did you know Annie snores?"

Nigel bestowed a hot look on his wife, causing her to blush furiously. Bess and Vicky noted the exchange, suddenly eager to leave the room.

"I say, er, who wants tea?" Bess sprang up and took Vicky's hand. "Where is Barnes when you need him?"

They faced each other, clutching hands as the door closed behind them. Their eyes were filled with hope but neither dared to voice what they were thinking about.

Chapter 17

Bess stuffed another mince pie in her mouth and took a bracing sip of Darjeeling, pulling up the collar of her coat. The family was having tea on the shaded portion of the terrace at Clemetine's insistence.

"What's the bally idea, Clem?" Nigel grumbled. "I can't feel my toes."

The cold weather had cast a pall on everyone, making them snap at each other. After Nigel nitpicked over a perfectly good pork chop that afternoon, Clementine put her foot down.

"That's it. We are having tea on the terrace."

She thought they needed to get out of the house and embrace the season. A little icy breeze never hurt anyone. Big fires were lit inside and a table was set up at the edge of the room with the doors thrown open. Clementine believed the fires would provide enough warmth and the fresh air would revive tempers.

Bess was glad they were not sitting under the oak tree in the garden, the spot where the family had afternoon tea in the summer.

"Shall we go in?" Annie asked gently. "There are so many things to get done before Christmas, Clem. For instance, have you finished shopping for gifts?"

A car appeared in the distance and roared up the drive, leaving clouds of dust behind. Clementine almost dropped her tea cup, exploding with anger.

"What on earth … I hope this is not one of those questionable young men you call friends, Bess."

Nigel had been following the car's progress with his eyes.

"Hold on, Clem. That looks like Dorian's car.

Is he expected?"

The car went out of sight as the drive curved around the house and they heard it come to a screeching stop. Barnes had already left to open the door. Bubbles rushed in a few minutes later, her hair in disarray, sans coat, with a hastily buttoned cardigan. Her wild eyes landed on Bess as they rove across the assembled group. With a tiny cry, she collapsed in a chair and leaned forward, her elbows on the table.

"You must come with me, Bess. Right this instant."

Clementine thrust a cup of tea before her and ordered her to calm down.

"What's the matter, Bubbles? Looks like you are back to disrupt everything."

Bubbles gulped her tea, coughing as it went down the wrong way. Clementine thumped her on the back.

"Cedric's been charged with murder!" Bubbles could barely speak. "Mother fainted and Momo is barely holding herself together. And Cedric … Cedric is terrified they are going to take him away."

Bess sprang up and came around the table, engulfing Bubbles in her arms.

"Everything will be fine. Why don't you calm down and tell us what happened? Did Constable Yates inform Sir Dorian?"

Bubbles drank her tea at Clementine's insistence. Finally, her hands stopped shaking and her pulse returned to normal. She took a deep breath and sat up straighter.

"DI Gardener summoned him. Cedric, I mean. They found his finger prints on the murder weapon, Bess."

A sob escaped her but she controlled herself.

"Things don't look good. The Inspector says this is irrefutable proof and they are preparing a warrant for Cedric's arrest."

Nigel and Annie were worried about Sir Dorian. Clementine sat with her arms folded in her lap, a mulish expression on her face. She had often said that Cedric Ridley would amount to nothing and come to a sticky end. There was a satisfied set to her mouth, since all her predictions were about to come true.

"Let's go right now." Bess pushed her chair back and stood up.

Annie swung a pleading look toward Nigel who began to splutter.

"What? I say, what? You are not going anywhere, Bessie."

The winter sun had long deserted them, apart from a few dying rays at the horizon. Twilight offered a soft glow but darkness would descend on them soon.

Vicky stepped in before Bess could object.

"This is for murdering Sir Lawrence?" she asked Bubbles. "Just Sir Lawrence?"

Bubbles shot her a malevolent look.

"Isn't that enough?"

"What about Wilma?" Vicky stressed.

Bubbles asked if she had lost her wits.

"Can you focus on the present, please? Who on earth is Wilma?"

Bess explained Vicky was talking about the poor maid who had been found hanging in the woods.

"Her name was Wilma McLeod, old thing."

Bubbles erupted with anger. How was she supposed to know that?

"I don't keep track of all the servants my father employs, Bess. The housekeeper does that. Anyway, I don't really live at Ridley Hall."

"We know that!" Clementine muttered under her breath.

Vicky remarked how eager Cedric had been to dismiss the girl's death as suicide. Had he been involved in her death too?

"Why should Cedric care about some lowly maid?" Bubbles argued. "And what do you mean involved? Don't beat around the bush. Say what you really mean."

Vicky was not one to be intimidated easily.

"I was trying to be subtle. What do the police say? Are they going to charge Cedric for Wilma's murder too?"

Bubbles slumped in her chair again.

"Look, I don't know. Cedric did not mention it. Are you going to help him or not?"

Bess was astonished to see her burst into tears. It was so unlike the flippant, headstrong woman she knew that she was speechless.

Vicky asked Bubbles if they should call Dr. Evans. "He can give you something for your hysteria."

It was the wrong thing to say. Bess tried to diffuse the situation.

"I say, Bubbles. I don't get it. The other day at Ridley Hall, you seemed convinced that Cedric was guilty. You even goaded him about it. What's come over you now?"

Bubbles confessed she was just making small talk.

"The whole idea was preposterous. You know me, Bess. I like to confront any problems head on. In my opinion, Sir Lawrence was asking for it. He's always been too pompous for his own good."

Vicky told her she was not helping anyone by making such statements. This prompted Bubbles to launch into another tirade against the unfairness of the situation.

Annie interrupted them.

"Will you all take a breath and think for a minute?"

Bess and Vicky stopped talking immediately and waited for her to continue.

"What about the fingerprints they found on the weapon?" Annie posed. "Does Cedric have any explanation for that?"

Bubbles deflated, admitting she had overlooked that.

"I came here the moment I heard the terrible news," she cried. "You make a valid point, Annie."

Bess told her all was not lost yet. "Don't lose hope, old girl. There might be a simple explanation for the prints."

Bubbles grasped the tenuous lifeline Bess offered.

"Sir Lawrence liked to boast about everything. He was a horrible braggart. What if he showed off his pistols to the men? Cedric might have handled it and left his fingerprints on them."

Nigel agreed with her. "That's a brilliant idea, Bubbles, and entirely possible."

Barnes had lit the lamps while they were engrossed in the discussion. Darkness had descended over the grounds and it was pitch dark. The fires in the room were dying and Clementine proposed they went inside.

"I can barely feel my feet."

There were cries of anguish as frozen toes and limbs came to life. Bubbles led the party to the drawing room and asked Nigel for brandy.

"Just two fingers, please, and we can be on our way."

"Nonsense!" Nigel cried. "I don't want my girls driving in the dark in this bad weather."

Bubbles gave a shrug, declaring she would go back on her own. Her family was depending on her and she could not let them down.

"I will telephone the Hall and talk to Dorian," Clementine announced. "Nigel is right, Bubbles. You can spend the night here."

Bess approved of the idea. It would give her and Vicky some time to come up with a plan of action.

"DI Gardener is a tough cookie," Vicky added. "It will be hard to convince him to see things our way." She shot a glance at Bess. "That is provided he gives us an audience."

Bess admitted they were persona non grata as far as the Inspector was concerned. She was afraid they had lost his trust.

Clementine pointed out it was time to dress for dinner. They were not expecting any guests, other than the vicar and his mother.

"It's just us tonight, but don't be late," she

warned. "We are having leg of lamb with turnip mash, game pie, salmon croquettes and bread and butter pudding."

Bubbles had no defence against such a fine spread.

"You do think Cedric will be fine?" she asked Bess. "I am counting on you, my dear."

Bess promised her she would spare no effort in proving Cedric's innocence. He may be a bit irresponsible but she believed there wasn't an ounce of evil in him.

"Two back to back murders in the same house don't look good. The police need to show they are doing something."

They parted at the landing, Bubbles going to the east wing, Vicky and Bess heading to their rooms.

"Don't make any false promises, Bess. What if Cedric is the actual killer? Are you going to shield him from the police?"

Bess told her to stop worrying.

"Of course not! Bubbles knows I will never lie for anyone."

"Why are you so sure about Cedric?" Vicky quizzed.

"Because, old bean, he has no motive."

Chapter 18

Vicky and Bess wracked their brains that night, trying to come up with valid arguments they could offer the Inspector. But the evidence of the fingerprints was something they could not refute. Finally, when a clock in the hall below struck midnight, they decided to call it quits.

"Maybe tomorrow will bring some new inspiration."

Bess bid Vicky goodnight and went to her room.

She woke early and dressed in record speed before going down for breakfast. Vicky was already there, buttering her toast.

"I thought we might get an early start."

Bess nodded her assent and picked up a piece

of toast. There was no kedgeree on the sideboard. A footman arrived with a fresh pot of tea for her. Barnes entered, holding a platter of kedgeree.

"Good morning, ladies. I thought you might want to get a head start."

"Oh Barnes, you are a dear."

Bess thanked him and loaded her plate, wolfing down big mouthfuls between cups of tea. Vicky told her to slow down, trying hard not to smile.

Bubbles had not made an appearance by the time they finished.

"We can start without her," Bess declared. "We will take our motor so we can get back when we want."

Nigel entered, followed by Annie and Clementine. All of them warned the girls to watch their back and be careful.

"Must you go?" Clementine complained. "Let the police handle this, girls. I think we have done enough for the Ridleys."

Bess told her to stop worrying. She had given her word to Sir Dorian and she could not renege now.

Dark clouds covered the sky and a mist hung in the air, making visibility difficult. Bess drove carefully with a steady foot on the accelerator, thinking the world around her looked as bleak as she felt. Neither of them spoke much on the way over, Bess claiming her mind was numb after thinking over the same things again and again.

Ridley Hall appeared in the distance and they braced themselves to face Sir Dorian. Hawk met them at the door and led them to a small dining room where the family was at breakfast.

Bess noticed the look of relief that flashed across Sir Dorian's face as they entered and she felt the weight of his expectations on her shoulders.

"Good morning." She began tentatively. "All is not lost yet, Sir Dorian. Remember, a man is innocent until proven guilty."

Vicky rushed to Lady Ridley's side and took her hand, trying to comfort her.

Momo came in, glad to see them.

"It's all up to you now, Bess."

"I say …" Bess was uncomfortable. "I am not a miracle worker."

Cedric was nowhere to be seen and Bess assumed he was still in bed.

"Our life is about to turn upside down and does that boy care?" Sir Dorian growled. "I find it hard to believe he is my son."

Lady Ridley whimpered, ready to burst into tears.

"Part of me wants to do the right thing," Sir Dorian railed. "I have never shirked from my duty, girls. I made the tough decisions but I never strayed from the path, always chose right over wrong. If Cedric shot Lawrence, he should hang."

Momo was the one who gasped this time. Bess was taken aback by how forthright Sir Dorian was. Any doubts she may have had about him trying to fudge evidence or bribe servants evaporated.

"It may not come to that." She soothed.

"But he's my son." Sir Dorian gulped. "No father wishes to outlive his offspring."

Bess told him to calm down and keep his chin up.

"You need to be strong for Lady Ridley and for Cedric too." Vicky was firm. "I never thought you were one to fall apart."

Her gentle tone must have made an impact because Sir Dorian sat up straighter and clenched his jaw, giving them a nod.

"We are going to do everything we can to prove Cedric's innocence," Bess assured him. "Now tell me, how on earth did his fingerprints get on that pistol?"

Sir Dorian turned red, something he did often.

"The blasted fool has no memory of handling that pistol."

Bess decided they needed to talk to the servants. She looked around and saw Hawk standing by the wall, staring straight ahead. No doubt he had been following their conversation.

"We can begin with you, Hawk. Let's go to your office and let the family continue their breakfast."

She had no intention of questioning him in front of everyone.

Vicky patted Lady Ridley's hand and they followed Hawk out of the room, eventually going downstairs through the back stairs to the butler's office.

"It is a sad turn of events, my lady." Hawk was grave.

Bess did not mince her words.

"Spill the beans, Hawk. Tell us everything you know about that bally pistol."

He seemed to hesitate before apologizing in advance.

"I do not mean to overstep, my lady."

Bess told him to be honest and upfront without worrying about anything.

"Upstairs, downstairs – all that doesn't matter, Hawk. This is murder we are talking about. Cedric's life is on the line here."

Hawk rushed to assure them Cedric was a good person.

"That Sir Lawrence, he had a certain personality, my lady."

"You mean he was an obnoxious, domineering braggart who liked to blow his own horn. We know that."

Vicky assured him they were well aware of Sir Lawrence's personality.

"Those pistols were his pride and joy. They were specially made for him, with ivory handles. The ivory came from elephants he had killed, you see?"

Bess could imagine One Eye Watkins taking pride in something macabre like that.

"Ghastly," Vicky muttered.

"He brought them out every chance he got," Hawk continued. "Especially when the men sat over their brandy or when there was some new male guest who had not seen them before."

"I bet he had a tall story about how he had hunted that elephant." Bess gave a snort. "Typical Sir Lawrence!"

Hawk told them Sir Lawrence insisted that everyone hold the pistol and see how perfect it was.

"One of a kind, he called them. Said whoever took a bullet from them would be one lucky bounder."

Bess realized the man had dug his own grave by making outrageous statements like that. No doubt he had sown the idea in his killer's mind.

Vicky tapped her arm and pointed out an important fact.

"In that case, the police must have found many other prints on the gun, not just Cedric's."

Bess sprang up from her chair, her eyes shining with excitement.

"I say! That's brilliant, Vicky. Let's call that crabby Inspector right now!"

Hawk gave a slight cough, seeking their attention.

"There is more, my lady. The pistols were cleaned twice a week."

Bess started figuring out what that meant. If Sir Lawrence had not shown the pistols to anyone since the last time they were cleaned, there would be no prints on them.

"The only fingerprints on the pistol would belong to the killer." Vicky summed up her line of thought. "This does not look good, Bess."

There was a nagging thought at the back of Bess's mind.

"We are forgetting something." She scratched a spot above her eyebrow, furious. "What is it, Vicky? It has to be about the pistols."

Hawk was mute as Bess tried to pace in the tiny room.

"Is it something about the path Sir Lawrence took?" Vicky asked. "Simon Watkins said …"

"Simon Watkins!" Bess cried. "What did he tell

us? He said Sir Lawrence did not carry any guns or weapons with him when he went for a walk."

"I don't follow." Vicky frowned.

"So how did this bally murderer put his hands on that pistol? I say, are the police really sure Sir Lawrence was shot with that same pistol?"

Vicky told her to cool down. The police would be sure about the murder weapon. It had been found in the woods, a short distance from Sir Lawrence. And they must have some way to establish what kind of gun killed him.

Hawk came to their rescue again. Sir Lawrence kept the pistols in his room, in a drawer in his wardrobe.

"Neither his room nor the wardrobe were ever locked, my lady. Anyone in the house might have entered and taken the pistols."

"Anyone including Cedric?" Bess felt deflated. "That would have worked in his favour, if only his prints had not been found on the gun."

Vicky wondered if Sir Lawrence had a valet. Hawk told them he had not brought one with him. Sir Dorian had offered the use of his own man but had been politely turned down.

"I bet he gave some lofty explanation about being used to roughing it in Africa," Bess chuckled. "Which of the servants might go to his room then?"

Hawk admitted he had been there on occasion when Sir Lawrence summoned him. The man had never taken ill and detested eating in his room so there had been no reason to send a footman with trays of food. Only the maids went in to lay the fire or clean the room.

"He liked to have a fire inspite of the central heating," Hawk told them. "Said he was used to a warmer climate."

Bess remembered the man had always been well bundled up. He must have felt the cold, after being away from England for twenty years.

"And who went in there to clean up, Hawk?" Vicky burst out.

Hawk told them he would need to talk to the housekeeper for confirmation but he was almost certain the same girl took care of all the guest rooms.

"Wilma McLeod, my lady."

Chapter 19

Vicky suggested a walk to clear their heads and Bess agreed. There was a lot of extraneous information floating around and she felt they needed to get rid of the chaff.

The cold air made her gasp at first. Bess took deep breaths, taking in the smell of pine mingled with smoke from burning leaves coming from a corner of the garden beyond a hedge. Rays of pale sunlight dappled the ground before them, adding a bit of warmth.

"We are in over our heads, Bess."

"How about meeting Grandmother and the aunts today, old girl?"

Vicky admitted she missed spending time with them. She had come to Buxley Manor hoping to meet her father but had discovered a whole new family instead.

They followed a meandering path, neither paying attention to where they were going. After a while, they realized they had entered the woods.

"Things don't look good for Cedric," Bess frowned. "We will have to convince the Inspector to consider other suspects."

Vicky thought they must have already done that. Clearly, they had not found anything incriminating.

"Nothing as bad as what they have against Cedric," she pointed out. "What's next, Bess. Shouldn't you be honest with the Ridleys? Why give them false hope."

Bess leaned against the bough of a dead tree and paused to catch her breath.

"We need to do two things, Vicky. First prove that just having the prints on the pistol does not make Cedric guilty."

"And come up with other viable suspects," Vicky summed up, always in tune with Bess. "Where do we begin?"

They walked deeper into the woods, noting how lonely the place was. Bess remarked how they had not come across anyone, wondering which path the servants coming to the hall from the village took.

"They must have come to work long ago," Vicky reasoned. "And there must be several paths through the woods. I think these paths form a criss cross pattern of sorts, Bess. A person may not even take the same path every day."

"I say, does this mean we have been going around in circles?"

Vicky pointed to plumes of smoke rising in the distance.

"Those are the Ridley Hall chimneys. As long as we walk back in that direction, we should be okay."

Bess wasn't taking any chances. She thought it was time they went back.

"Let's think about motives. Cedric had none."

Vicky reminded her about the poor opinion Sir Lawrence had about Cedric. Bess brushed it off.

"Young men like Cedric are thick skinned. Their primary goal in life is to eat, drink and be merry. I doubt he would pay attention to an old fogey like Sir Lawrence."

"He would if the money well dried up," Vicky argued.

Bess thought Cedric would borrow from friends or run up debts in town before he thought of killing anyone.

"The main point being, there is not a single coherent thought in his mind. Men like Cedric don't think, Vicky."

She thought they should follow the money trail.

Simon Watkins stood to gain a lot since he was heir to everything Sir Lawrence owned.

"He might appear warm and friendly but I am sure he has not been upfront with us."

She had asked the Inspector to check Simon's background but had no idea what he had found.

"If only he was talking to us!" she sighed. "You think he would tell us if there was anything not right with Simon Watkins?"

Vicky believed they could not completely dismiss him as a suspect.

"He went on those walks with his uncle so he must know the routes Sir Lawrence took. And he knew the poor man was unarmed."

Bess moved on to Edwin Brindley, the man from Africa.

"We know nothing about him."

"I am not convinced he is honest."

"Who crosses a continent to extend an invitation? He could very well have sent a telegram or a letter. Or telephoned."

Vicky thought Sir Dorian might know him well since he had let the man stay in his home.

"That means nothing, old bean." Bess gave a shrug. "That's the way of things. Even if someone is a friend of a friend, we give them a meal and a room. I could not count the number of such remote acquaintances who have spent the night at Buxley Manor, partaken of our hospitality."

Vicky scrunched up her nose.

"Aren't you people supposed to be uptight?"

Bess took umbrage at that.

"We both come from the same stock, you silly girl."

"Yes, but I am an American and always will be."

The Hall was in sight and they saw Sir Dorian's car in the distance. It came to a stop before the entrance and Bubbles got out. The front door opened and Hawk came out, greeting her with a bow.

"I say, she's taken her own good time, hasn't she?"

Vicky was not surprised. She had never seen Bubbles exert herself for the sake of another. It was a miracle Bess had turned out to be so kind hearted, considering how much she looked up to the woman.

Tea was being served in the drawing room. Cedric had made an appearance, sitting beside Lady Ridley with one leg folded over the other, arms behind his head, the picture of nonchalance.

"What ho!" Bess called out. "I trust you slept well?"

"Do I detect something caustic in your tone, young Bess?" He was unaffected by the sarcasm. "Have a biscuit."

Lady Ridley ordered coffee for Vicky and told Momo to pour a cup of tea for Bess. There was a platter of sandwiches and some crumbly cake on offer.

Vicky took a cucumber sandwich and asked about Sir Dorian.

"Hiding in the study," Bubbles smirked. "He can't stand the sight of his own son."

If she had wanted to get a rise out of Cedric, she did not succeed.

Bess sipped her tea and nibbled on some cake, glad to be in the warm room. Vicky nodded at her after she finished her coffee and they both stood up.

"We need a word with Sir Dorian," Bess informed the company. "Toodles."

Hawk materialized and led the way to the study. He knocked once and announced them, closing the door after them.

"Good morning, my dears." There was an expectant look in his eyes. "Have you found something?"

Bess felt like a heel as she shook her head and apologized.

"We just had a few questions."

"What do you know about Edwin Brindley?" Vicky began. "Did he really come here to invite Sir Lawrence for a hunting contest?"

Bess voiced her suspicion. "Seems farfetched. What?"

Sir Dorian seemed amused.

"You think old Edwin shot Lawrence? Where on earth did you get the idea?"

Bess explained what they were thinking. They

needed to provide the police with other strong suspects to get them off Cedric's back. Edwin Brindley was the obvious choice. Who would believe he came to England just to extend an invitation?

"Something about him doesn't ring true."

"You are barking up the wrong tree." Sir Dorian told Bess to stop moving and take a seat. "He's a pukka gentleman. Lawrence had tremendous respect for him and so do I."

Sir Dorian told them Sir Lawrence and Edwin Brindley were two of a kind. Although Edwin was somewhat younger, they saw eye to eye with each other on everything.

"Edwin first came to Ridley Hall several years ago. Lawrence brought him. They were both eager to explore Africa and make something of themselves. Edwin is highly esteemed in Kenya. He's one of the richest men over there."

"So money could not have been his motive?"

Vicky quizzed.

Sir Dorian laughed heartily.

"My dear, his estate is worth ten times that of Lawrence's."

Bess commented on Sir Dorian's generosity, inviting a stranger into his home.

"But we have known each other for yonks," Sir Dorian protested. "Edwin visits us every time he is in England."

Unlike Sir Lawrence who had stayed away for twenty years, Edwin Brindley had made frequent trips back home. He advised them to speak to the man again.

"He's the most forthright man I know. I am sure Edwin will answer all your question, girls."

There was a loud banging in the distance, followed by the clomping of several boot clad feet. The study door opened and Hawk peeped in.

"Detective Inspector …"

DI Gardener entered before Hawk had finished announcing him, accompanied by Constable Yates. He must have brought more men with him because Bess could hear some angry exclamations in the distance.

"We have a warrant to search these premises, Sir Dorian. Any resistance will not work in your favour."

"I would never come in your way. Do what you will, Inspector."

James sat down, directing the constable to keep an eye on the group in the drawing room. Bess was itching to call his bluff but Vicky quelled her with a warning look. Ten minutes later, a constable who was not familiar to them rushed in, brandishing a piece of rope.

"We found this in Mr. Ridley's room, Sir."

Cedric was summoned. His veneer had finally cracked and he was looking flustered. Bess felt sorry for him.

"Does this rope belong to you?" The DI asked Cedric.

"I say, er, yes. Yes it does."

"May I ask what you needed it for?"

Cedric told them he had taken up mountaineering as a hobby. It had all begun as a lark at his club but he took a genuine liking to it.

"I was born with a heart defect, you know," he explained. "Never played cricket and stayed at home when all the fellows I knew went off to war."

Bess found it necessary to say something.

"DI Gardener did not fight in the war either, Cedric. As far as I know, there is nothing wrong with his health."

James flashed her a sardonic grin, urging Cedric

to continue.

"Well, I climbed a small hill with the chaps earlier this summer, in the Lake District. I felt fine so I saw a doctor in Harley Street. He says there is nothing wrong with the old ticker. Isn't that marvellous?"

Sir Dorian wanted to know the point of the story.

"Cedric takes up a new hobby every few months. What of it?"

The Inspector asked about the rope in Cedric's room.

"I was practicing knots. Need to be fit before I attempt climbing the Alps next summer."

He struggled with them, having fat fingers.

"That's not against the law, is it, old chap?"

The Inspector congratulated him on his lofty goal.

"The only problem, Mr. Cedric, is this is the exact rope that was used to hang Wilma McLeod."

Cedric turned white. Sir Dorian closed his eyes and leaned back in his chair, looking like a man condemned.

"I say …" Bess cried. "How can you be sure of that? There must be several lengths of it lying around the estate."

"You are right." DI Gardener leapt to his feet. "I pride myself on being thorough."

She knew what he was leaving unsaid. The police would prove the two ropes were the same.

"Here is what I think," he told them. "The maid witnessed Sir Lawrence's murder or found some evidence linking Mr. Cedric to it. So he had to silence her."

"Good God, man!" Cedric exclaimed. "You are mad!"

The Inspector promised he would return with a warrant for Cedric's arrest. He spun on his toes and stomped out, followed by the constables.

Cedric wrung a hand through his hair, looking like a cornered animal. Bess realized he was now accused of murdering two people.

"That poor girl," Sir Dorian murmured, his eyes red. A tear trickled down his cheek and he looked like a man who had lost everything in the fraction of a second. "Do you realize what you have done, Cedric?"

Chapter 20

Bess and Vicky were having tea with the aunts and the Dowager Countess in the west wing of Buxley Manor.

"Considering the events of yesterday, I thought it was time the Nightingales regrouped," Bess explained. "Sorry you had to come here on such short notice, Grandmother."

Louise brushed off her concerns. The Dower House was barely a quarter of a mile away from the manor and it was no trouble to telephone and ask Barnes to send the chauffer to pick her up.

"We did wonder how you two were getting on."

Hortense fanned herself with a handkerchief. Her cheeks were red with the heat from the roaring fire. It was a marked contrast from the blistering wind moaning outside the windows.

Bess and Vicky gave them a brief account of what had happened. Everyone agreed things looked bad for Cedric.

"He's being framed," Louise declared.

"Framed." Perpetua agreed with her. "Scapegoat."

Hortense thought the killer must know Cedric well and had assumed the indolent young man would not do much to defend himself.

"I say, that's ridiculous." Bess disagreed. "Cedric didn't ask for this but what can he do?"

The ladies asked the twins if they had a plan.

"What is your next step going to be?" Louise asked. "It's time you gave it some thought before haring off in different directions."

Bess admitted she was out of ideas.

"Sir Dorian thinks we can work miracles, Grandmother. And looks like we are going to disappoint him. It's a terrible thought."

Barnes came in and cleared his throat. Louise presumed he had come to check on them.

"Another pot of tea, please, Barnes."

He bowed and promised to send one up right away.

"Lady Ridley has arrived," he announced. "She is requesting to meet Lady Bess and Lady Vicky."

Louise and Hortense glanced at each other and nodded. Bess offered to go down and escort her to the west wing.

"I will get some more refreshments, my lady," Barnes announced.

Lady Ridley looked worse than she had two

days ago. She had lost weight and looked pale with scarcely any colour in her cheeks.

"This is a terrible time for us, my lady." She sat on a sofa facing Louise. "Dorian hasn't left his study and refuses to touch his food."

"You have to be strong for him." Louise was firm. "We are going to try our best to save Cedric."

Lady Ridley could not hold back her tears. The tea arrived with a platter of sandwiches and mince pies. Bess poured a cup and added plenty of sugar on Louise's instructions and handed it to the poor woman.

"Do have a sandwich, Lady Ridley." Vicky coaxed her to eat something.

Bess offered the mince pies, eating two herself, keeping up with some inane chatter. Lady Ridley gulped her tea and nibbled on some food, discovering she had an appetite. She finally calmed down.

"Why did you trouble yourself, my lady?" Bess asked. "If you had just left a message via the telephone, Vicky and I would have come over to meet you."

Lady Ridley had wanted to get away.

"Momo is smothering me with her concern while Bubbles pains me with her lack of it. I am so glad I came here, my dear."

The police were excited about the piece of rope they had found in Cedric's room but she was not convinced.

"It's like a smoke screen. Some evil man is trying to frame the poor boy."

Just like the prints on the pistol, the piece of rope was another nail in his coffin. Cedric had been bragging about his latest hobby, declaring his intentions to climb the Alps next summer.

"Nothing is hidden from the servants," she sighed. "I have no doubt this latest obsession has caused plenty of comment downstairs."

She told them Cedric found it hard to knot the rope and had been working on developing the skill for the past few months. He was a good sport about it, telling one and all about his shortcoming in a self-deprecating manner that drew plenty of laughs.

"You think one of the servants is mixed up in this?" Vicky mused.

"Either that or they must have said something in the presence of the villain." Lady Ridley gave a shrug. "I should not say this, being a mother, but I am afraid my Cedric is a bit lacking in brains."

Louise stifled a laugh, clearing her throat.

"Last I heard, that was not a crime."

Bess had been deep in thought while Lady Ridley shared her woes. Louise asked her opinion.

"The rope is relevant only if Cedric killed Sir Lawrence." She waited for the others to catch on. "But if he has no connection to the first crime, he had no reason to kill Wilma McLeod. There is no motive."

It was possible that the maid's death had nothing to do with Sir Lawrence. In that case, Cedric's innocence in the first crime would absolve him of the second. But she did not mention that.

Vicky thought they needed to consider that Wilma McLeod might have shot Sir Lawrence. She had been in the dining room when Bess talked about having evidence of the crime. Afraid of being unmasked, Wilma had gone to the spot where Sir Lawrence had died, looking for anything she might have left behind.

"She went there to search for something that might incriminate her."

Hortense dipped her handkerchief in a basin of lavender water, shaking her head.

"Are you saying she was so consumed by guilt, she took her own life?"

"That, or she was afraid of facing the consequences," Louise offered. "She might have taken the rope from Cedric's room."

Bess approved of the theory. Wilma must have known where Cedric kept a length of rope since she cleaned the rooms.

Vicky did not believe her. That would mean Wilma had gone to the spot where Sir Lawrence died with the purpose of taking her life.

"It all sounds too dramatic. Do you remember how flustered she was when she dropped the coal scuttle in Hawk's room, Bess? No, that girl was afraid of her shadow. If she wanted to take her own life, she would have done something easy, like eat a poisonous herb for instance."

The ladies grew quiet once they realized they were getting nowhere.

"Lunch," Perpetua announced. "Find out more about the girl."

As if on cue, Barnes arrived to inform them that lunch was being served in the dining room. Louise insisted Lady Ridley stay to partake of the meal.

"Go to Ridley this afternoon," she told Bess and Vicky. "Try the ale in the local pub." She gave them a broad wink.

They headed to the dining room at a stately pace, looking forward to some respite. Clementine had learned of Lady Ridley's arrival and had asked Mrs. Bird to rustle up one of her favourites.

Bess and Vicky ate quickly and set out for the village of Ridley. Their first stop was The Crown, the local pub. They chatted up the landlord, praised the mulled wine he served them and tasted the spiced biscuits his wife offered.

"That poor girl." Bess leaned forward on her stool, speaking in a hushed tone. "I don't suppose you knew her?"

The couple caught on at once and there was no need to specify who they were talking about. Orphaned at an early age, Wilma had found a home with some relations until she arrived at Ridley.

"Spoke her mind, she did," the wife confided. "But there weren't a bit of guile in her."

"Skittish as a kitten," the man reported. "Afraid of her own shadow."

They needed no prompting to reveal where the girl had lived. After offering fulsome praise, Bess and Vicky walked out of the pub, eager to learn more.

They crossed the village green and headed toward a cluster of cottages situated behind the local church. Set on a rise near a gushing stream, they offered a nice view of rolling greens merging into a row of elms. Bess pointed at a rough path that disappeared into the woods, guessing it eventually led to Ridley Hall.

"This is the route she must have taken," Vicky mused.

A thin line of smoke rose from the chimney of the largest cottage. Bess knocked on the door, hoping they would be welcome. A young woman who was about their age answered, a snotty child on her hip.

"Did Wilma live here?"

The woman pointed at a cottage two doors down, openly curious.

"She was a good girl, no matter what they are saying at the hall." She shifted the child to her other hip.

Bess assured her she only wanted to help.

"I am going to find out who hurt her. Can you tell me anything about the last few days of her life?"

The woman admitted she hadn't known her very well.

"She was worried about her job at the hall. That's what Edna told me."

Edna was the girl Wilma had shared a room with. She was visiting her sister in a neighbouring village.

"And when will Edna come back?" Vicky asked. "Do you know?"

The child began bawling, prompting the young mother to lift him in her arms and coo at him. She answered them with a shrug and went inside. Bess and Vicky realized they would not get any more out of her.

They walked back to the car, mulling over the latest piece of information.

"Nobody mentioned Wilma was going to be let go." Vicky quirked an eyebrow at Bess. "The housekeeper must have looked out for her."

"But Wilma might have believed that, my dear. What if Cedric threatened her?"

Vicky pursed her lips, trying to visualize what might have happened.

"You mean she helped Cedric in acquiring the pistol? Cedric must have warned her to stay quiet if she wanted to keep her job."

Bess expanded on the theory. Already under duress, Wilma had been terrified when the twins declared they were going to unmask the murderer. She might have gone to Cedric and urged him to come clean. He realized she was going to be a stone around his neck and decided to silence her.

Vicky stared at her, eyes wide. They had stopped by the side of the village pond, engrossed in their conversation. A mallard glided to a stop near them and let out a huge quack, startling them.

"What a load of crap!"

Bess defended herself.

"I say, no need to be so beastly about it, old

girl. It could have happened like that."

Vicky shook her head, telling Bess it all defied belief.

"Did Cedric even know the girl? Based on what I have heard, he spends most of his time in the city."

"There's an easy way to find out."

They reached the car and drove to Ridley Hall. Hawk was at the door, looking nonplussed.

"I believe Lady Ridley has gone to Buxley Manor to meet you."

"We are here to ask you something," Bess replied.

He led them to his office and offered tea. Bess thanked him and proceeded with her questions. Hawk could not have faked his surprise.

"Wilma was new, my lady. Mrs. Macdonald was hoping to train her to be a parlour maid and then the housekeeper before she retired."

"So there was no problem with her work?" Vicky asked.

Hawk admitted he had found the girl outspoken, but she was young. Mrs. Macdonald was sure the girl would learn to curb her impulsiveness with time.

"And Cedric?" Bess rushed ahead. "Did he often complain about her?"

Hawk allowed himself a smile.

"I doubt Master Cedric knew who she was. He rarely pays attention to the servants."

Vicky asked if he was sure. Hawk told them he was ready to stake his pension on it. Cedric Ridley had never exchanged a single word with Wilma McLeod.

Chapter 21

Another meeting of the Nightingales was in full swing. It was a bitterly cold December day. Bess and Vicky had spent the morning in Chipping Woodbury with Annie and Nigel, doing more Christmas shopping.

Annie insisted on visiting the jeweller again. The necklaces she had commissioned for the girls were ready. Bess stared at the diamonds and emeralds glittering under the bright lamp, awed by her mother's generosity.

"This is too extravagant, Annie. I cannot accept this."

"It's a mother's prerogative, my darling." Annie smiled in dismissal. "You already have the Maharajah of Burma's ruby necklace but it is to be shared between you and Vicky. I think the emeralds go really well with your eyes."

"But …"

Bess had noticed the jeweller's assistant was lapping it all up, no doubt eager to gossip about them with his friends. She gave a slight shrug and thanked Annie, deciding to talk to Nigel about it.

Annie addressed the thoughts racing through her mind when they stepped out of the store into the deserted street.

"I am not trying to buy your affection."

Vicky laughed, told Bess she was being silly, and that was that.

Barnes had given her the message when they got home. The ladies were expecting them in the west wing for tea.

"Are you done day dreaming?" Louise asked Bess. "Shall we address the matter at hand?"

The older ladies shared a smile.

"Who are his people?" Perpetua rapped. "Not our sort, is he?"

Bess pretended she did not hear. Vicky took the bait.

"What do you mean, Aunt Perpetua?"

"That Inspector," Hortense trilled. "Bess has a thing for him."

Vicky could not help laughing, knowing there was a grain of truth in what she said. Bess glared at all of them.

"That man, that pompous stuffed shirt is not even talking to me. How on earth can you think I feel anything for him?"

More laughter ensued, causing Bess to turn red.

Louise steered them back to the purpose of their meeting. She wanted to know more about the maid. Mollified, Bess gave a brief account of what they had learned at Ridley the previous day.

"Wilma McLeod was a liar."

Vicky added another possibility. The girl might have been mentally ill.

Louise shook her head and told them to take a minute and think.

"You are missing the obvious, my dears. Someone was feeding her all this nonsense, misleading her."

"But why?"

Hortense crumpled her handkerchief and told them they had to go back to the village.

"Find out more about her," Louise added. "That girl she lived with might be able to tell you something."

The twins decided they would go back to Ridley the next day, hoping she had returned.

Barnes arrived with the tea, much to everyone's relief. Bess loaded her plate with tiny ham and cheddar sandwiches and mince pies, always eager to replenish herself. Tea was poured and there were moans of pleasure as they savoured the hot drink, marvelling at the bleak weather outside.

With renewed vigour, Louise brought up the other objective of their meeting.

"What about our main goal, girls? It seems you have lost sight of it amidst all this confusion."

"Nothing of the sort, Grandmother." Bess was indignant. "We talked to Sir Dorian."

Vicky admitted they needed to pick up speed. They would talk to the servants again and see if they had remembered anything since the last time they talked.

"We are asking different questions this time, Grandma."

The meeting broke up. Bess and Vicky left the west wing, debating how to pass the time until dinner.

"How about a walk, old thing?"

Vicky pointed at the sleet outside, hitting the roofs of the many sheds and outbuildings in a staccato rhythm.

"Nasty," Bess yawned. "How about going downstairs to talk to the servants?"

They reached the ground floor and headed to the green baize door. Barnes came out of the dining room and hailed them.

"May I help you, my lady?"

Vicky asked for a few minutes of his time, entering the parlour. She nodded at Bess, aware her sister had known Barnes for a longer time and had a good rapport with him.

"We have been trying to reconstruct the day of the hunt, Barnes. Did anything out of the ordinary happen at that time?"

Bess was expecting him to offer his apologies. She was surprised when his face broke into a smile.

"Funny you mention that now, my lady. One of the footmen told us about a cat on his family farm. His aunt has been poorly since last week and the little beast – the cat, not the aunt – refuses to eat. That has become a problem since she is a mouser and …"

Bess wondered if Barnes was becoming senile. Had he misunderstood her?

Vicky was more patient, realizing he was trying to make a point.

"Something similar happened twenty years ago?"

Barnes bobbed his head in assent. Philip had a strong attachment to his horse and showered a lot of attention on him.

"Everything had to be just so. A special variety of oats were ordered for him from Scotland. Lord Philip had laid out specific directions for his care. Why, he even brushed the horse himself, claiming the horse recognized his touch."

Bess was becoming impatient again.

"We have heard all that before, Barnie. This magnificent horse, what was his name?"

"Zeus," Barnes prompted.

"Right. Philip was crazy about Zeus. Now can you please get on with the story?"

Barnes gave a deep sigh, as if trying to reason with a stubborn child.

"Zeus died, my lady."

Bess and Vicky had already known that. But Barnes surprised them by what he said next.

"Three days after the master."

"What?" Bess exclaimed. "Zeus died three days after Philip? But how?"

Barnes gave a shrug. The manor was plunged

in grief after Philip's sudden death. Momo had been inconsolable. The villagers were in shock. Everyone had loved Philip and he had been too young to die. Nobody thought of the horse.

"It was a while before we found out," Barnes admitted. "Some said the poor horse died of grief."

Bess thought the idea was ridiculous but she said nothing. Vicky commiserated, saying the same thing had happened to someone she knew in America. They thanked Barnes and went up to their rooms.

Dinner was another quiet affair and Bess went to bed early, rising with the sun the next morning. She was relishing a plate of kedgeree when Vicky entered the breakfast room.

"We are going to Ridley," Bess told her. "Eat up, old girl. We may not be back for lunch."

The winter sun warmed their faces and a pleasant breeze promised a milder day. Bess drove through the receding fog and they reached the village of Ridley in good time.

"What was the name of that girl?" Vicky asked as they set off toward Wilma's cottage. "Etta?"

"Edna, I think."

They spotted the open door from a distance and were hopeful. A mousy girl in a faded frock came out with a basin of potatoes and sat down on the steps. She began peeling them, discarding the peels in a cardboard box that must have served as a rubbish bin. Her lips moved and Bess thought she was talking to herself. As they drew closer, she realized the girl was humming.

"Hello!" Vicky hailed her, a friendly smile lighting her face. "Are you Edna?"

The girl smiled back and nodded, her curious gaze taking in every detail of their appearance.

"You must be the ladies from the Hall."

"I say, can we talk?" Bess charged. "We have

some questions about Wilma."

"That poor soul!" Edna sighed and stood up, heaving the basin of potatoes.

She went inside, summoning them with a tip of her neck.

The place was neat and tidy and well cared for. Edna walked through a cosy drawing room into the kitchen and offered them tea. A kettle slung over the fire whistled and she began adding sugar to three mismatched stoneware mugs.

Vicky thanked her and accepted one, taking a polite sip. They heard a rattling cough in the distance. Edna explained her mother was an invalid.

"Let me take this tea to her."

She was back soon and finally took a seat, offering to replenish their cups.

"Do you work on the Ridley estate?" Bess asked.

Edna explained she was a dairy maid but was currently out of work. She had given up her job at a local farm to care for her mother. Money was tight so when Wilma came along with Mrs. Macdonald, looking for a place to rent, they welcomed her with open arms.

"Did she come from Scotland?" Vicky asked.

"She had a 'ard life, poor Wilma. Lived in them 'ighlands until she was nine. Mrs. Macdonald's sister was her neighbour. Then Wilma's Ma died first, then her Pa. She was sent to live with some relations in Yorkshire."

Wilma had big dreams and wanted to see the world. A young man she had been in love with was going to take her to America but he died in the flu epidemic. She had become despondent after that, losing her interest in life. The cousin she was living with knew Mrs. Macdonald was the housekeeper at Ridley Hall and had been a friend of Wilma's mother. He brought her to Ridley and left Wilma in the woman's care, hoping the change of scene might help her overcome her grief.

"And it worked!" Edna began peeling potatoes again. "She loved working at the Hall. Used to say she was just a maid now but would become housekeeper one day."

Vicky asked if she had been having problems.

"That woman with the child next door mentioned Wilma was afraid of losing her job?"

Edna's face clouded.

"It was just bad luck."

She muttered over how misfortune seemed to follow Wilma.

"That one eyed fellow had it in for her."

"Sir Lawrence?" Bess was amazed. "I say, are you talking about the man who died in the woods?"

Edna told them he had made Wilma's life hell.

"She cleaned his room, see? He claimed things had gone missing and blamed her." Edna's chest rose with indignation. "He told people Wilma was a thief."

Bess and Vicky stared at each other, mystified.

"And was she?" Bess called Edna's bluff. "She must have faced a lot of temptation, working at a place like Ridley Hall. Who can blame her if she picked up a shiny bauble or two?"

Edna's cheeks had grown pink.

"Is that what you think of us, your ladyship? We are poor but we are 'onest."

Vicky tried to soothe her.

"I am sure Wilma was a nice girl, Edna. Was she very disturbed about this?"

"Fit to be tied," Edna sniffed. "You would be too if anyone called you a thief."

The girls took their leave, realizing they would

not get much more out of Edna that day. Their direct hit on Wilma's character had offended her and it would be best if they gave her some time to cool down without probing any further.

Bess was quiet on the way back, thinking about Wilma's state of mind.

"Do you think all this was in her head?" she asked Vicky.

"Grief does strange things to people. Dr. Evans can give us a medical opinion."

Bess reminded her the girl was already dead. The doctor could not examine her or talk to her so whatever diagnosis he gave would be speculative.

"Her actions are more important. And I am beginning to think Wilma McLeod had a screw loose and hung herself."

Chapter 22

Bubbles was on the telephone, complaining about the weather.

"What a terrible bore, Bess. Do you fancy a trip to London? You can meet that Inspector chap and ask him what he is up to. Poor Cedric is on tenterhooks, expecting the police to come and arrest him any minute."

Bess had tried to reach DI Gardener a few times. He was away working on another case. Or he was evading her on purpose. For a minute, she was tempted to go up to London and march into his office at Scotland Yard, demanding he attend to her. But her good sense prevailed. Vicky would have talked her out of it anyway.

"Are you thinking of coming here?"

"Momo is getting homesick too so you might see us at Buxley Manor anytime soon. I don't want to miss Mrs. Bird's mince pies."

"But what about Lady Ridley?" Bess asked. "And Sir Dorian? They need your support. I think you should stay there and cheer them up."

And this might be the last chance Momo and Bubbles had to spend some time with Cedric but she didn't mention that.

"Mama will be devastated if we leave now," Bubbles agreed. "At least come here for tea or something."

Bess promised to visit Ridley Hall soon.

"Toodles, darling. Momo wants to say hello."

They talked for a few more minutes, Bess assuring Momo that everything would be fine.

Clementine was lunching with Louise at the Dower House and Nigel and Annie had left right after breakfast on a mysterious mission. Bess and Vicky decided to go to the pub.

"Tell Mrs. Bird she can put her feet up for a change," Bess told Barnes, sharing a grin with him.

They both knew she would do nothing of the sort.

The drive to the Buxley Arms was short but invigorating. Dark clouds covered the sky and a light drizzle began as they entered the pub. Harvey, the proprietor, offered an effusive greeting. His wife came out when she heard their voices.

"Are you here for lunch, my lady? Pie will be ready in ten minutes."

Vicky rubbed her hands and confessed she had been craving the delicious steak pie Mrs. Harvey was known for. Bess hoped there was apple crumble.

They chose a table near the window and sat

down, glad they were out of the cold. The scene outside the window was depressing as a steady downpour began. But the pub enveloped them in its cosy warmth. A fire crackled in the big fireplace, adding a golden glow to the place.

Mrs. Harvey brought the pie and gravy and stayed until they each took a bite.

"Marvellous!" Bess gave her a thumbs up.

They ate well, scraping the dish clean. Vicky opted for cream with her apple crumble. Constable Potts came in when she was debating over a second helping.

"Ladies." He stopped in his tracks when he saw them. "Nasty weather, what?"

Bess and Vicky wished him a good day. He chose a table farthest from them, making Bess giggle. Mrs. Harvey brought them a pot of tea.

"We should ask him about Philip, Bess. They must have called the police."

Bess thought it was a capital idea.

The constable was just about to dig into Mrs. Harvey's pie. He shrank back in his seat as they approached him.

"I gave the Inspector your message, my lady," he blurted.

Vicky spotted the sweat glistening on his brow and felt sorry for him.

"Don't worry about that, Constable. We wanted to talk about something else."

Potts nodded, leaning back in his seat with a sigh. The girls decided it was an invitation to sit.

"This is about the day Philip died," Bess began. "Do you remember that day, Potts?"

"Like it was yesterday." Potts levelled a thoughtful gaze on them. "You know what they say, my lady. Let sleeping dogs lie."

Bess told him she was not going to rest until she proved her father was innocent.

"Are you implying there was foul play?" Vicky quizzed. "Why are you reluctant to talk about it?"

Potts clasped his hands together, pressing his lips.

"It's just a feeling I had over the years, my lady. I cannot explain it."

Bess asked him to tell them everything he remembered.

"It was a dreary autumn day, my lady. There was big excitement in the village about the hunt. Lord Buxley, that was Lord Philip at the time, bought a few rounds for everyone when there were folks at the manor. He was very generous like that."

Vicky urged him to begin his meal. Potts gave her a grateful smile and began eating. The hunt was supposed to end around two or three in the afternoon. People started trickling back long before that. Finally, Philip was the only one who had not returned.

"Did they raise an alarm then?" Bess prompted.

Tired and hungry, the group from the hunting party ate and drank their fill, swapping stories. One of the grooms arrived, gasping for breath. Philip's horse had come back without him.

"Your father formed a search party," he told Bess. "They sent a message to the pub, calling on the villagers to help."

People headed off in different directions, some taking the trails Philip was known to frequent. Potts joined one such group. They had come across the body two hours later, lying under a tree.

"His head was cracked open." Potts ate with relish. "The poor man bled to death."

Bess asked about the cause of death.

"It was obvious he fell from his horse," Potts replied. "His shoulder was bruised and his arm was at an odd angle. Dr. Evans called it an accident."

Vicky wanted to know when the doubts began. What had made people say that Philip had been murdered?

Potts admitted it was hard to pinpoint. One or two people asked what if he had been deliberately killed. The rumours started and became stronger with time. A police investigation began and Nigel had been thoroughly questioned. They could never find any proof against him and he was released.

"The rumours should have died after that," Potts mused. "But they became louder. I don't know, my lady. Every time it feels like people have forgotten the incident, they begin again."

As if someone was keeping watch, feeding the fire when needed, Bess realized. It made her sit up.

They left Potts to his meal and went back to their table. The tea was cold and Harvey offered to bring them a fresh pot.

"We'd rather go home," Vicky told him. "Thank you for a lovely meal."

The drive home did not take long. Barnes stood at the door to welcome them back.

"Lady Buxley is home," he announced. "She would like to see you."

Bess understood he was talking about Momo. She rushed to the east wing with Vicky, wondering what had brought her back in such a hurry.

Momo sat in her parlour, reading a book. Her face lit up when she saw the twins. Bess was glad to see her.

"I say, you are back early, Momo."

She admitted she had missed the manor. Lady Ridley had grudgingly agreed to let her go for a day or two, provided Bubbles remained at Ridley Hall.

"Bubbles is not happy," Momo laughed. "I promised to go back the moment she telephoned, in case something went wrong."

Bess crossed her fingers and told her to be positive.

"I have a feeling we have turned the corner. Everything will be fine from now on."

"Why, do you mean you have found the culprit?" Momo asked.

Bess collapsed in a chair and shook her head.

"Not yet. But Sir Lawrence was an outsider and so was that girl Wilma. They had nothing to do with us."

She saw the doubt on Vicky's face and hesitated. But Momo was looking relieved. A little prevarication would help her sleep better.

"Do you mind if we talk about Philip?"

Momo gave them a sad smile.

"He is never away from my thoughts, girls. I welcome any chance to talk about him."

Vicky told her they were gathering details of the fateful day.

"Do you remember the last time you met him?"

Momo told them she would never forget that day.

"Philip loved having people around. He was so excited about the hunt. All his friends had been invited. The manor was filled to bursting."

"When did you say goodbye?"

A big breakfast had been arranged at the manor.

"Mama and Papa were given a room. Bubbles was already here. Some of the guests from the nearby area started arriving by seven."

Bess realized it had been a crush.

"I doubt you got a chance to talk to him."

"We had a big argument in the hall," Momo laughed. "In front of all the guests too. Mama was scandalized." She tucked a strand of hair behind her ear. "I wanted to go, you see? But Philip was adamant. Dr. Evans had advised me to rest and Philip made me promise I would not ride that day."

Vicky asked her when they said goodbye.

"We almost didn't," Momo chuckled. "Philip left with the others but came back for his coffee."

Bess nodded. Several people had told them how Philip preferred coffee.

"It was a specific type from France," Momo replied. "I had ordered the kitchen to have a flask ready for him. We had both calmed down by the time he returned. He took the flask from me and promised to be back soon."

Vicky noticed Momo's eyes were moist. She tapped Bess on the knee, sending her a silent message. It was time they changed the subject. But Momo wasn't done.

"I didn't visit the stables for ten years. Just the thought of going near a horse made me break out in a cold sweat."

Bess asked her when the doubts about his death began. Momo had no idea. She was immersed in her grief. Her world had turned darker when she lost her unborn child a few weeks later.

"It's because he was such a good rider, I suppose." Momo shrugged. "Some people refused to accept his death was an accident."

They sat in silence for a few minutes, mulling over their thoughts.

"Have you done any Christmas shopping yet?"

Vicky asked. "Why don't we go to Chipping Woodbury tomorrow?"

Momo rallied around. She needed to buy gifts for everyone.

"Let's have some good times while we can. Who knows when your Inspector will come and arrest Cedric, Bess?"

Chapter 23

It was like the calm before the storm. Momo went back to Ridley Hall. Nothing much happened and the Nightingales urged Bess to contact the Inspector and ask for an update. Vicky told her to set her ego aside.

"It's not like that." Bess sulked. "We know he doesn't want us anywhere near his investigation."

"Is that going to stop you though?" Louise asked. "The Ridleys are like family. You should worry more about their welfare than what some policeman thinks, my dear."

Bess knew her grandmother was right. She decided to go for a walk to clear her head.

"Are you coming?" she asked Vicky.

The twins stepped out of the front door and climbed down the steps, deciding to stick to the paved road. Bess suggested going over all the people who had been residing at Ridley Hall at the time of Sir Lawrence's death.

"We are back to that?"

"I believe Wilma's death is related to the first murder. We need to tackle that first."

Vicky pointed out they had not questioned Sir Lawrence's friend from Africa. Sir Dorian might think him above suspicion, but they needed to get a firsthand impression.

"But do you think he will talk to us?" Bess was uncertain.

"Why shouldn't he? If he's innocent, he has no reason to be afraid of us."

Bess did not want to waste any time once they had decided on the next step. She proposed going to Ridley Hall right away.

"Lady Ridley will give us lunch. If not, we can eat at The Crown."

Vicky couldn't help bursting into laughter.

"You are so particular about your meals, Bess. How does it matter if we skip lunch and eat something later?"

Bess told her she had been brought up to stick to a certain routine. Meals were served at stipulated times and there was tea in between if one felt in need of sustenance.

"I can't imagine not starting the day with a hearty breakfast."

Vicky rolled her eyes but said nothing.

Barnes raised his eyebrows when he learned they planned to leave for Ridley Hall.

"But lunch will be served in forty minutes, my lady." He stared at Bess. "Perhaps a hamper from the kitchen …"

"We don't have time for that," Bess replied. "Don't worry, we can eat at the pub."

Vicky mentioned the mince pies. Barnes summoned a footman and gave him precise instructions. By the time the chauffer brought the motor around, he appeared with a wicker basket and loaded it in the boot.

"Mrs. Bird added some sandwiches, my lady," he beamed. "Just in case you got hungry."

Bess thanked him and told Barnes they would be back soon.

"Will you tell Papa I am taking the Rolls? I would rather not drive in this miserable weather."

Barnes assured her he would relay the message.

Vicky dozed on the way to Ridley Hall. Bess occupied herself by thoughts of a certain Inspector who was incommunicado. The dark clouds threatened to burst any second, doing nothing to lighten her mood. She was down in the dumps by the time they reached their destination.

Their arrival was welcomed with effusive warmth by the ladies. Bubbles punched Bess in the arm, looking pleased.

"Isn't this marvellous?" she gushed. "You are just in time for lunch."

Lady Ridley inquired after everyone at Buxley Manor. Bess could hardly get a word in but was glad to find them in high spirits.

The dining room was half full with Sir Dorian and his guests. Cedric was present along with Simon Watkins and Edwin Brindley. Bess found herself seated between them. Vicky was directly opposite her.

The soup arrived, a rich and creamy leek.

"Your fame precedes you, my dear," Edwin Brindley spoke to Bess. "We could use an intrepid gel like you in Kenya."

He wanted to know if she had ever been out of the country.

"France," Bess replied. "And parts of Belgium, I think."

She did not tell him it was during the war, letting him assume it had been for some frivolous purpose like shopping or on holiday.

He addressed Vicky next.

"You are American, aren't you? I bet you are more fearless than Lady Bess here." He cut a piece of pheasant doused in sauce. "Life in the colonies is amazing, isn't it? Never a dull moment."

Vicky told him America had stopped being a colony over a century ago. He guffawed, admitting his mistake readily. Bess found him easy to talk to and thought he appeared forthright.

"Can you spare us a few minutes after lunch?" She buttered a roll. "Vicky and I have some questions."

He nodded and they agreed to meet in the library.

Cedric did not speak to anyone during the meal, devoting himself to savouring the meal. Bess wondered what was going through his mind. His usual effervescence was missing and she felt sorry for the predicament he found himself in.

Lady Ridley stood up after the pudding was eaten. Bess and Vicky followed her to the parlour and excused themselves.

"We have requested an audience with Edwin Brindley."

She made them promise to look in on her before they left. Bess knew the way to the library and knocked on the door before going in. Edwin Brindley sat in the middle of a green velvet sofa facing the hearth, chewing an unlit cigar.

Bess and Vicky took a chair on either side of him. His eyes twinkled as his gaze swivelled between them.

"This feels awfully like an ambush."

"I say, nothing of the sort." Bess hastened to assure him. "It's just that I have been fascinated by this hunting contest of yours. Won't you tell us more about it?"

"Have I told you about my pet lion?" Brindley tucked the cigar in the pocket of his jacket. "We call him Leo. Not very original, I am afraid."

Bess tried to hide her irritation as Brindley went on to detail the lion's schedule in excruciating detail.

"And the contest?" Vicky prompted when he finally paused to take a breath.

Brindley confessed he rarely found an appreciative audience.

"This is a one of a kind hunting competition, my dears. Happens only once every ten years and takes place on a global scale. Every hunter from America to Russia wants to win the coveted crown."

He felt that Sir Lawrence was supremely qualified to win the contest.

"Edwin, he said to me, I have given many decades of my life to this wild country but it's time I went back to my estate and settled down."

The contest should have taken place three years ago but had been postponed, first due to the war and then because of the flu pandemic. Sir Lawrence had given up hope of realizing his lifetime ambition and come to England for a visit.

"I say, you took a lot of trouble, travelling such a distance to tell him about it." Bess watched his face, hoping he would betray his emotions.

"The telegraph must not be available in

Kenya," Vicky probed.

Brindley roared with laughter.

"I see what you are doing there, ladies." He pulled the cigar out of his pocket and put it in his mouth. "My daughter thinks she is smart but she doesn't hold a candle to you."

Bess folded her arms, her mouth settling in a frown. Brindley was under no obligation to provide them with any explanation.

"Do you really think I came here to kill Lawrence?" He stared into the fireplace. "Why on earth would I do that?"

"To get rid of your rival, of course!" Bess exclaimed. "If this contest is so important, you must dream of winning it."

Edwin Brindley answered with a grimace.

"There was a time when it meant a lot. But dreams change as one grows older."

He told them he had built a veritable empire for himself in Kenya. But his real wealth was his family. His foremost wish was to ensure his wife and children were happy and taken care of.

"I do not wish to risk my life at the hands of some beast, my dear."

Bess was not ready to believe him.

"Let me tell you a secret," he continued. "I have these white patches in my eyes that obscure my vision. There is no way I could participate in a hunting contest now."

Vicky gave her head a slight shake, getting Bess's attention.

"That means you would not be able to shoot well with such an inaccurate aim."

He could not have killed Sir Lawrence, Bess realized.

"Will you be honest with us?" she pleaded.

"Clearly, you did not come here to invite Sir Lawrence to the contest. You might have written a letter or telephoned."

"Why did you come to Ridley Hall?" Vicky pressed.

Edwin Brindley flung the cigar aside, oblivious to where it landed. He stood up and added another log to the fire.

"Lawrence and I knew each other since Eton," he began. "He went to Oxford and I went to Cambridge. We lost sight of each other for a while. Then we met up again in Africa."

They had both been young, intent on a life of adventure. Brindley tired of it in a year and started working on building a business. Sir Lawrence had chosen to be a professional hunter, heading deep in the wilds of Africa wherever he was needed.

"I made my home in Kenya. Lawrence had an open invitation to visit and he began to treat it as his base."

They had both fallen for the same girl. She in turn was attracted to the both of them.

"I am not sure I can go into detail here, ladies. Much of what happened later is not meant for delicate ears."

Bess assumed an air of nonchalance.

"We have both seen thousands of dead men on the battlefield. Nothing you say can shock us."

Brindley hesitated, then resumed his tale. The girl wanted stability. She could not live in constant fear, dreading when some wild animal would tear her man apart. But Sir Lawrence had not been ready to give up hunting.

"His goal was to kill a hundred lions in a year, or something equally silly."

Bess and Vicky could guess what had happened. The girl chose Edwin Brindley.

"We got married, Suzie and I," Edwin Brindley summed up. "I have never regretted it."

He was still very much in love with his wife. Sir Lawrence had given them his blessing and been the best man at their wedding. Bess wondered if Sir Lawrence had repented giving up the girl. Unwittingly, Edwin Brindley addressed her question.

"What is the one thing Lawrence wanted, even hankered for?" he asked them.

"To win this grand competition?" Bess took a guess.

Vicky shook her head. "An heir."

Edwin Brindley clapped his hands and gave her a slight bow.

"Capital, my dear. You are absolutely right."

Bess waited with bated breath, sure he was going to reveal something momentous.

"I apologize for being indelicate," Brindley continued. "You see, er, Lawrence has one. And I thought it was time he was made aware of it."

One of Brindley's boys had actually been fathered by Sir Lawrence. He did not go into the details of how that had happened, what impact it had made on his marriage or when he had found out.

"It is the kind of news one does not impart in a letter," he sighed. "Do you see why I had to come here in person? I had to let Lawrence know about his own flesh and blood."

Bess stared at Vicky, stunned. This changed everything.

"Did you tell him?" she asked Brindley, eager to know if Sir Lawrence had known about his son before he died.

He nodded, his eyes filled with sadness.

"At least Lawrence died a happy man."

Chapter 24

Edwin Brindley took their leave after his startling revelation, claiming he could not miss Sir Dorian's excellent port. Bess rubbed her eyes, trying to come to grips with what they had just heard.

"I say, what in the blazes …"

"It must have been a pleasant shock." Vicky spoke under her breath.

Sir Lawrence had been very vocal about finding a wife. He had even joked he was looking for a young woman of child bearing age who would give him a son. There was no doubt he hankered for an offspring of his own in the autumn of his life.

"What's the first thing he might have wanted to do?" Bess quizzed.

"Go to Kenya and meet his son. Actually, he must already know the boy since he was often a guest of the Brindleys."

Bess was considering more worldly matters.

"He would change his will, old girl. Make sure his son was taken care of."

Vicky wondered about the legalities. Was an illegitimate son allowed to inherit? Bess wasn't sure.

"I think he may not be able to claim the title but he would get all the money and any property that is not entailed."

"Don't hold back. You think Simon Watkins heard them talking about this."

Bess tipped her head in assent.

"Anyone in his position would be devastated. He has been slogging on that estate all these years, thinking it was all coming to him. I say Simon Watkins would be very angry and I don't blame him."

Vicky thought it was all conjecture.

"He told us he had great respect for his uncle and I believe he was telling the truth."

"It would evaporate in a second if he learned the same uncle planned to leave him penniless."

"You are being cynical, Bess. I think he's a straightforward man who would never hurt a fly."

Bess was not convinced.

"Here's what I think happened, old bean. Simon heard Sir Lawrence and Brindley and saw all his dreams vanish. Time was of the essence. He needed to act before Sir Lawrence got an opportunity to change his will." She paused, suddenly feeling parched.

"You can drink tea later."

"Simon told us Sir Lawrence did not carry any gun or pistol when he went for his walk. So he knew the poor man was going to be unarmed. He grabbed his chance, Vicky. Took his uncle's pistol, followed him into the woods and shot him in cold blood."

Vicky did not believe it was so cut and dried. They would need evidence to prove it. Bess dismissed her concerns and carried on, growing more excited by the minute.

"And don't forget this, Vicky. He was present at the dinner when we announced we knew the killer. That made him panic although I don't know why he would kill that poor maid. I haven't figured it out yet."

She rang for tea. Hawk arrived a few minutes later.

"Say, Hawk. Can we talk to the servants now? It's important."

Hawk assured her the servants were willing to do anything for Cedric. He offered to send them to the library one by one, starting with the housekeeper.

"Do you mind if we talk to all of them downstairs?" Vicky asked. "Perhaps in the kitchen?"

Bess approved of the idea. That way, they would cause the least amount of disruption and if one of them tried to prevaricate or embellish, the others would correct him immediately. Hawk left, requesting they come to the kitchen after ten minutes.

"I trust you can find your way there, my lady?"

Bess had visited the Ridley Hall kitchen plenty of times, begging the cook for treats. She laughed at the memory, telling Hawk he was right.

"Why didn't you order tea?" Vicky asked after the butler left.

"No need."

They sat in silence for some time and walked out of the library. A hum of conversation accompanied by the clacking of balls indicated some of the men were using the billiards room. The parlour was empty and Bess assumed the ladies had retired to their chambers. She walked down the hall and took a few turns until they reached the green baize door, pushing it open to enter a different world.

Vicky followed her down a set of stone steps, passing the butler's and housekeeper's offices. A group of servants were seated at a long, scuffed pine table. A teapot resided on it, along with two cups and saucers and a three tiered stand loaded with dainty sandwiches, cakes and biscuits.

Everyone struggled to their feet when they saw the girls. Bess greeted the old cook like a long lost friend.

"You make the best jam biscuits, Cook." She popped one in her mouth and took a cucumber sandwich next.

Hawk offered to pour the tea. Vicky declined, looking around the table. She served herself a piece of cake and waited for Bess to take the lead.

"I remember some of you," she began. "Maybe you can tell us your names again."

Apart from Hawk, Mrs. Macdonald and Cook, there was a maid and two footmen. All of them professed they were eager to help.

Bess thanked them and promised she would not take too much of their time.

"Cedric's fate hangs in the balance," she reminded them. "You can make a difference to the family and Sir Dorian will make sure you are suitably rewarded."

Mrs. Macdonald spoke up, her voice gruff.

"We don't care none about the money, Miss. That poor Wilma never hurt a soul. What is it you need from us?"

Bess brought up Simon Watkins. She wanted to learn about his movements. What his routine was, where he went or who he met. The tiniest detail could be relevant.

"Did you notice anything peculiar about him?" She observed their faces, alert for the slightest reaction. "Maybe a queer habit, for instance."

Cook glanced at Hawk and waited until he gave her a nod.

"The kitchen window looks out over the path that goes into the woods."

She told them there was a side door in the hall upstairs that opened on this particular path. Simon Watkins often took it, either with Sir Lawrence or alone.

"I see him on most mornings but I cannot be certain if he went out there on the day that poor man died."

Bess was disappointed. None of the other servants had anything more to offer. The maid, a stout, rosy cheeked girl with a thick neck had tears in her eyes.

"Did that Mr. Watkins kill Wilma?" She pulled out a handkerchief and blew her nose. "Why does he keep going to the woods?"

Cook apologized for not being of much help. Vicky tried to set her mind at rest.

"It's not your fault, Cook. I expect all the days before the murder run together. Sometimes, the mind tries to block an unpleasant memory. Maybe it will come to you if you stop thinking about it."

Bess accepted several days had passed since the incident.

"But he still goes out there," Cook interrupted. "Sometimes two or three times a day."

One of the footmen finally spoke up. He had seen Simon Watkins on the path Cook mentioned two days ago. He had been staring at the ground, muttering to himself.

Bess drained her cup of tea and stood up, trying hard to suppress her excitement. They finally had a new piece of information that might lead somewhere. Eager to discuss it with Vicky, she thanked the servants and promised to put in a good word with Sir Dorian.

"You have all been most helpful. I will make sure Sir Dorian learns about this."

Hawk stood up to see them out but Bess told him not to bother. They went up the uncarpeted steps and exited through the green baize door. The hall was deserted and no sound filtered out of the billiards room.

"Wonder where they all are." Vicky asked Bess if she wanted to meet Simon Watkins.

"Not yet. Let's not spook him."

Hawk had been prompt about sending a message to their chauffer. He had brought the motor around and climbed out to hold the door open for them. Vicky and Bess got in, eager to discuss everything they had heard.

"Why do you think he keeps going into the woods?" Vicky breezed ahead. "Is he nostalgic, trying to relive the time he spent there with his uncle?"

Bess thought she was being gullible.

"You can be so naïve. I think he dropped something there and is afraid it will implicate him."

"Like what? A cufflink?"

"Or a button. Maybe he got into a scuffle with Wilma and did not realize he had lost it."

Vicky thought Bess had assumed a lot of things in that sentence.

"So you believe Simon Watkins is responsible for both murders."

"He shot Sir Lawrence because of the will. Then he kept going back to search for something. Either the maid saw him shoot Sir Lawrence or she suspected him and called his bluff. He could not risk getting caught so he called her there on some pretext and swung her up that rope."

Vicky shivered at the vivid picture Bess painted.

"We need to contact the Inspector now. There is a lot of new information and I think it is our duty to inform the police about it."

Bess grimaced, agreeing with her.

"I don't think he knows about the new will."

Chapter 25

They reached Buxley Manor just in time for tea. Clementine gave them a grudging smile of welcome, happy they were back in time.

"Mama and the aunts want to see you." She poured a cup of Darjeeling for Bess and slid a plate of mince pies toward her. "You can go to the west wing after tea."

Barnes came in with a silver pot of coffee for Vicky.

"Where are Mom and Pops, Aunt Clem?"

Bess realized they had not spent much time with their parents lately.

"They went for a walk," Clementine supplied, her brow setting in a frown. "Should have been back by now."

Bess allowed herself to feel hopeful. Annie was feeling very much at home, based on her actions. And she and Nigel had set the past aside to focus on the present. Could they continue on the path and decide to grow old together? She looked up and quirked an eyebrow at Vicky, receiving a shrug in response. Only time would tell.

"What are you getting us for Christmas, Aunt Clem?" she teased. "Not another of your ugly hand knitted jumpers?"

"That's enough cheek from you." Clementine gave her a playful slap on the arm. "Now run along!"

Louise sat in the middle of a sofa, wearing a hat that could only be called colossal. Decorated with twigs and fallen leaves interspersed with apples, it set off her light brown eyes, eyes that were sparkling with annoyance.

"You took your time," she grumbled when the twins entered.

Hortense dabbed her forehead with a lavender scented handkerchief, agreeing with a sigh. Perpetua said nothing but her glance told them she was miffed.

Bess sat next to her grandmother in a move to appease her.

"We have a new suspect in Sir Lawrence's murder. I think we may be able to save Cedric after all."

Her announcement was met with silence.

"What's the matter, Grandma?" Vicky was concerned. "Have I done something to offend you?"

The fight went out of Louise. Her eyes softened and she patted the empty seat next to her, inviting Vicky to sit.

"We were talking …" she waved a hand to include Hortense and Perpetua. "It looks like we are losing sight of our goal."

"More important than Cedric Ridley," Perpetua quipped.

Bess and Vicky understood at once and felt guilty.

"We haven't been idle, Grandmother." Bess hastened to bring them up to date. "As you see, we haven't learned anything concrete."

Vicky admitted they were going around in circles.

"I don't get it. When we spoke to Constable Potts, he told us it was all cut and dried. Philip had taken a bad fall and died in an accident. So why was our father implicated?"

Louise gave a deep sigh, her eyes growing moist.

"It was that cad Miles Carrington. His account did not match your father's. Poor Nigel denied it all till he was blue in the face but the seed of doubt had been planted."

Bess was enraged. "So Miles lied for no reason."

Vicky reminded her he had been a wicked man. During the course of their investigation in his death, they had found many instances of his immoral behaviour.

"We will just have to dig deeper. I am sure there are things about that day that we haven't uncovered yet."

Hortense told them she remembered the flask Philip carried with him everywhere. Momo had been besotted with him and made sure it was always filled with fresh, hot coffee.

"She was a young bride in love with her husband. Poor girl hardly got a chance to be happy."

Louise told them she remembered hearing about the horse's death. Momo had kept the saddle as a keepsake.

"You mean the one that artisan slaved over for

the better part of a year?" Being a horse lover, Bess was curious about it. "Can we have a look at it, Grandmother?"

Louise told her they needed to talk to Momo. That reminded her of the Ridleys and their plight.

"Let's talk about Cedric now, girls. I hope Dorian is aware of the effort you are taking. Don't take any insults from him."

Bess assured her he was being very gracious and cordial.

"Not like the ogre he used to be. Doesn't matter, Grandmother. We are doing this for Cedric."

The older ladies asked about the new developments at Ridley Hall. They were astounded to learn that Sir Lawrence had fathered a son.

"Not unheard of in our circles," Perpetua claimed.

Hortense fanned herself and stated the girls were now old enough to know about the facts of life. Illicit liaisons had occurred since time immemorial. The Happy Valley in Kenya was infamous for them.

"That old fool!" Louise spat. "He would have spoilt the boy until he grew as pompous as him."

Bess told them what Brindley said. Sir Lawrence had watched the boy grow up and spent a lot of time with him, albeit as a favourite uncle.

"Do you think a new will would make a difference to Simon Watkins, Grandma?" Vicky asked.

The ladies discussed the Watkins family. They were known to be among the richest of the landed gentry around Kent. Simon Watkins had a reputation of being a hard working family man devoted to taking care of his estate.

"He is rarely seen in town," Louise mused. "I

know his aunt, his mother's sister. She is a viscount's daughter and eloped with a baron. It was quite the scandal when we came out. Spoiled her poor sister's prospects of course, so she had to marry a land owner."

Bess halted her trip down memory lane.

"That's ancient history, Grandmother. How can it help us?"

Louise told them her friend Maud had not been blessed with children. She doted on Simon and her letters were filled with praise for him.

"She might leave him a generous fortune."

Vicky gave a low whistle.

"So Simon Watkins is not short of money." She gave Bess a knowing look.

Even if Sir Lawrence had written Simon out of his new will, it would not make much of an impact.

Louise promised to contact her friend and ask about Simon's financial condition. She advised the twins to concentrate their efforts in and around Ridley.

"For instance, have you found out everything about the maid? Another trip to the village might help you unearth more information."

Bess and Vicky both admitted they felt sorry for Wilma McLeod. She had been a poor orphan who would not be missed much. Apart from the housekeeper who felt a certain amount of guilt for bringing her to Ridley Hall, not a single person would cry on her grave.

"Enough!" Perpetua ordained, glancing at a clock on the wall. "Time to dress for dinner."

As if on cue, the dressing bell rang and the group broke up. Louise declared she was tired and was going back to the Dower House. Hortense and Perpetua were going down since their sister Cordelia was coming for dinner.

"Oh good!" Vicky cheered, expecting she

would come with her son, the vicar. "Cecil is always good company."

The twins encountered Barnes on the way to their rooms. He was holding a silver tray containing a brown envelope.

"For you, Lady Vicky."

Bess noted the rush of colour on her sister's face and hoped it was the news they had all been waiting for.

"What?" she asked after they sped up the stairs and reached the landing that led to their rooms.

Vicky had already torn it open and was skimming the lines within.

"They want to meet in the new year."

The sisters let out a whoop and embraced each other.

"I say, jolly good, old girl."

Vicky made her promise to keep it under wraps

for the moment. Nothing was final yet.

They washed and dressed, glad to meet Nigel and Annie when they went to join everyone for drinks. Dinner was a sumptuous affair, beginning with a thick pea soup, culminating in apple pie. Bess realized she was exhausted and surprised everyone by going to bed early. She slept like a log and did not stir until the maid came in and opened the curtains, flooding the room with bright sunlight.

"What a glorious day!" She gave a wide yawn and thanked the maid.

The door opened and Vicky came in, freshly bathed. She had big plans for the day.

"Please!" Bess pleaded. "Not before breakfast."

The breakfast room was redolent with the aroma of eggs and bacon mingled with kedgeree. Annie was cutting into a stack of pancakes drenched in syrup while Nigel gazed at her with an indulgent smile.

Barnes pulled out a chair for Bess.

"Constable Potts telephoned, my lady. The Inspector is expected to arrive at 11 AM."

"Capital!" Bess thanked him and beamed at Vicky. "We will go and wait for him there."

He would not be able to brush her off that easily.

Bess had her fill of kedgeree and drank two cups of Darjeeling, glad to see Vicky enjoy her pancakes. They set off in the motor a few minutes before ten.

"It would be just like him to turn up early," she told Vicky.

Her intuition proved to be right. The familiar red Hispano Suiza was parked outside the tiny police station. Bess and Vicky dashed in and looked around, hoping the Inspector hadn't taken off somewhere on foot.

"Good morning, ladies!" DI Gardener grunted.

"Are you here to report a crime?"

Bess told him they had important matters to discuss with him.

"You will have to excuse me," he drawled. "I am here on police business. The real one, not the one you like playing at."

Bess turned red and was about to let off a string of expletives but Vicky beat her to it.

"No need to be nasty, Inspector. I bet you have no idea about what we are here to tell you."

He set his pen down with a sigh and pointed at the chairs before him. Bess collapsed into one and glared at him, her arms folded. Vicky took the chair next to her, trembling with tension. She rarely raised her voice at anyone.

"Well?" he prompted. "Go on. Enlighten me."

They told him about their meeting with Edwin Brindley. If the Inspector was surprised to hear about the illegitimate son, he did not show it.

Bess brought up the will. She explained how Sir Lawrence had to be killed in a certain window of time, before he had a chance to name a new heir.

"That's not all." Vicky told him about the cook's observations. "We think Simon Watkins lost something in the woods. He must have tried hard to search for it."

Bess delivered the final judgement.

"That maid Wilma must have seen him and realized what it was. She confronted him and he got rid of her, thinking she had connected him with Sir Lawrence's murder."

The Inspector clapped his hands. Constable Potts had been standing a few feet away, listening to the whole story.

"Bravo, ladies! Have you ever tried your hands at writing crime novels? You will make a packet."

Bess felt a blush steal over her cheeks.

"I say!" She glowered at the Inspector. "You don't have to be such an ass."

He explained how tenuous their theory was, based on the big assumption that Sir Lawrence wanted to make a new will.

"Are you aware such a will exists? Did he intend to make a new one?"

"But can't you see?" Bess cried. "He never had the time. This evil murderer shot him before he could take action."

With a deep sigh, the Inspector admitted they had uncovered a vital piece of information. But they had no real evidence. He quashed their hopes with a single terse summation.

"You don't have a leg to stand on, Bess."

Chapter 26

The visit with the Inspector put Bess in a bad mood.

"Why is he being so terrible?" she grumbled on the way back to the manor.

Vicky urged her to see reason. Unlike them, the police needed to follow certain procedures. And they acted based on evidence. Cedric's fingerprints on the pistol were incriminating. They needed to find something similar to implicate Simon Watkins.

Clementine looked surprised to see them.

"Not eating at the pub then?"

"I am sorry Aunt Clem, did you want us to go back?" Bess snapped, then immediately felt contrite. "I say, that was horrible. Please forgive me."

Clementine brushed off the apology with a smile and told them lunch was in an hour. The girls promised to be on time and went to the library.

Polo started barking when they were a few feet away, jumping up to greet them as soon as they pushed the door open. Nigel and Annie sat on the sofa, perusing old photo albums.

"What ho, Papa! Annie!" Bess frowned.

Vicky rushed to give her mother a hug.

"So you remember this is your home?" Nigel quipped. "Have a good lunch, girls. You are helping your mother fill the Christmas baskets after that."

Bess mentioned going to Ridley. Nigel quelled her with a stern look.

"The Countess of Buxley always oversees the Christmas baskets. Your mother never got a chance to do that. You know how the tenants look forward to them, Bessie!"

Annie's eyes shone with excitement.

"We have done a lot of shopping. I had some ideas, you see."

Bess hoped she didn't have too many newfangled notions. Christmas was all about tradition. Vicky's face fell, sensing an argument brewing but Annie did not bat an eyelid.

"It's all right and proper, my dear," she laughed. "You will see."

Determined to make an effort to get along with her mother, Bess gave her a grudging nod. Nigel and Annie talked about a surprise they were planning for the girls.

"Is it a new motor?" Bess was hopeful. "The Vauxhall is a bit dated now, Papa."

Vicky hoped it was something the four of them would do together. That set Bess off. The group tossed a dozen ideas back and forth but Annie and Nigel refused to divulge their plans. They were surprised when Barnes arrived to announce lunch.

Clementine had conjured mutton curry, making Bess break into a big smile.

"This is marvellous, Aunt Clem!" she beamed.

The aunts had made it down to the dining room, lured by the prospect of curry. They ate with gusto, finishing with bread and butter pudding and warm custard.

Annie led the girls to the ballroom after that. The twins gaped at the scene inside. A row of tables had been arranged in the centre of the cavernous room, lined with dozens of baskets. A bushel of oranges marked one end. There were boxes filled with sundry items like socks, handkerchiefs and other goods.

Clementine told them Annie had come up with some brilliant ideas.

"We send them a goose, of course. And the baskets have the usual goodies – socks for the children, pencils, candles, a pound of tea and mince pies."

Nigel was a generous landlord and the family went all out on Christmas to make sure the tenants were warm and well fed for the holiday. Bess felt a surge of pride for her father, knowing he had taken care of the village for the past twenty years. She did not know if Philip would have been a better earl but Nigel was a pretty good one.

"What else have you bought for them, Mom?" Vicky asked Annie, picking up a fragrant block wrapped in colourful paper. "Smells like lavender."

"Scented soap for the women," Annie gushed. "They have been so kind to me, girls. All of them welcomed me with a smile and told me how pleased they were to see me back here."

Bess rifled through the bars of soap, noting each was different. She could smell rose and sandalwood among them.

"I say, that's a marvellous idea, Annie."

Something stirred in her heart when her mother flashed her a thousand watt smile.

"I got lace handkerchiefs too," she told them eagerly. "What do you think?"

Clementine was full of praise for Annie and told the girls to start by adding three oranges to each basket. They lost track of time as they worked in unison, dashing into each other, making mistakes, laughing their heads off.

Barnes arrived with the tea trolley and it was time for a break.

"This is hard work," Bess complained, picking up a cucumber sandwich. "But it is worth the trouble."

Vicky agreed with her.

"We donate to a lot of charities back home but

this feels personal."

Bess assured her it was. "Papa delivers the baskets himself. I suppose Annie will accompany him this year."

Clementine told her she was right.

"It is time the Countess of Buxley took her rightful place."

The shadows lengthened outside and servants came in to light the lamps. Bess straightened when a bell rang in the distance.

"Gosh. Is that the dressing bell? I am ready to call it a day."

Annie proposed a halt, declaring they had done enough. She had been tying pretty bows to the handles, adding another special touch.

"Thank you for doing this, girls. We had fun, right?"

They concurred, finally sitting on the chairs the

footmen had brought in while they were working. Fires blazed in four giant fireplaces around the room, adding a golden glow. Clementine told them to ignore the bell.

"Barnes must have rung it out of habit." She smiled. "Or to give us a bit of warning."

"About what?" Vicky asked.

The ballroom doors were flung open and Barnes came in, followed by a procession of maids and footmen. They spread blankets on the floor in front of a fireplace, adding plenty of cushions. The maids began setting out the food.

Clementine revealed they were having a picnic.

"Marvellous!" Bess shrieked. "You have outdone yourself, Aunt Clem."

Nigel came in, followed by a footman bearing a tray of champagne. Mrs. Bird had sent up a fine collation. There was an array of cold meats, pickles, fruit and cheeses along with Annie's favourite fried chicken. They had just finished loading their plates when Louise arrived, accompanied by Hortense and Perpetua.

"Mama!" Nigel stood up to welcome her. "You came!"

The family had a merry time that night. Bess was in high spirits when she said goodnight to Vicky later.

"We go to Ridley Hall tomorrow, old bean. Cannot put it off, what?"

Vicky smiled in acceptance.

The next morning saw them hurtling toward the village of Ridley after breakfast, bundled in heavy winter coats and mufflers to protect against the bitter cold. Winter was making its presence known with a vengeance.

Bess proposed going to the pub first.

"We can warm up with a cup of tea, or coffee." She rubbed her hands together. "Never hurts to gossip."

Vicky believed the man at the pub was keeping something from them so she supported the idea.

A scrawny girl wearing a stained apron was cleaning the tables. The pub was empty but the owner stood with his elbows on the bar, calling out instructions. He nodded a greeting at them, his smile unctuous.

"What will it be, my lady?"

Bess asked for a pot of tea and chose a table the girl had already cleaned. The man served ginger biscuits with the tea.

"I thank you for your business, your ladyship." He stood there, feet planted apart, gracing them with a smile. "The pub's doin' well since toffs like you started coming."

Sir Dorian had always come in to share a pint with the men or eat the beef stew his wife made, but the ladies had made a difference.

"Women come in for tea." He seemed bewildered by the fact. "The missus wants to make those tiny sandwiches and fancy cakes, turn this into a tearoom …"

Vicky assured him it was a grand idea. They had not realized their patronage made such a difference.

The landlord gulped, becoming distressed.

"Actually, it's not just you, my lady. I think Miss Gertrude really made a difference. Folks are happy to see her back in Ridley, like."

Bess put her cup down with a clatter.

"Bubbles comes here?"

"She and that Wilma McLeod were like this." The landlord crossed his fingers. "Came to meet her. They sat in that corner and twittered like sparrows. Well, mostly Miss Gertrude spoke and that Wilma listened."

Vicky's mouth had dropped open at this

unforeseen confession. Bess was brimming with excitement. She paid up and wished the landlord a good day. They managed to suppress themselves until they burst out of the pub.

"Golly!"

"This is bonkers!" Vicky agreed, shaking her head in awe. "Do you think he was fibbing?"

"He has no reason to."

"Bubbles is a snob. She barely notices the servants."

There was no need to discuss their next course of action. Bess pointed the motor toward Ridley Hall. The butler Hawk stood on the front steps, waiting to escort them to the parlour. Lady Ridley sat alone, working on a piece of embroidery. She looked pleased to see them.

"Good morning!" Bess glanced around. "Where is everyone?"

Lady Ridley gave them a brilliant smile.

"The children have gone to the woods to select the Christmas trees. We have at least ten, you see, for different places across the estate."

It was a Ridley family tradition that had been observed for generations. It had taken a backseat this year in turn of the unfortunate events. Cedric had broached the subject and convinced his sisters to join him.

"His time with us might be limited." Her mouth drooped again. "My boy is trying to live in the present and make the most of it."

Bess glanced at Vicky, disappointed. She had been eager to confront Bubbles.

"What about Sir Dorian?" Vicky inquired. "Do you think he can spare some time for us?"

Lady Ridley told them they would find him in his study.

"He will be pleased to see you, my dear. We are

grateful for your efforts."

Bess thanked her and followed Vicky down the hall to Sir Dorian's study. She felt a pang of discomfort at the look of hope that entered his eyes when he saw them.

"Do tell me you have some favourable news," he pleaded.

They told him about Simon Watkins and his possible motive.

"Lawrence had a son? By Jove! It was his fondest wish."

He was impressed to learn that they had already apprised DI Gardener. The police were going to look into Simon's background for any nefarious activities he might have indulged in.

"You have given me hope, dear girls," he boomed, sounding like his former self.

Bess warned him they had nothing concrete against Simon Watkins but he chose to be optimistic, urging them to stay for lunch.

"The children will be back soon. Momo has been talking about going back to Buxley Manor."

Bess hesitated before asking him the next question. Vicky took the plunge.

"Have you deputized Bubbles to help you in estate matters?"

Sir Dorian admitted he was puzzled. Bubbles barely spent any time at Ridley Hall. She had never taken an interest in helping him.

"The proprietor of the Crown mentioned she has been going there often," Bess began. "Talking to Wilma McLeod."

"The maid who died," Vicky elaborated.

Sir Dorian stared out of the window, his eyes glassy.

"Bubbles rarely goes downstairs or notices the

servants. So we presumed she must be carrying a message for you." Bess could not imagine why Sir Dorian would want to directly communicate with the maid. If he had any concerns about her work, Hawk or the housekeeper Mrs. Macdonald would handle them.

Vicky noticed Sir Dorian had turned white. She poured out a generous measure of brandy from a crystal decanter she saw on a side table and made him drink it.

"Are you eating well?" The nurse in her took over. "You must be under a lot of stress, Sir Dorian. It is important you eat nourishing food and get some fresh air."

He tossed back the brandy and gave her a wistful smile.

"Nigel is a lucky man, my dear. Twice as much."

Hawk came and announced lunch. Bess and Vicky urged Sir Dorian to join everyone in the dining room. The drone of cheerful voices they heard suggested his offspring were back from their mission.

Momo cried in delight when she spotted them. Bubbles wore a smirk as Cedric entertained Lady Ridley with an account of how they had spent the morning.

"It was a terrible bore." Bubbles gave a yawn.

Cedric looked stricken, not used to her callous behaviour. Momo looked resigned. Bess realized it was her usual reaction to anything Bubbles said.

Lunch was not the languorous affair it was at Buxley Manor. All the Ridleys dispersed in different directions after Bess announced they needed to go home.

Bubbles stepped out with them.

"Tell me when we can go up to London, girls. I've had enough of this mausoleum."

Bess cranked up the motor and tackled her.

"Why did you meet Wilma McLeod in the village, Bubbles? I am surprised you knew her."

Bubbles twisted her mouth in a grimace, showing her irritation.

"It was Papa's idea. He thought I could take her to London as my lady's maid."

Chapter 27

Bess woke up with a headache the next morning. She had tossed and turned all night, barely getting any sleep, agonizing over why Bubbles might have lied to her. So she was in a foul mood when she went down to breakfast.

"Where is the kedgeree, Barnes?" She queried after a glance at the sideboard revealed the staple was missing from the buffet.

"I am afraid you will have to do without, my lady. Mrs. Bird sends her apologies."

That did not improve her disposition.

"What on earth? This is a crisis of dire proportion. I hope you will try to resolve it at the earliest, Barnes."

A footman placed a rack of toast before her.

She picked one up and started buttering it with a vengeance. Vicky, who had been watching all this while munching her toast and marmalade, laughed.

"It won't kill you to eat a boiled egg once in a while."

Bess knew she was right, of course. But she felt entitled to a tantrum. She poured herself a cup of Darjeeling and declared it wasn't hot enough. The fragrant brew soothed her senses and by the time she had consumed a good amount of toast slathered with butter and marmalade, she felt human.

"What are we doing today?" she asked Vicky.

Barnes had been watching over them, directing the footmen as needed. He cleared his throat.

"The Dowager Countess has requested your presence in the west wing, ladies."

Bess pushed her chair back and sprang up.

"Grandmother is here? Let's go, Vicky."

They dashed out of the room, eager to meet the Nightingales.

"I say!" Bess spoke. "Do you think they found something?"

Vicky gave a shrug and picked up her pace. They would learn soon enough.

The Nightingales reclined in their favourite chairs, sipping tea. Louise did not blink when Vicky swooped down to embrace her.

"Good morning, Grandma! We came as soon as Barnes gave us your message."

"I directed him to wait until you finished eating." Louise quirked an eyebrow at Bess. "You look out of sorts, young lady."

Hortense offered a lavender soaked handkerchief when she learned Bess had a headache.

"It will make a world of difference, child."

Bess thanked her and slid lower on the sofa, closing her eyes and placing the dainty lace handkerchief on her forehead as Hortense instructed her.

"There was no kedgeree at breakfast. Can you imagine?"

Louise asked her how many times she had gone without the dish in her lifetime.

"Almost never." Bess groaned. "Not unless Birdie's sick or something." She sat up with a start. "Is she?"

Lousie gave her a knowing look.

"Has Dr. Evans been called?" Bess cried. "I acted like such a beast. Why didn't Barnes say something?"

"Calm down, my dear." Louise smiled. "The doctor has been to see her. Mrs. Bird caught a cold and it will have to run its course. She is resting now so don't go barging in on her."

Bess breathed a sigh of relief. Vicky asked the older ladies if they had anything to report. Had their sources come up with any information on Simon Watkins?

Louise gave a smug smile.

"Better than we hoped, my dear."

Simon Watkins had been allowed to have certain expectations. For the past two or three decades, the entire Watkins family had accepted that the chances of Sir Lawrence marrying anyone were slim to none. The hunter himself had communicated that several times via his letters. So Simon Watkins allowed himself to have lofty dreams and he took steps to ensure they were fulfilled.

"But what does that mean?" Bess cried. "Is he a gambler? Has he run up debts in the city, Grandmother? Or has he been spending more than he can afford?"

Louise admitted she felt sorry for the man. His ambition had made him go overboard.

"He has worked diligently to maintain the family estate in Kent," she explained. "And for the past decade or so, he came up with plans for expansion."

Simon Watkins had borrowed money to put his plans into action. They would take some time to come to fruition.

"Of course, he did all that assuming the estate would be his one day. He was building a legacy for his sons."

The long and short of it was that he owed a lot of money, Louise told them. He would be in dire straits if Sir Lawrence did not bequeath everything to him as promised.

"That's a strong motive!" Vicky exclaimed. "Time was of the essence. Simon had to get rid of his uncle before he changed his will in favour of the new-found son."

Bess wanted to call the Inspector immediately but Lousie held her off.

"Have you found anything new at Ridley?"

Vicky told the ladies what they had learned at the pub. Bess felt her headache return.

"Bubbles has never lied to me." She crossed her arms and sulked. "Why would she start now?"

Louise raised her eyebrows and shared a knowing look with Hortense.

"Blind." Perpetua snapped.

"You have always had a soft corner for Bubbles, dear," Hortense elaborated. "But she is not infallible."

Bess remembered that most people at Buxley Manor had lied to her about her mother. Louise read the doubt on her face correctly.

"None of us is perfect, Bess."

"But why would Bubbles lie?" Bess was not ready to give in yet. "And that too, about talking to a maid? It's natural she will hire a lady's maid when she goes to live in London. All of our sort do."

Vicky pointed out the flaw in her statement.

"Sir Dorian did not ask Bubbles to go and speak to her. I think Bubbles was lying through her teeth. She would never hire an inexperienced girl such as poor Wilma."

Bess looked stunned. She realized Sir Dorian had not confirmed the statement.

"Do you remember how shocked he was when we mentioned that?" she asked Vicky. "You had to ply him with brandy."

Louise and the ladies wanted to know more. Vicky gave them an almost word by word account of what they had said and how Sir Dorian had responded.

"And he said nothing?" Lousie mused.

"Curious! Dorian is rarely at a loss for words."

Bess pointed out he had been involved in some subterfuge.

"I don't know why he asked Bubbles to speak to that maid. But it must be something underhand. He never expected us to find out."

"If that's true, Dorian and his daughter are both hand in glove," Louise stated.

Hortense provided her opinion.

"I say Bubbles is lying. She has never bothered to mingle with the servants. In fact, she goes out of her way to be nasty to them. I simply do not see her taking the trouble to spend time with a maid, even if it is to interview her. The butler or housekeeper would be expected to do that."

Bess nodded unconsciously. She had thought the same.

"And as for Dorian," Hortense continued. "He

is under a lot of pressure. It must have taken a toll on him."

Perpetua agreed with her sister.

"The servants are our responsibility, girls. They trust us implicitly and believe we think about their welfare. Having that young maid lose her life in such a tragic way – it's bound to affect Dorian."

Bess leaped up from the sofa and walked to the window. Dark clouds covered the sky and the landscape stretching before her was bleak. Suddenly, she longed for the emerald green lawns of summer.

"I give in. So Bubbles was lying to us. Why would she do so?"

Louise declared she had no intention of wasting her time thinking about it.

"That girl has never listened to reason. Nor has she ever displayed any regard for another. I have no idea what motivates her."

They proposed to meet again in a day or two. Louise declared she was famished and was going back to the Dower House for lunch. Hortense and Perpetua had been invited to go with her.

Bess and Vicky wished them a good day and began the long walk back to the main hall. They had to telephone the Inspector.

Constable Potts told them the Inspector was not available and offered to pass on a message. Bess disconnected the call and placed another one to Scotland Yard. Another constable answered and asked her to wait while he tried to locate the Inspector. She had almost lost her patience when he came on the line, slightly out of breath.

"What is it, Bess?"

Miffed at the abrupt tone, she told him everything about Simon Watkins. It was a waste of time.

"We know all that," he quipped. "We have

been checking his background and the word on the street is that Simon Watkins is neck deep in debt."

Eager to press an advantage, Bess blurted out the next thing that came to her mind.

"Bubbles met Wilma McLeod at The Crown. Several times."

"And that is relevant because?" The Inspector sighed.

"She never talks to the servants."

"Listen carefully, Lady Bess." He laid unnecessary stress on the word Lady. "Every minute I spend talking to you takes me away from the real investigation. So please stop wasting my time with inane gossip."

Chapter 28

Bess thought the day grew from bad to worse. Lunch was a quick affair, cold meats and cheeses with other things from the larder. Concerned about Mrs. Bird, she finally went down to the kitchen and visited the cook in her quarters. It was a set of two cosy rooms adjoining the kitchen. Bess had spent many afternoons there as a child, hiding from her governess or evading Clementine.

"Don't come near me," Mrs. Bird croaked. "I might pass on this nasty cold to you."

Bess assured her she was blessed with an iron constitution.

"Can I get you anything?" She took the old lady's hand in hers, worried to see how pale she was. "Some beef broth? Or willow bark tea?"

Mrs. Bird assured her she was being cared for well. Mrs. Jones looked in every hour and Dr. Evans was going to come back for a visit later that evening.

"This is a bad time to be sick, my lady," she moaned. "Why, Christmas is around the corner and there is so much baking to be done."

The housekeeper peeped in and shooed Bess away.

"She needs to rest, my lady. You can talk her head off when she's better."

Bess wished Mrs. Bird a speedy recovery and went upstairs, at a loose end. Barnes informed her the others were in the ballroom.

"Lady Buxley requested your presence."

"I suppose Papa's with her," she muttered, debating taking a nap in the library.

Polo appeared and put his paws on her knees, barking his head off. She picked up the poodle and nuzzled her face in his fur.

"Ball room it is then."

Nigel and Annie sat at a table, painting pine cones. Vicky was mixing silver paint. It was a domestic scene the like of which Bess had rarely encountered before. She felt a sudden lump in her throat and swallowed.

"There she is!" Nigel saw her and exclaimed in delight. "Which one do you like most, Bess? Your mother is partial to the silver."

She allowed herself to be pulled into the banter. The afternoon passed in a pleasant daze. Momo arrived with the tea.

"I was homesick," she admitted. "And I am longing for my own bed."

Clementine was pleased to have her back.

"We want you here for Christmas. This is your home, my dear. It's where you belong."

The group broke up soon, Annie claiming she needed her beauty sleep before dinner. Bess and Vicky followed Momo to the east wing, hoping to tackle the matter of the old saddle.

"This might be painful," Bess began. "Please ask me to shut up if I cross a line."

Momo turned pale, guessing what was coming next.

"Is this about Philip?" She squared her shoulders. "Can you not stop digging in the past, Bess?"

Vicky explained they were doing it for Nigel.

"It's our only hope if we want to see our parents united."

Momo gave in, promising to do whatever necessary for Annie and Nigel. Bess convinced her it would allow her to move forward.

"And where am I going?" Momo smiled. "This is my life, Bessie. I am surrounded by family and well cared for. I contemplate living out my days here, playing with your children."

Bess threw back her head and laughed.

"You are so dramatic, Momo! Our vicar would marry you in a heartbeat, only if you show him the slightest encouragement."

Vicky stared at her, bewildered.

A deep blush spread across Momo's face.

"Tell me what brings you here."

Bess turned serious. "Grandmother told us you had Philip's old saddle."

Momo frowned, nonplussed.

"I am drawing a blank at the moment." She bit her lip, trying hard to remember. "Oh yes, the saddle." Her eyes grew dull. "Grandmother is correct. I couldn't take my eyes off it for several years. Kept it on that table over there, made sure it was polished regularly. Frankly, I was sort of obsessed."

Bubbles had made her see the error of her ways.

"She told me I had to get rid of it if I wanted to let go of the past."

The saddle had been removed. Momo had no idea what had happened to it. She admitted she hadn't given it much thought in recent years.

Bess rang for Barnes. He paid minute attention to what happened in the manor and was well informed.

"What happened to the saddle Momo had here?" she asked when he entered.

"It was sent up to the attics, my lady," he replied instantly. "I presume it is still up there."

"Excellent!" Bess approved. "I knew you could be trusted to know about it, Barnes."

He gave them a slight bow and left, turning

back at the door with a twinkle in his eye.

"May I advise caution, my lady? We do not know what might be lurking in the dark corners up there."

Buoyed by the prospect of an impromptu adventure, the ladies giggled as they contemplated braving the attics. Vicky had never visited that part of the manor.

"Don't tell me you are scared, Momo?" Bess challenged. "We played hide and seek there, remember?"

She regaled Vicky with her childhood exploits as they began the long climb to the top of the manor. The final set of stairs were a bit steeper and they were huffing by the time they reached the top. To their disappointment, there was not a single cobweb in sight.

The gigantic space stretched before them, dimly lit by a few rays of the setting sun filtering through a skylight. There was no electricity there so Bess carried a hurricane lamp. She turned the wick up and a golden light filled the space around them.

"This is all so methodical." Vicky walked through the rows of chests that were labelled with different decades, set at close intervals through the centre of the room. The walls were lined with pieces of heavy furniture from a bygone era.

"What did you expect?" Bess laughed. "Aunt Clem cracks her whip here too."

They had to make two rounds of the entire space before Momo found the old saddle. It was tucked under a walnut table piled with chairs.

"That's the one!" she exclaimed, falling to the ground to pull it out, causing the stack of chairs to collapse.

Bess caught them just in time.

"I say, be careful, won't you? We can't let anything happen to you, Momo."

Vicky helped her remove the chairs one by one. Finally, they tugged at the saddle and slowly pulled it out. There was a fine layer of dust on it. Momo pulled out a white lace handkerchief from her person and began wiping it down.

"It will have to do for now," Bess told her a few minutes later, noting the tiny square of lace had turned black. "One of the maids can give it a thorough cleaning."

There was nothing remarkable about the saddle.

"I have seen many finer pieces back home," Vicky told them. "My own saddle was made in Texas. It has silk stitching and rhinestones."

Momo stroked the leather, her eyes vacant. Bess realized she was lost in some old memory.

"We heard Philip hired an artisan to make a special saddle for him," she began. "I must say, we have many other saddles like this one in the stables now."

Momo wrapped her arms around the dusty leather.

"This is the one Philip used that day. One of the grooms brought it over for me."

Had Philip been taken in by the so called artisan, Bess mused. He had been quite young at the time and may have easily fallen for a sales pitch. Everyone proclaimed him to be an excellent rider and lauded him for being a kind landlord. Maybe he had taken pity on a man in need and provided him with a place to stay and good pay. Then he had spread the word about him being a good artisan.

"Would Philip buy something just to help someone?" she asked.

Momo nodded, a smile lighting up her face.

"He did that a lot, rather than just hand money to the indigent. Every man has his pride, he said. But the downtrodden and poor needed encouragement. It was his duty to bolster their spirits since he was blessed with so much."

Bess gave up hope of ever finding a flaw in Philip's personality. The man had truly possessed an impeccable character.

Vicky had been examining the saddle while Momo and Bess talked about the past, mainly interested in how different it was from the western saddles she used in America. She came across a frayed bit and cried out in surprise.

"This leather has been cut."

Bess scrambled to see what she meant.

"You mean the buckle is missing?" She turned the saddle over. "Or the girth?"

They may not have sent every little part of the saddle since Momo just wanted it as a keepsake, she reasoned. Vicky insisted the cut in the leather was deliberate.

"This would cause the saddle to slip no matter how well it was cinched," Vicky argued. "I smell a rat, Bess."

Momo had a wild look in her eyes. She grabbed the saddle from Vicky and looked at the straps.

"I think Vicky's right. Why would anyone do this, Bess?"

A stunned silence filled the attic. Had the broken saddle been the reason Philip fell off? If the straps fastening the saddle to the horse's body had been partly cut through, they would eventually give way on a long ride, unseating the rider. However good a rider Philip was, he would be thrown off the beast if caught unaware.

Bess felt her vision blur and realized her eyes had filled with tears.

"We have always suspected Philip was murdered. Now we know how it was done."

Chapter 29

Bess telephoned the Dower House right away, expecting her grandmother and the aunts to share in her excitement. Her hopes were dashed when Louise refused to meet and discuss the latest find.

"We have been invited to dine with the Carringtons tonight. Didn't Clementine tell you?"

As if on cue, Clementine appeared in the hallway, demanding why she was not dressed yet. Bess placed the receiver in the cradle and faced her.

"Nobody told us, Aunt Clem."

Happy to reunite with the Carrington girls after a long time, Bess and Vicky enjoyed the chance to spend time with people their own age. The food was delicious and plentiful and the party was ready to turn in by the time they came back to Buxley Manor.

Exhausted by the hectic day, Bess slept well and woke with a purpose, determined to call a meeting of the Nightingales. Louise was already at the breakfast table when she went down, flanked by the great aunts.

"Eat quickly." The grand old lady ordered. "We have much to discuss."

The group marched to the west wing later, accompanied by Nigel and Annie. Louise had insisted on their presence.

"What are we doing here, Mama?" Nigel complained as soon as everyone took a seat. "Annie and I are going into Chipping Woodbury."

Louise quelled him with a sharp look.

"You have played Romeo and Juliet long enough. The time has come to pay attention to more serious matters."

Prodded by her, Bess recounted what they had found the previous evening.

"Good God!" Nigel sprang up. "So Philip's death was definitely not an accident."

He sat down again and placed his hand in Annie's.

"Your father would never commit such a dastardly act," she told Bess. "How are you going to prove it?"

Louise had worked out their next steps. The old stable master had retired a few years ago and lived in a cottage on the estate.

"You will go and talk to him," she instructed Bess and Vicky. "Show him that saddle and ask him to explain."

The twins nodded, eager to get started.

"One more thing," Louise warned. "Watch

your back, dears. Our family has already suffered much. What happened in the past cannot be allowed to affect your safety."

Nigel and Annie echoed her sentiment. The twins promised to be careful and exited the west wing, their hearts racing with excitement. Bess wanted to make a detour to the kitchen.

"Let's just check on Birdie. It won't take long."

Mrs. Bird sat in a chair at the servants' table, directing the kitchen maids.

"What are you doing out of bed?" Bess grumbled. "Where is Mrs. Jones?"

"Don't you make a fuss now, imp," Mrs. Bird rasped. "I am not going to let a silly cold keep me down."

After extracting several promises from her to retire the moment she felt ill, Bess and Vicky left the kitchen, munching on mince pies.

Barnes was ready with their coats and mufflers.

"A nasty wind is blowing in from the north, my lady," he warned. "You will take care?"

Bess told him to stop fussing and slid her gloved hands in mittens at his insistence. Vicky laughed and did the same, claiming she had braved much worse in New York.

The chauffer had brought the Rolls around. They huddled in and asked him to drive toward the pensioned servants' cottages.

"We are looking for Jonah White," Bess told him. "Do you know where he lives?"

"The old stable master?" The chauffer asked. "Will have you there in two shakes of a lamb's tail, my lady."

They reached their destination fifteen minutes later. The chauffer knocked on the door and went back to the car. He heaved the old saddle out of the boot and lugged it inside.

Jonah White was a short man with a sparse head of hair and a wiry build. He peered at them through rheumy eyes, trying to recognize them.

"Lady Bess and Lady Vicky," the chauffer whispered, making him spring to attention.

He took off his cap and stared at them, a hint of a smile appearing on his face.

"'Tis true what I heard at the pub, then."

Bess did not wait for him to elaborate what he meant.

"Do you remember the special saddle Philip commissioned?" she rushed ahead.

"Aye," Jonah answered. "A thing of beauty it was. Took the better part of a year to make."

Bess and Vicky looked at each other, sceptical.

The chauffer directed Jonah to examine the saddle they had brought. He took one look and turned to them with a smirk. "This ain't it, ladies."

"Are you sure?" Bess prodded. "They say Philip paid a lot of money for this, although I fail to see what is so special."

Jonah told them it was the wrong saddle. The one Philip commissioned had a lot of intricate detail, the kind of workmanship that had taken months. Vicky asked him to describe it and Jonah went into excruciating detail, highlighting the fine aspects of the legendary item.

"I may have bad eyesight but I can tell this is not the same one," he insisted.

A woman came out, bearing a tea tray. She was at least a foot taller than Jonah and double his girth. Bess thought she looked familiar.

"You have grown into a fine woman, Lady Bess," she praised. "Been a while since I bobbed you on my knee."

A much younger version of the woman flashed before Bess.

"Nurse White!"

The woman's face broke into a smile. Martha White had looked after Bess after Annie left for America. She stayed at the manor for five years until a proper nurse and governess were hired. Bess remembered a gentle woman who sang lullabies and stayed with her until she fell asleep.

Martha poured tea and ordered Jonah to pass the cups around.

"Lord Buxley has been good to us," she beamed. "He made sure we had this cottage and gives Jonah a good pension. Dr. Evans takes care of us when we are ill, all thanks to your father."

Bess nibbled on the ginger biscuits Martha provided and watched Vicky listen in rapt attention as Martha recounted some anecdotes from their childhood.

"I was never blessed with my own babies, see? So I made the most of looking after you."

The conversation finally turned to the saddle.

"What is this about Lord Philip?" she quizzed Jonah. "You make sure to tell them every little detail."

He nodded his head, staring into space.

"I remember the saddle now. It belonged to Lady Buxley, Lord Philip's widow."

"Momo?" Bess and Vicky burst out at once. "But how is that possible?" Bess continued. "Why would Philip use a different saddle?"

Jonah White made a startling revelation.

"He took Lady Buxley's horse, didn't he? That lad Joe Cooper saddled him. I saw it with my own eyes."

Bess wasn't sure if they could trust the old man's memory. Nothing he said was making any sense.

"Do you remember Zeus? Philip's horse?"

Jonah White bobbed his head, his expression

mulish.

"Of course I know who Zeus was? Looked after him since Lord Philip brought him home to Buxley. He did not trust anyone else with him."

Vicky asked a simple question, hoping to placate the old stable master.

"Why did Philip not ride Zeus that day?"

"He got sick that morning, that's why. Poor mite could barely open his mouth or walk two paces. Lord Philip wanted to stay back and look after him but most of the hunting party had already left. There were no spare horses so young Joe offered to saddle Lady Buxley's horse for him."

Vicky showed him the leather strap. Jonah began muttering under his breath.

"This has been cut," he cried.

Bess asked him how it would affect a rider.

"I reckon it was not cut all the way through at first, my lady." He pointed out the obvious. "Otherwise, the saddle could never be cinched to the horse."

Had Joe Cooper made a mistake, Bess asked. Jonah gave a shrug saying it was possible. Joe was very ambitious and a quick learner but he had been young then.

"Was walking out with a scullery maid at the time," Martha supplied. "Couldn't wait to muck the stalls so he could go meet her by the trout stream."

They thanked the old couple and went back to the Rolls, speechless. Neither spoke until they reached the manor and the chauffer deposited them near the front steps.

"Can you make any sense out of this, old girl?" Bess asked as they trudged up the steps.

Vicky thought Zeus had been poisoned. The idea was to make him go berserk so Philip would be unable to control him and get thrown off.

"But the plan backfired and Zeus could barely move. Joe Cooper must have acted at the last minute, cutting through the cinch so the saddle would come off and unseat Philip."

Bess thought it was a wild theory. Why would Joe Cooper harm Philip? Had he held some kind of grudge against his master? Or had someone bribed him to commit the horrible act?

Chapter 30

Brakes hissed and screeched as the train pulled into the railway station. A mass of holiday revellers rushed to board it. Thankfully, none of them entered the first class carriage Bess and Vicky sat in, dressed in woollen frocks and thick winter coats, their heads bundled in cashmere.

"Stop sulking." Bess pouted. "We are going to have a good time."

"I don't fancy stomping around in this weather."

"But I do want to get something special for Annie, especially after I have been so beastly to her."

Vicky gave a sigh and stared out of the window.

A whistle blew and the train began to chug out of the station. They were going to London in search of the perfect Christmas gift. At least that's what Bess believed. Vicky thought a gift was symbolic, just a means to convey your regard for someone.

"Mom is hungry for your approval, Bess. Not some expensive trinket you can buy in a city store."

"It's a pair of handmade shoes made with fine Italian leather," Bess argued. "No woman can resist them."

As always, Bubbles had influenced Bess. She had telephoned from London the previous evening.

"I am here to interview staff, darling. Why don't you make the best of it? Come up to the city tomorrow and we can go shopping."

Bess admitted she was feeling a bit boxed in due to the weather. A jaunt in London sounded like just the thing.

"Will you give us lunch?" she asked. "We can spend the afternoon shopping and take the last train to Chipping Woodbury."

"No you won't! You will stay here at the flat with me. We can visit a few nightclubs and paint the town red."

Vicky had shaken her head, sure Bubbles was talking Bess into mischief.

"I say," Bess hedged. "We can decide all that tomorrow."

Bubbles guessed what she was saying.

"If Vicky's going to be a spoilsport, she can stay at home."

Bess kept the last part to herself. She couldn't hold back her excitement.

"Please say you will come," she had pleaded. "It will be fun."

Vicky gave in. They were to meet Bubbles at

the Savoy Grill for lunch.

The train pulled into Paddington station thirty minutes later. Bess and Vicky waded through the crush of humanity on the crowded platform and hailed a taxi.

Bess rubbed her hands with glee, anticipating a lavish meal at the Savoy Grill.

"We will have oysters, of course. I should go easy on the champagne though, if we are to spend the afternoon walking from store to store."

Vicky smiled and maintained a diplomatic silence.

They received a warm welcome at the Grill. A window table had been reserved for them. A waiter brought champagne and told them the meal had already been ordered.

"Mom loves this place." Vicky allowed herself a sip of champagne and gazed outside. "Bubbles is late."

The oysters arrived with no sign of their hostess. Bess was not worried.

"She needs more time to primp and get ready. Dear Bubbles!"

When the waiter arrived with the chops, Vicky decided to say nothing and enjoy the meal. They were digging into a lemon souffle when Bess was summoned to the telephone. She came back, looking crestfallen.

"That was Bubbles. She's stuck interviewing the staff. One of them was very late, it seems. She wants us to go ahead and start without her."

They stepped out of the hotel and huddled close, struck by a vicious gust.

"I am sorry, Bess." Vicky grinned. "You had your heart set on that cobbler."

"Shoe maker," Bess corrected. "And all's not lost, old bean. Bubbles gave me directions. That man is expecting us."

Vicky asked if she had brought the outline of their mother's shoe. Bess patted her coat pocket.

"Bubbles says he prefers to directly measure the foot. We will have to convince him to make an exception."

They started walking down the Strand, away from the Savoy.

"Are you sure we can't take a taxi?" Vicky asked

Bess shook her head. Bubbles had given her intricate directions. She took a left after some time and they walked on until Bess decided it was time to take a right turn. The street grew narrower as they walked on and a foul smell hung in the air.

"That's the river," Bess informed Vicky. "We are close."

She wasn't sure what they were close to but she dared not admit it. The area grew seedier. A dirty urchin with barely any clothes on snatched at Vicky's purse but she pulled her arm away, threatening to go after him. He laughed and ran off.

"I think we should go back."

"Just a bit longer," Bess urged. "Look, we take a left here and that will …"

She stared at a dirty grey arch that ended in a garbage heap. Dark forms huddled around it, some asleep under threadbare blankets, others warming their hands over fledgling fires.

A grubby crone flashed them a toothless grin while a one eyed man with sunken eyes and a red scar across his chin leered, stretching his hand to touch Bess.

Vicky grabbed her arm and pulled her away. Bess was rooted to the spot, staring at the abject poverty displayed before her.

"Let's go!" Vicky hissed.

Bess finally moved and they fled out of there, finally stopping to catch their breath. She looked around, trying to get her bearings.

"I think we are lost."

Two girls wearing heavy perfume and dark red lipstick stood under a broken staircase, smoking cigarettes. The skirts they wore stopped at their thighs. One of them offered Bess a cigarette.

"Are you lost?"

Bess explained what they were looking for. The girls stared at each other and burst into raucous laughter.

"This is Villiers Street, dearie. Ain't a place for posh people like you."

Vicky stepped in and asked how they could get back to the Strand. She listened carefully and thanked the girls, pulling out a five pound note from her handbag and offering it to her. The girl took it and tucked it into her bodice.

"The poor can't afford pride," the other girl told them. "Look sharp, now."

They thanked the girls again and took off, eager to reach familiar surroundings. The stench from the river began to fade and they could hear the horn of a motor, indicating they were getting close to the main thoroughfare.

Despite the warning, they relaxed a bit and must have let their guard down.

Bess felt something poke her in the back. An arm came around and a hand clamped over her mouth. There was an ominous click that sounded awfully like a switchblade springing open. Bess squirmed, trying to free herself from the deathly grip. Something stung her cheek but she ignored it, trying to jab her elbow in her assailant. Footsteps sounded behind her. The hold around her body lessened and she whirled around to see a masked figure go flying in the air. It landed on the ground with a thud. She turned to see who had helped her, expecting Vicky, only to come face to face with a tall, bearded stranger with dark grey eyes.

He grabbed her arms and asked if she was alright, handing her over to Vicky who had appeared behind her, slightly out of breath. The man looked around and ran down the street, presumably in hot pursuit of her assailant who was nowhere in sight.

"You are bleeding!" Vicky cried and pulled out her handkerchief. "What happened? I thought you were right behind me."

Bess dabbed her cheek with the hanky, astonished to see it turn red.

The man came back, panting. His eyes were full of concern.

"He got away, the rascal." He took a step back and hesitated. "Have you lost your way, ladies?"

Bess noted he spoke in a cultured voice and had a regal bearing. She introduced herself and

Vicky and admitted they had wandered in search of the perfect gift.

"Looks like someone played a trick on you. There is no shop like the one you mention anywhere around here."

He offered to escort them to the Strand and would not take no for an answer.

"You haven't told us your name," Vicky spoke after they had taken a few steps.

"Sheldon. Robert Sheldon."

Bess asked if there was a rank he was leaving out.

"Captain Robert Sheldon," he admitted, staring at his feet. "That was a long time ago."

Bess had a dozen questions but she held herself back, after a warning look from Vicky. They reached the Strand five minutes later.

"You should be safe here," Captain Sheldon

remarked. "I will take your leave now, my lady."

Bess asked him to join them at the Savoy for a drink.

"I need a large brandy after that ordeal."

Captain Sheldon laughed and pointed at her cheek.

"You should put a plaster on it and have a doctor take a look. I am afraid the Savoy does not admit the likes of me, my lady."

"But you are with me," Bess protested.

Vicky took her arm and thanked the soldier.

"I think you saved my sister's life today, Captain. It's a debt I will never be able to repay. But do look in on us at Buxley Manor if you are in the area. It's near Gloucester."

He gave her a sheepish smile, telling her he had heard of the place.

"Fellow I fought with, Barton, talked about it."

"Not Giles Barton?" Bess exclaimed. "He's our cousin."

Sheldon gave a deep bow and started walking away from them. He was soon lost in the crowd. Vicky and Bess stared after him, each wondering why a well educated army officer was living in such reduced circumstances.

They entered the Savoy Grill and Bess headed to the ladies' room to wash her face. One of the attendants procured some antiseptic and Vicky dressed the wound, covering it with some gauze and tape.

They ordered brandy at the bar and submitted to the solicitous care of the maitre'd. Bess began to shiver as she came out of shock, realizing the magnanimity of what had happened to her.

"I say we go to Mayfair right now and confront Bubbles. What on earth was she thinking?"

Vicky put her foot down.

"We are taking the next train home, my dear. Don't even try to argue with me."

Bess gave in, eager to return to the manor. She wanted to get into bed and stay there for a long, long time.

Their arrival caused the expected hue and cry at Buxley Manor. Barnes was the first to voice his concern. His eyebrows shot up when he spotted the bandaged cheek and his shoulders drooped.

"My lady!" He placed a hand on her shoulder.

Bess stretched her lips in a smile, trying to ward off tears. The stoic figure of Barnes had made her emotional.

"It's not as bad as it looks, Barnie."

Vicky propelled her toward the stairs, calling instructions to Barnes.

"Tell Mom and Pops we are home. Call Dr. Evans. And let Aunt Clem know too."

Barnes was already hurrying to the telephone.

Vicky helped Bess change into her pyjamas and watched her climb into bed. She was propping pillows around her when Clementine rushed in.

"Tea was an hour ago, girls. You might have …" The rebuke died on her lips.

She sat on the bed and stared at Bess, taking her hand in hers.

"How did that happen, child? I better call the doctor."

Vicky told her Barnes was taking care of it.

Nigel and Annie entered the room next, their eyes wide with fear.

"What?" Nigel sputtered. "My dear Bessie …" He was at a loss for words.

Annie kissed Bess on the forehead and told her

husband to calm down. She looked at Vicky and gave a slight nod.

"Tell us everything."

"I say!" Nigel erupted. "What was Bubbles thinking, sending you to Villiers Street?"

Clementine played devil's advocate.

"Bubbles has always been harum scarum. I doubt she had any idea what she was doing."

Bess tried to remember her conversation with Bubbles.

"Maybe I misheard the directions. There was a lot of disturbance on the line."

Annie advised her to stop thinking about her day.

"You are staying in bed for the next few days, sweetie. Clem will order your favourite meals from the kitchen and your father, Vicky and I will sit here, on guard. So don't even think about sneaking out."

Bess felt her eyelids droop. She finally stopped resisting and fell asleep, lulled by the voices of her loved ones.

Chapter 31

Bess let herself be pampered for the next three days. She had to admit Annie was making an effort to make her feel special and she basked in the warmth of her mother's love. Annie came up with several ideas to keep her entertained. They made Christmas cards, wrapped presents and consumed plenty of mince pies with tea. Mrs. Bird was hale and hearty once again and back in the kitchen, churning out kedgeree and spicy dishes for Bess.

Vicky took off the tape on her cheek two days later. The wound had almost healed but it could leave a scar.

"People can easily tell us apart now," Bess joked.

She had telephoned Bubbles in London the

next day. There was no response.

"I hope nothing's happened to her, Vicky. What if she lost her way on that awful street, just like us?"

Vicky rolled her eyes but said nothing.

"She could have telephoned to ask about us."

Momo informed them that Bubbles was back at Ridley Hall. Bess wasted no time in telephoning her.

"I say, Bubbles, you abandoned us! That's just not cricket."

"Darling, don't be such a bore. I waited a whole hour for you at the shoe maker's. He was horrible. Made me pay a fine because you missed your appointment."

Bess explained everything to Vicky later.

"We took the wrong turn. Bubbles says we had to go north on the Strand. No wonder we ended up on that ghastly street."

The Nightingales appeared grim when they visited Bess in her room.

"We are getting closer to our adversary, girls," Louise proclaimed. "This attack on Bess is proof."

Hortense fanned herself with her handkerchief and gave her assent.

"Yes." Perpetua was brief as usual.

Vicky and Bess stared at them, wide eyed.

"What are you saying, Grandma?" Vicky cried. "You think someone followed us in London?"

Louise nodded. The assailant must be keeping an eye on them and had cornered them in London, taking advantage of the crime ridden area they were in.

"But who knew about our plans, Grandmother?"

Hortense told them it had to be someone close to them.

"Someone in Ridley or Buxley, of course," Louise agreed.

Sir Lawrence had been killed at Ridley Hall so it made sense that his murderer was from the area.

"Well, whoever he is, he knows more than we do," Vicky sighed. "We still have no solid proof against anyone."

Louise asked what excuse Bubbles had given for lying to them about Wilma.

"You are being unfair, Grandmother," Bess bristled. "I believe Sir Dorian is the one who lied. I can clearly imagine him foisting a local maid on Bubbles. Probably wanted the girl to spy on her."

Vicky suggested talking to Cedric again. He might be willing to own up to a lesser crime, like flirting with the maid. Maybe she was in a delicate condition and had taken her life.

Louise guffawed and shook her head. The post mortem had not revealed anything of the nature.

"But how do you know that?" Bess quizzed. "DI Gardener has not let anything slip."

Vicky lauded her grandmother for being resourceful.

"I guess Dr. Evans has come through for you again, Grandma."

Clementine came in to inform them they were late for dinner. A maid followed her with a tray for Bess.

"I am not an invalid, Aunt Clem!" Bess insisted on accompanying everyone to the dining room.

They had retired to the parlour after an excellent roast of mutton when Barnes peeped in, holding the silver salver he used for the mail. He cleared his throat and waited for their permission, looking apologetic.

"Go on, Barnes," Louise snapped. "Don't just stand there like a pole."

Bess picked up the piece of paper and handed it to Vicky. It was a bit greasy and had been folded several times.

"What does it say?" Annie asked, stirring sugar in her coffee.

Vicky frowned as she read the missive.

"It's a bit strange. According to this, Bubbles told Wilma McLeod that Sir Lawrence was after her job. Even urged her to act fast."

Momo rushed to her sister's defence, claiming the note was a load of rubbish.

"Where did you find this, Barnes?" Louise boomed.

It had been slipped under the kitchen door. The scullery maid had almost stepped on it and picked it up. She gave it to Mrs. Jones, the housekeeper.

Louise shared a look with the great aunts. They all turned toward Bess but were silent.

"I see something's cooking among you," Clementine bristled, standing up. "No need to tell me anything."

She bid them goodnight and stalked out.

Annie was next. She kissed Bess and Vicky and begged them to be careful. Momo left with her but said nothing.

"I think a trip to Ridley Hall is the first order of the day tomorrow," Louise grunted. "Now we know why Bubbles was meeting that poor girl."

Bess doubted the veracity of the note.

"I think someone in the village has a grudge against Bubbles. You know she's a bit of a snob."

Vicky said nothing but Bess gathered she wasn't convinced.

The group broke up, bidding each other a good night. Bess and Vicky waited in the hall with Louise while the chauffer arrived to take her to the Dower House.

"Remember, my dears … keep your eyes and ears open and be careful."

Bess and Vicky went up, barely able to keep their eyes open. The night passed quickly and Bess woke with a purpose, bracing herself to tackle Sir Dorian. He had played a good game, trying to flatter her with plenty of compliments. But how could she forget his aversion to her all these years?

Vicky convinced her to have a quick breakfast. Bess wolfed down her kedgeree in record time, drank a single cup of Darjeeling and stepped into her motor, ready to brave the elements. There was a sprinkling of snow on the ground but the air was crisp and fresh, just what Bess craved after being stuck indoors.

Vicky was pensive, staring at the passing scenery. She did not make any comment when Bess pressed her foot down on the accelerator, taking a few sharp turns at high speed.

"A penny for your thoughts." She gave a nervous laugh when Vicky did not respond. "How about a bet? Winner wears the rubies at Christmas."

Vicky clenched her lips, giving a shrug.

"Wilma was almost our age, you know. Nothing can bring her back."

"You are right, old girl." Bess felt like a heel. "I can be so thoughtless."

She was quiet for the rest of the drive, speaking up only when they turned into the grounds at Ridley Hall.

"Let's confront them at the same time. We will ask Sir Dorian to summon Bubbles to his study."

Vicky gave a silent nod, leaning forward in her seat in surprise. Bess saw the vehicles lined up in the drive.

"What's going on here?"

They had both spotted the red Hispano Suiza standing next to a police wagon and a battered two seater.

"He's here." Bess gasped. "That could only mean one thing, Vicky. Cedric is going to be arrested."

Sir Dorian would be sad, Vicky said. They had disappointed him.

"We didn't live up to his faith in us."

The girls ran up the front steps, pausing at the threshold. The front door was wide open and Hawk, the butler, was nowhere in sight. They could hear a woman wailing in the distance.

"Sounds like Lady Ridley," Bess muttered, striding down the hall, Vicky right behind.

They headed for Sir Dorian's study. Constable Yates stood outside, along with another policeman who was not familiar. He barred their way.

"You cannot go in, my lady."

"Where is he?" Bess demanded, placing her hands on her hips. "Tell the Inspector he is making a grave mistake."

Vicky asked if they had found any more evidence against Cedric.

Yates lowered his eyes but said nothing. The door opened and DI Gardener came out, his face set in stone.

"You can't stop me from seeing Sir Dorian," Bess railed.

He forbid them from going in the study, demanding they follow him.

"For once in your life, Bess, do as you are told."

She opened her mouth to protest but Vicky took her arm and pulled her away. She had seen the anguish in the Inspector's eyes.

"What has happened?" she ventured as they entered the small parlour.

"Brace yourself, ladies." DI Gardener took a deep breath. "I am sorry to report Sir Dorian is dead. He was shot and succumbed to his wounds."

Bess collapsed on a sofa and leaned against Vicky, feeling light headed.

"When … when did this happen?"

They would not know until the post mortem but according to his estimate, the accident had occurred in the early hours of the morning.

"Accident?" Vicky probed. "Did the gun misfire?"

The Inspector's expression became stony. Bess realized he would not divulge any more information but he surprised them.

"One of the maids caught Cedric red handed. He was standing over the body, holding a gun in his hand."

Bess asked if he had confessed to the crime. The Inspector sighed and shook his head. Cedric maintained he was innocent.

"He says he found Sir Dorian at his desk, already dead. He had just picked up the gun when the maid came in to light the fire."

Vicky asked what he thought.

"I will have to act on the facts as they are presented to me. Cedric will have to accompany us to the station for questioning."

He stopped mid sentence, staring at Bess.

"What happened, Bess?" There was a dangerous glint in his eyes.

Vicky told him about them getting mugged in

London.

"On Villiers? What possessed you to go there?"

There was a knock on the door and a constable entered. He gave a smart salute and announced the doctor was asking for the Inspector.

"Does Lady Ridley know?" Vicky asked.

The household was plunged in grief. Hawk appeared, white in the face. He told them Lady Ridley had just woken up. Bubbles had given her the sad news and was trying to console her.

"Perhaps the doctor can give her something to calm her down?" he requested.

Vicky offered to go up while Bess took up the task of telephoning Buxley Manor. She spoke to Clementine first, knowing she would take charge and handle the situation with aplomb.

"Momo!" she cried. "She will be devastated, Aunt Clem!"

Annie came on the line and Bess realized she felt a lot better after talking to her.

"We will start for Ridley Hall right away, sweetie," she promised.

Bess requested Hawk to send some tea to Lady Ridley's chamber and finally braved the stairs.

Vicky sat on the bed, trying to comfort Lady Ridley, gently stroking her back. Bubbles stood by the window, staring outside.

"I say!" Bess rushed to embrace her. "My deepest condolences, Bubbles."

She turned around, levelling her glassy eyes on Bess.

"Don't be silly, darling! He never cared much for me." Her lips stretched in a gruesome smile. "I suppose we can say goodbye to the Christmas ball."

Chapter 32

The news of Sir Dorian's death spread like wildfire. Neighbours and friends arrived, among them the Carringtons of Oakview and Rosehill. Clementine had reached the hall first with Nigel, Annie and Momo. Lord and Lady Morse were on their way.

Dr. Evans came and gave Lady Ridley a sedative. He offered the same to her daughters. Bubbles scoffed at him, claiming she was made of sterner stuff.

Bess and Vicky sat in the big parlour with everyone, drinking tea and coffee, listening to the exclamations of awe and surprise. There was a general sense of disbelief.

"Three murders in a matter of weeks!" Lord Morse thundered, looking around the assembled company. "That defies belief!" He stared at Bess. "My dear, I have full confidence you will get to the bottom of this soon."

DI Gardener had just entered the room, wanting a word with Cedric. His expression hardened when he heard Lord Morse.

"I advise everyone to let the police do their job. We don't want a fourth body on our hands."

One of the Carringtons swooned and there was a scramble for smelling salts.

Bess yearned to question the servants but it was impossible until the police left. Vicky caught her eye and quirked an eyebrow, of similar mind.

They ran into the Inspector in the hall.

"Won't you please listen to me, Bess?" he pleaded. "I cannot assign a man to look over you."

"You mean a bodyguard?" she smirked. "I need to stretch my legs and it's too cold outside."

Vicky went up the stairs and Bess followed, itching to do something. Maybe they could take a tour of the house.

"All the Ridleys have rooms on the first floor," she explained. "Even Bubbles and Momo, although they don't really live here. Cedric is the only one who has a suite on the second floor."

They paused on the first floor landing, debating looking in on Momo. Clementine stepped out of a room and spotted them.

"Why are you loitering here?"

Bess gave her a wave and ran up to the second floor, urging Vicky to follow her.

"Most of these are guest rooms," she explained, pointing at a corridor stretching in both directions. "I say! Where are Simon Watkins and Mr. Brindley?"

"In their rooms?"

They knocked on the doors one by one, venturing in when there was no answer. All of the rooms were empty.

"They have been cleaned," Bess pointed out. "The beds are made and the fires are laid out. I think our birds have flown."

"The police must have let them go," Vicky reasoned. "Do you realize what this means? Neither of them can be suspected of Sir Dorian's murder."

"You are right, old bean."

A low growling emanated from the far end of the corridor. Bess thought it sounded familiar.

"Is that …" She ran ahead. "The corner suite is generally reserved for special guests."

"Like Sir Lawrence?"

Bess pushed the door open and shrieked as a

furry form enveloped her and almost knocked her down.

"303! You poor darling! Did someone lock you in?"

The German Shepherd who followed Sir Lawrence like a shadow barked joyfully, wagging his tail. Bess and Vicky cuddled and stroked him until he finally calmed down.

Vicky went in and found a basin half full of water. There was another bowl containing the remnants of meat. So the servants were making sure the dog was fed but he must miss his master.

"I think he's lonely."

Bess nodded, thinking the same.

303 entered the room and walked over to a chair by the window. He laid his head on the rug and closed his eyes but sprang up as soon as they began to exit the room.

"I think he wants us to stay." Vicky sat down and stroked his back.

"We have nothing better to do." Bess began to sit on the bed but changed her mind. She started pacing around the room. "Is it awfully indelicate to say I am hungry?"

Vicky pointed at a clock on the wall. It was past their lunch hour.

"They might have put out some food in the dining room."

303 sat up and whined.

"Why don't we stay here a bit longer?" Bess sighed, looking around the room.

She began pulling out drawers, shutting them when she realized they were not empty.

"Looks like all of One Eye's stuff is still here."

Her eyes landed on a writing desk placed below a far window. She walked over and sat down, fiddling with an ink pot, rifling through a stack of hunting books and putting them down.

"The man was obsessed," she muttered, giving a low whistle at a drawer full of old letters. "I say!"

Vicky stared at her but said nothing.

"He's not going to object," Bess laughed. "I know this is highly improper but maybe it will reveal something we don't know."

"Like a clue?" Vicky brightened. "Why didn't we think of that before?"

Bess began searching through the mail with renewed vigour. There were some letters from Edwin Brindley, apprising Sir Lawrence of his arrival. A firm of solicitors had written confirming an appointment. She set them aside, along with a bunch of hunting related periodicals. Her eyes fell on a faded envelope tucked at the very bottom, yellowed with age.

"What's this?" Bess murmured and picked it

up.

The postal stamp was very familiar. Her mouth fell open when she realized it was the Buxley post office. Everything made sense when she turned it over and saw a flamboyant scrawl, stating the sender.

"Golly! This looks like a letter from Philip, Vicky."

"Impossible!"

"Not really. It's frightfully old, look. And it's addressed to Sir Lawrence."

"But that means it was written over twenty years ago, Bess."

What was Sir Lawrence doing with a letter that old?

"He must have kept it as a memento, the sentimental fool. It must be the last letter Philip wrote."

Vicky frowned, trying to analyse this latest piece of information.

"This may be his last letter, Bess. But they met after that. Sir Lawrence came to Buxley for the hunt, remember?"

Bess pulled the letter out, heeding Vicky's warning to be careful. Why had it meant so much to Sir Lawrence?

It was dated in the beginning of 1901. Sir Lawrence must have been in Africa at the time. The tone of the letter was apologetic. It was clear early on that Philip was sorry for what he had done.

Vicky came around and stood over her shoulder so they could read it together. Bess heard her gasp and realized her own pulse had sped up.

"I say! What is this colossal mistake Philip is supposed to have committed?"

"No, no." Vicky corrected her. "He says

although it felt like a mistake, he came to terms with it later and was now expecting a happy event."

The twins stared at each other, wide eyed.

"Happy event?" Bess cried. "Do you think he's referring to Momo being pregnant with his child?"

Vicky thought so.

"This is a reply to the letter Sir Lawrence sent him. We don't have that but we can guess a bit. Apparently, Philip chose his duty over his feelings and married Momo because both the families wanted it. He agrees he chose the easy option."

Bess agreed with her.

"So Sir Lawrence castigated him for being dishonourable and leaving an innocent in the lurch and Philip agrees. It can only mean he made false promises to some girl and later deceived her."

This was hard to digest. Every person they spoke to, whether master or servant, had maintained what an upstanding, honourable man Philip was. And here he was, accepting he had acted like a scoundrel.

"You realize what this means, Bess? We might finally have a motive. Philip could have been murdered by a scorned lover. This is the chink in his armour we have been looking for."

Bess warned her against drawing hasty conclusions and started reading the rest of the letter.

"He says Sir Lawrence has been a father figure to him, etc. etc. And he cannot fathom losing his respect. There is an invitation for the autumn hunt. If Sir Lawrence forgives him, he will come to Buxley and allow Philip to make amends."

Vicky mentioned what they knew about Philip. He and his cronies had been infamous for leading a profligate lifestyle. It followed that he had consorted with a lot of women during the time.

"Remember our vicar? Cecil had no idea he had fathered a son."

"You can't believe the same thing happened to Philip? That would be too much of a coincidence."

Vicky took the letter from Bess and read through it again. Were they attaching too much importance to it?

"Why do you think Sir Lawrence kept this letter for twenty years? He did not strike me as a romantic."

303 had come over and parked himself by Bess. She ran her hand through his fir, pondering over Vicky's question.

"Not in public. He had a stiff upper lip, like any self respecting Englishman. Maybe he planned to give it to someone."

Chapter 33

The Nightingales gathered in the west wing of Buxley Manor after breakfast the next morning. The previous day had passed in a blur and it was late in the evening when everyone returned from Ridley Hall, weary in body and mind. Dinner had been cancelled in favour of trays in the bedrooms. The twins barely had an opportunity to reveal their findings to anyone.

Bess was glad for the respite. She had been mulling things over in her mind long into the night and had telephoned Louise first thing in the morning.

"We need to meet, Grandmother." She was brief. "Sooner the better."

Whatever the crisis, breakfast was never forgone at Buxley Manor. Bess was happy to fortify herself with kedgeree. Nigel had picked on her, unable to hide his worry.

"I say, Bess, this is a terrible business, what?" He turned to give Annie a helpless look. "I mean … just terrible."

Bess and Vicky stopped eating, waiting for him to gather enough courage to put his point across. He tended to be tongue tied when something bothered him.

"Your father wants you to be careful, girls." Annie was stern. "And I agree."

"Drop it." Nigel mustered. "Drop the whole thing. Let the police take care of it."

Cedric had been arrested the previous night. He had given Bess a pleading look, insisting he was innocent.

"I promised Sir Dorian," Bess reminded her parents. "Vicky and I both did. Shouldn't I keep my word?"

Clementine handed her a cup of tea and shook

her head.

"He's gone. Nobody's holding you to that promise. Enough is enough, Bess. Nigel has been too lenient with you. Think of the family. You don't want your shenanigans to affect us, do you?"

Vicky assured her she was not in danger.

"How do you know?" Clementine pounced. "There doesn't appear to be any rhyme or reason for all this mayhem. I will be glad to say farewell to 1921. It's just been a series of shocks, one after the other." She glanced at Annie and Vicky and smiled. "Some of them have been pleasant, though."

Louise came in, escorted by Barnes.

"Are you teaching your daughters to be dishonourable, Nigel?" she glared. "For shame."

Bess and Vicky sprang up, declaring they were done.

"See you later, Pops, Mom." Vicky went around to embrace her parents.

Louise followed them out and the group headed to the west wing.

"You arrived just in time, Grandma." Vicky took her hand. "I feel bad for defying them. Pops is looking stressed."

Louise told them it was high time they put an end to the matter.

Hortense and Perpetua had eaten in their quarters and sat in their usual chairs, waiting for them.

"Speak." Perpetua ordered before Bess had a chance to settle on her favourite chaise. "No time to waste."

The twins took turns telling the Nightingales about what they had discovered in Sir Lawrence's room. There was a stunned silence.

"So Philip was culpable after all," Louise spoke.

"He was human," Hortense reasoned. "Young men of our sort often have these dalliances. It may have no bearing on the present."

Bess told them to be patient while she outlined her theory.

"This may sound outlandish. Vicky and I gave this a lot of thought and we decided to focus on the facts. The things that we know for sure happened."

She looked around to make sure she had everyone's attention.

"It leads to a gruesome picture, Grandmother. Something so fantastic we could never have imagined it."

Hortense dipped a fresh handkerchief in a basin of lavender water and moaned. Louise and Perpetua told Bess to get on with it.

"Let's start with Philip," Vicky began. "We embarked on this quest by assuming he was murdered."

Bess pointed out the astonishing facts that had stayed hidden all these years.

"Philip was not riding his own horse. What's more, the saddle he was using had been tampered with. We agree something spooked the horse. The cinch must have broken and Philip got thrown, hitting his head on a stone."

Vicky pointed out who had made sure the saddle was broken.

"Joe Cooper, who is now dead. So we have no way to ask why he did it."

The older ladies glanced at each other and shrugged.

"Someone paid him off," Perpetua nodded.

Bess talked about Nigel.

"Someone had to be framed to take the attention away from the real killer. So Papa was accused of murder. Who made sure he did not have an alibi?"

"Miles Carrington," Vicky supplied, before the aunts replied. "He made Pops look like a liar and branded him as a murderer for life."

Louise had turned ashen.

"Miles was a maniac who did a lot of things just to be contrary. But we will never be able to ask him now."

Bess banged her fist into her palm, springing up to go to the window. The sun was peeping through the clouds, blessing the landscape with pale light.

"And now for the motive to kill Philip. Apparently, he committed a grave sin, one we can only guess at. But only Sir Lawrence knew about it."

Hortense dabbed her hanky on her forehead, flustered.

"But he's dead. They all are."

"Exactly!" Bess and Vicky exclaimed in unison.

"The three men who could have shed light on Philip's murder are all dead."

The older ladies stared at them, their eyes wide with dismay, mouths hanging open.

"What kind of harebrained theory is this, Bess?" Louise thundered. "All three men died at different times. And they were killed by different people for different reasons. The men who murdered Miles Carrington and Joe Cooper are in prison. They could not have shot Lawrence."

Bess conceded the point.

"But why did all these three men die in the space of a year? It's too much of a coincidence, Grandmother."

Vicky asked them to consider what was common among all the three men.

"They were present at Buxley Manor at the time of the hunt, when Philip died. We think they were involved in his murder."

Perpetua asked how they had come to the conclusion.

"According to you, there is a criminal mastermind who has been orchestrating all this, controlling people like puppets. Or is it possible that someone wants to avenge Philip's murder?"

"But who is it?" Hortense burst out, white faced. "Have you figured it out?"

The twins proceeded to reveal what they had deduced.

"Good God!" Louise exploded. "That is diabolical."

Hortense was not ready to believe them but Perpetua nodded her head slowly, turning it over in her mind.

"Suddenly, it all makes sense."

Bess and Vicky huddled together on the sofa, feeling the hair stand up on their arms.

Although they had been confident they were right, hearing it out loud had chilled them.

"And to think we have harboured this fiend in our bosom." Louise paled. "This is what you are going to do now, Bess." She held up her hand to ward off any objections. "You will go and report all this to James Gardener. Let the police handle this now."

Bess recognized the wisdom in her advice and gave in. She had her own ideas for unmasking the killer but she would need the Inspector's help for it.

"No time like the present," Louise quipped. "And ring for tea on your way out."

Bess yearned for a strong cup of Darjeeling herself but she ignored her craving. There would be enough time for all that later.

She and Vicky strode into the main hall and ran into Barnes. He informed them the motor had been brought around, just as instructed.

"En guard, ladies!"

They promised to take extra care. Bess found herself touching the wound on her cheek. Had it been a failed attempt to get her out of the way? She owed Captain Sheldon her life.

The roads were clear of ice and they reached the tiny police station in the village shortly, heartened to see the Hispano Suiza parked outside.

Bess scampered up the stairs with Vicky right beside her. DI Gardener was looking through a big file while Constable Potts stood at attention a few feet away.

"You need to release Cedric Ridley at once," Bess roared. "He is innocent."

To her immense surprise, the Inspector gave her a slight bow.

"Your wish is my command, my lady. He was released an hour ago. Constable Yates escorted him back to Ridley Hall in a police vehicle."

Deflated, Bess flopped down on a chair before him.

"Does that mean you have figured out the whole thing?"

"Not exactly." His face fell. "Just that Cedric did not shoot his father. We questioned the servants thoroughly and there is no way he could have managed it."

"We can tell you who did it." Vicky burst out.

Once again, they outlined their deductions, starting at the beginning. The Inspector's eyes threatened to bulge as the story unfolded. He folded his arms and shook his head, making Bess turn red with anger.

"You don't have a shred of proof, Bess. As you said, all the witnesses have been eliminated."

"And that is exactly why we have come up with a plan." Vicky was calm. "Just hear us out."

Now it was the Inspector's turn to lose his

temper.

"Absolutely not, ladies." He shook his head vehemently. "What on earth are you thinking? There are a million things that might go wrong."

Once Bess made up her mind, it was hard to make her budge from her position.

"You admit this case is more complex than anything you have encountered? Solving this will add one more feather to your crown."

DI Gardener had earned the moniker of Bulldog Gardener for solving the Dockyard Doxy case. He was used to facing danger himself but could not risk a civilian's life.

"Absolutely not!" he repeated. "Can't you see what you are proposing is dangerous? Too many lives have been lost."

"You will be there," Bess pointed out. "And as many policemen as you can summon. This is the only way."

Vicky seconded her, weaving her arm through hers in silent support.

"We trust you, Inspector."

Chapter 34

A sizeable crowd had assembled in the ballroom at Buxley Manor. Apart from the entire Gaskins clan including the churlish dowager Beatrice, Philip's mother, the vicar Cecil Chilton and his mother had also been summoned. Lord and Lady Morse were present with their offspring, so were the Carringtons. Lady Ridley had needed some convincing but she had agreed to come when the Inspector promised to reveal Sir Dorian's killer. Dressed in black, she was flanked by her children, Cedric, Momo and Bubbles.

The upper servants had been allowed to attend. Barnes insisted.

A generous buffet was laid out on a side table, with stacks of sandwiches, ginger biscuits and mince pies. Tea and coffee had been served.

All the chairs were arranged in a semicircle. James Gardener sat facing them, along with Bess and Vicky. There were footmen standing to attention at the numerous doors. Unknown to the assembled company, plenty of policemen stood on guard behind them, ready to apprehend anyone who tried to escape.

People spoke in loud whispers, wondering what the police were up to. DI Gardener ordered them to be quiet. Bess waited for the buzz to die down and addressed the group.

"Thank you for coming here at such short notice. I am especially sorry to drag you here, Lady Ridley. This is a sad time for all of us."

Lord Morse encouraged her to go on.

"Is this about Dorian, girls?"

Vicky nodded.

"You got that right, Sir. It's about Miles Carrington, Joe Cooper, Sir Lawrence Watkins, Sir Dorian Ridley, and above all, Philip."

Beatrice stirred in her seat, ready to lash out.

"I say, Bess! What is this new palaver? I won't let you disparage my son."

Nigel and Annie had been kept in the dark, along with Clementine.

"Let her speak, Bea," he chided. "Why must you always censure her?"

Bess decided to plunge in before she lost everyone's attention.

"We are here to solve not one, not two, but six murders."

A buzz broke out but DI Gardener silenced everyone with a quick warning.

"It begins with Philip. Although the police ruled his death as an accident, there has always been an element of uncertainty around it. Rumours abound, flaring up every few months, accusing Papa of killing his cousin to come into the title. Well, today I am going to eliminate all the doubts." She paused to make sure everyone was listening. "Philip was indeed murdered. The crime was planned in meticulous detail and my Papa had nothing to do with it."

"I say …" Nigel stirred, at a loss for words.

"He was a victim of circumstances, just like my mother." She smiled at Annie and took Vicky's hand in hers. "And us. But I am not going to harp on that."

She explained how Joe Cooper had played a part in Philip's death by providing a damaged saddle. Miles Carrington had been convinced to provide a false alibi. Sir Lawrence alone knew the motive that had sparked the murder.

"All three people maintained their silence for twenty years, ensuring the truth never saw the light of day. Sir Lawrence did it by being out of the country, of course. But something must have changed in the past year or two. Something that prompted Philip's killer to silence anyone who could rise against him."

Cedric Ridley wanted to know how his father had fallen victim.

"I will come to that," Bess promised.

Nigel finally found his voice.

"Miles was killed by Peter. And that bone digger fellow murdered Joe Cooper. We already know that, Bess. But what about Lawrence?"

Vicky told them Wilma McLeod shot Sir Lawrence.

"She was manipulated, just as the other two were. Wilma McLeod was sure she was going to lose her position at Ridley Hall. She was a poor orphan who had nowhere to go. But someone managed to convince this timid girl that Sir Lawrence was a threat to her. Was it Cedric?"

"Please!" Cedric Ridley burst out. "I barely knew the girl. Haven't I told you that?"

DI Gardener confirmed Bess was right. The

police had found more than one set of finger prints on the pistol that was used to shoot Sir Lawrence.

"That is why we did not arrest Cedric at the time. Wilma McLeod's fingerprints were on the gun."

"And she committed suicide after this heinous act, I suppose?" Beatrice spoke up. "Good riddance."

Bess shook her head. Poor Wilma had also been murdered.

"This is when things started going downhill for our killer. Wilma might have confessed easily and been arrested, just like the other two. But Cedric's fingerprints on the gun muddied the waters. Wilma was a loose thread the killer could not afford. Just like Sir Lawrence."

Vicky talked about the letter they had found in Sir Lawrence's room.

"Some of this is conjecture, of course. But it was clear Philip wronged someone. He apologized for it again and again. So it was clear several people not known to us had a motive to kill him. Sir Lawrence was the only one who might have identified these people. So he had to go."

Bess explained his arrival in England earlier that spring could have triggered the killing spree. As long as he was far away in Africa, he posed no threat. That changed when he turned up to upset the cart, reminiscing about Philip at every party.

Lord Morse wondered why Miles had been killed first. Bess assured him it was all part of a grand plan.

"Joe Cooper brainwashed Peter into killing Miles. And Sir Lawrence influenced the architect who murdered Joe. Then Wilma was manipulated into shooting Sir Lawrence."

Three of the people who knew the identity of Philip's murderer had thus been taken out of the picture.

"Unfortunately, Wilma had to be killed too. So far, our master criminal had managed to use others to do his dirty business. That changed with Wilma."

Lady Ridley had been sobbing into her handkerchief. There were other sniffs around the room from the Carrington ladies.

"What about Dorian?" Nigel asked.

Vicky gave a shrug.

"He figured it all out. So he had to go."

A deathly pall hung over the assembled group. Annie broke the silence.

"I know you left this out, sweetie, and I am sorry if this hurts you. But all those nasty insinuations about me and Miles …"

Vicky told her she was right.

"That was also part of the plan, Mom. We may

never know the reason but I think this person wanted to break our family. It was as if he could not bear to see anyone happy."

Nigel found his voice.

"But how did this person know Peter hated Miles? Or that Joe Cooper was blackmailing the bone digger?" His eyes grew round in astonishment. "I say, Bessie, it must be someone from our circle."

"That's a marvellous deduction, Papa. He must have intimate knowledge of everything that has happened here for the past twenty years, and even before that, actually."

Beatrice sprang up from her chair, her eyes red.

"Who is it, Bess? Unmask this fiend and I will be your slave for the rest of your life. Who murdered my poor Philip?"

Vicky flung a finger toward the Ridleys.

"That's them right there. Momo and Bubbles.

Snakes in the grass, both of them. Living among us, plotting our demise all this time. You harboured them in your home, Pops. But their time's up."

The group scraped their chairs and craned their necks, trying to land their eyes on the accused. Momo had turned white and Bubbles was purple, bristling with anger.

"My little girls!" Lady Ridley sighed. "Surely not …"

"What in the blazes do you mean, Bess?" Cedric thundered as Lady Ridley fainted.

One of the footmen rushed forward with a jar of smelling salts.

Bess knew the moment of reckoning had come. She had to summon all her inner strength to get through the next few minutes.

"Momo never loved Philip. She confessed as much when we went on a ride this summer. You did her a grave wrong, Lady Ridley."

Cedric was apoplectic. Lady Ridley, who had begun to stir, fell into another faint. Dr. Evans appeared to check on her. He had been waiting in the wings to take care of any medical emergency.

"Momo submitted to family pressure to marry Philip. But she did not care for him. In her defence, I will say she tried hard. But Philip was obsessed with his tenants and his horses with no time to spare for her."

Momo let out a gasp.

"He was doing his duty, living up to family expectations. It's what a good landlord is supposed to do."

Bess frowned, giving her a pitying look.

"But he ignored you, and of course you could not bear that. So you silenced him forever. And Bubbles was your accomplice in all this, of course. She was the dutiful younger sister, carrying out your plans, following your command."

She paused, letting Vicky continue.

"We couldn't do that for each other, even as twins."

They began clapping, their gaze pinned on the Ridley girls.

"Bravo, Momo! You have been hiding your light under a meek persona. Even DI Gardener admits a genius planned all these murders."

"Momo was the mastermind behind all this, of course," Vicky explained to the stunned audience. "She planned everything meticulously, beginning with manipulating Peter. Fed his anger so he would kill Miles."

Nigel sputtered, barely managing to say a word.

"Joe Cooper's greed was a boon. With the help of Sir Lawrence, she let that poor archaeologist chap believe it was fine to murder a man to achieve his ambition. That was just smashing, Momo!" Bess praised.

"Shedding skin after skin like a snake," Vicky chuckled. "Changing colour like a chameleon. Who would've believed it of her?"

The twins went on to extoll Momo's virtues, mentally crossing their fingers, hoping their hyperbole would have the desired effect.

A shrill scream erupted, startling every person in the room. They stared at the Ridleys, trying to figure out why Bubbles was shrieking like a banshee.

Chapter 35

"Genius? Criminal mastermind?" Bubbles guffawed, holding her sides. "Momo?"

She howled again, unable to control herself. Dr. Evans gave her a resounding slap. Bubbles pressed her cheek, her eyes flashing fire.

"This ninny can't say boo to a goose. You think she is capable of a single intelligent thought?" She paused, her chest heaving. "*I* did all this. Me alone. Without anyone's help, I might add. Especially not this numbskull's."

"Gotcha," Vicky whispered under her breath.

Bess held herself back. She still had a part to play. They needed Bubbles to confess everything without any coercion.

"Why are you taking the blame for what your

sister did?" she pleaded. "Just admit you were misled and DI Gardener will go easy on you."

Bubbles fell hook, line and sinker.

"You know me, Bess. I am not afraid to go after what I want."

Vicky coaxed her. "And you wanted Philip?" They were just guessing this part but Bubbles told her she was right.

"Philip and I loved each other." She looked at her mother, who was staring at a far wall, dazed. "You never took the trouble to find out, Mother, did you? It was all Momo this and Momo that. Momo was the one destined to be Lady Buxley. Well, I was going to change all that."

Beatrice looked like she had aged ten years.

"My Philip could never love a monster like you."

"Oh, but he did, Aunt Bea!" Bubbles laughed.

"It happened in the south of France the previous year, on the Riviera. I was there with Aunt Griselda, remember?"

Momo and Bubbles were supposed to spend the summer at their aunt's villa in France but Lady Ridley had fallen ill at the last moment. Momo stayed behind to care for her.

"I wasn't out then," Bubbles sighed. "Philip was there, visiting friends. I had known him all my life so Aunt Griselda allowed me to talk to him. We spent a lot of time together, going on drives in the country or visiting beaches."

They had fallen in love. Philip promised to talk to his parents as soon as they returned home. Sir Dorian and Philip's father had hatched a different plan in their absence. There was a tacit understanding between the friends that Momo would marry Philip when she came of age. They announced the engagement, catching Philip unawares. Then Lord Buxley, Philip's father, died suddenly.

"Philip became earl," Bubbles continued. "A

lot earlier than planned of course. But I couldn't complain. I was ready to be Lady Buxley."

Philip decided to honour his father's word, stick to the commitment he made to Momo.

"What about the promises he made to me?" Bubbles growled. "All those declarations of love, of spending our lives together?"

Despite several entreaties, Philip did not listen to her. He apologized handsomely but he was torn. Momo became Lady Buxley and came to the manor. Around this time, Bubbles discovered she was expecting a child. She had been sent north to a distant relative.

"They did not even let me hold the babe in my arms. I never knew if it was a boy or a girl."

Momo clutched Cedric's hand, her eyes filling with horror as the tragic story unfolded.

"My parents were complicit in all this," Bubbles fumed. "I could not bear to stay a single minute with them."

She began spending more and more time at Buxley Manor. She saw Momo and Philip grow closer. Then she noticed a familiar spark between them. Love.

"Philip said he would marry Momo for the sake of duty but she would never have his heart. I was the only one he loved. It was all a lie, of course. I was a fool, believing him when he had already deceived me once."

Bess glanced at DI Gardener, acknowledging his nod.

"Tell us about the day of the hunt," she prompted. "How did you convince Joe Cooper to tamper with the saddle?"

Bubbles laughed.

"He was just a boy. It wasn't hard." Her eyes gleamed. "Joe cut into the cinch, leaving just a tiny bit. The saddle was bound to come off at some point. Any other groom would have noticed it but Joe saddled the nag himself."

Nigel wondered why Philip had not spotted it.

"He would have noticed something was amiss, long before the saddle came off."

Bubbles told them he was drugged. She had gone to the kitchen to fetch his coffee flask for Momo, then added something to it.

"And Miles?" Bess prompted. "He knew?"

Bubbles grinned. Miles wanted to shine in the hunt so he threw a snake in the horse's path, believing it was a silly prank. Philip was a skilled rider who could handle his horse. Later, Miles promised he would never say a word.

"Philip was his biggest rival and I think they had some boyhood grudge. He said he was glad to see him dead."

Nobody blinked at this. They knew Miles Carrington had been a villain.

Bess asked what had prompted her killing spree.

"Why now? After all these years?"

Joe Cooper started blackmailing her after he came back from the war. She had been paying him for his silence but his demands grew every few months.

"He was a loose end and had to be silenced," Bubbles explained. "So was Miles, of course. And Sir Lawrence. I had to plan all their deaths so none of them were linked to me."

Pudding had not uttered a single word that day. She suddenly sat up.

"What did Sir Lawrence do?"

Bubbles told them he was her biggest threat.

"He was there, in the South of France. He saw it all happen and tackled Philip."

Philip had assured Sir Lawrence he had the

best intentions. He intended to marry Bubbles. But then he had reneged, creating a rift between them.

"That's what the letter was about," Vicky nodded. "Philip was apologizing for hurting you. Sir Lawrence must have cared about you."

Bubbles smirked. He had forgiven Philip soon enough and come to Buxley for the hunt. "He told me I would fall in love with someone else, get married."

It had never happened. And twenty years later, Sir Lawrence reappeared, making subtle jabs at her, asking if she missed Philip.

"Of course I missed him. He was the love of my life."

Joe Cooper's blackmail, Sir Lawrence's knowing looks, it had all been too much for Bubbles. She wasn't going to take any more risks.

DI Gardener asked how she had coerced

Wilma.

"She was like putty in my hands. I told her Sir Lawrence was telling all kinds of stories about her. Papa would turn her away without a reference."

Bubbles had fed her all the information, knowing her mind would absorb everything like a sponge. She made her feed 303 in the kitchen so he would not make a fuss when she confronted Sir Lawrence in the woods. She had not cleaned the pistol, also on her instructions.

"And you killed her too," Bess prompted. "Why?"

"She was a loose end, of course," Bubbles shrugged. "I could not have any peace of mind, knowing she was roaming free."

She had seen Cedric practise his knots and bought a similar rope, intending to throw suspicion on him.

Bess was feeling drained. Although she had

solved the murders, hearing Bubbles confess to everything left a bitter taste in her mouth. This woman had been her role model most of her life. Was she such a poor judge of character?

DI Gardener flashed her a sympathetic look.

"Why did you murder your father, Miss Ridley?"

"He was on to me, of course. Spouted some drivel about how I had gone too far." Bubbles giggled. "Gave me an ultimatum. Poor Papa! He wanted me to confess everything to the police, save my soul."

He had been going on and on about how she would rot in hell when she shot him point blank. Lady Ridley groaned, levelling a shaky finger at her.

"I rue the day I gave birth to you."

Cecil Chilton stood behind Momo's chair, his hands on her shoulders, comforting her. Louise and the great aunts were stoic, their eyes hard as they digested the harsh truth. Nigel and Annie sat close, hand in hand. Beatrice was on her own, her face blotchy with tears.

"How can you claim you loved my son?" she sobbed. "You killed him in cold blood."

Bubbles finally broke down. A single tear rolled down her left eye, and the deluge started.

"He wasn't supposed to die that day." She pointed her finger at Momo. "I planned it for her, you see. But Philip took her horse at the last minute, riding off with the bad saddle. Then Miles threw a snake in its path."

After Momo's death, Philip would have no reason to not marry her. She would become Lady Buxley and bring their child home. But the plan had gone astray.

Later, Bubbles remained at Buxley Manor, believing it was her right. She acted like a lady of the manor, dominating her docile sister. But nothing could bring Philip back.

"He loved me!" she screamed, as the constables came in to handcuff her. "Only me!"

Epilogue

The household plunged in shock after Bubbles made her startling confession. DI Gardener arrested her on the spot, determined to ensure she paid for her crimes. He had been hard at work tying up loose ends.

Lady Ridley stayed on at Buxley Manor for a few days at Nigel's urging. She had been stoic, maintaining a tenuous control over her emotions until Sir Dorian's lawyers arrived one morning to apprise her of the contents of his will. Two hours later, they were gone, leaving everyone stunned.

Cedric inherited the entailed property as expected. There was generous provision for Lady Ridley for the rest of her life. Sir Dorian had divided the rest of his considerable wealth into four portions, one each for his offspring and one for his estranged granddaughter, none other than Wilma Mcleod. There was a letter explaining that she was the child Bubbles had given birth to all those years ago. Lady Ridley fainted again while Cedric plunged his fist in a wall. There were several exclamations across the room.

"That poor man!" Annie cried. "How he must have suffered!"

"Bubbles killed her own daughter in cold blood." Clementine voiced what everyone was thinking.

Bess inferred Sir Dorian had been aware of Wilma's identity. Vicky wondered why he had taken her on as a servant.

"What if he had told everyone who she was?" She argued when the Nightingales met in the west wing later. "Bubbles might have been united with her child. Who knows, she might not have gone on this killing spree."

Perpetua shook her head while Hortense

dabbed her face with a cool handkerchief.

"We would never have solved Philip's murder," Louise pointed out. "The past cannot be undone, child."

Wilma had been a Gaskins, Bess realized, being Philip's daughter. But her life had been far different from theirs.

A pall settled over the manor for the next few days until Clementine took everyone to task one morning.

"The Christmas party is a week away. I say we go to London for some shopping."

Nigel stopped crumbling his toast and protested, giving Annie a mute look.

"The invitations have already been sent, darling." She patted his hand. "It has been a sad year but the veil of misfortune that hung over this family has finally lifted. It is time to celebrate."

Bess found herself agreeing with her mother.

"Mom's right, Papa. We need to buck up."

All eyes in the room swung toward her and Annie gave a small shriek, springing out of her chair and coming around to envelop Bess in a hug.

"I say." Bess turned red. "What is all this palaver?"

"You called her Mom!" Vicky beamed.

"Well, I considered Mother or Mama but I think it's less confusing if we both refer to her as Mom."

Nigel began clapping and everyone followed.

"Does this mean you have finally come to your senses, Bessie?"

"Something like that." Bess bit her lip, wrapping her arms around Annie's. "I was such a beast. Can you forgive me?"

Louise cleared her throat and the great aunts followed. Clementine reminded Bess they were still in England.

"Are you going to be a watering pot now, Bess? Where is your stiff upper lip?"

The twinkle in her eye belied her stern tone.

Bess looked up to see Barnes give her an approving nod. She looked around the table, glad to see all the happy faces. Aunt Clem was right. They needed to shrug off the gloom and get into the spirit of Christmas.

The days flew by as everyone got busy preparing for the grand party. The ladies spent a couple of days in London, acquiring new dresses for the event. Every inch of the manor was dusted and polished until it shone. Menus were planned, extra staff was hired from the village and the finest champagne was ordered. Finally, the big day arrived.

The entire Gaskins clan was assembled in the breakfast room. It was three days before

Christmas and spirits were high. Nigel was looking forward to welcoming their friends and acquaintances. They had much to celebrate. Finally absolved of having a hand in Philip's death, he suddenly stood taller, looking like a much younger man.

A buffet had been set up, catering to every taste and whim. Bess had a plate of kedgeree before her, along with a steaming cup of her favorite Darjeeling. Vicky sat next to her, buttering toast. The women in the family watched them with adoring looks and indulgent smiles, the three Dowager Countesses of Buxley among them.

Louise, Beatrice and Momo sat opposite the twins, plying them with cake and biscuits. The great aunts sat beside Louise, picking at their food. Nigel sat beside Vicky and Bess was next to Annie, while Clementine looked on with pride.

"When do the Carringtons get here?" Bess asked. "Mabel's going to be so jealous of my dress!"

Barnes told her they would be there for tea. The Morses were already on their way.

"Good old Pudding," Bess chuckled. "Don't let her give you a hard time, Vicky."

Their tickets for America had arrived the previous day. The entire family would set sail for the western continent the next summer. Annie could not wait to show them around.

"Make sure you are on your best behavior tonight, girls," Clementine warned. "Act like the well brought up young ladies you are."

The twins giggled and dissolved into laughter. Nigel followed and everyone joined in one by one, including Clementine.

Everyone headed in different directions after that. The day was bright and sunny but bitterly cold. Bess talked Vicky into going for a drive, promising to be back soon. She was true to her word, returning in time for a light lunch. The shadows had lengthened by the time she woke from her nap and then it was time to get ready.

They wore identical dresses in a deep sparkly red and bickered over who would wear the Maharajah rubies. Annie arrived with a solution.

"You wear them for the first half of the evening, Bess. Vicky will have her chance after that."

Arm in arm, they walked out of the room and down the hall to the top of the grand staircase. Nigel stood at the bottom, a wide smile lighting up his face. Annie went down first, followed by the twins.

"My lady," Nigel murmured as he offered his arm to his wife. "You look ravishing."

Bess reached them and wove her arm through Annie's, clearing her throat.

"I say, Papa. You are not going to embarrass us, are you?"

Nigel ignored her and moved closer to his wife. Vicky laughed as she took his other arm.

"This is what we dreamed of when we met on that battlefield in France, Bess. Mom and Pops together again."

They agreed it was the best Christmas present anyone could ask for.

**

Don't forget to check the complete list of Leena Clover books at the end. You will find many more gripping mysteries featuring strong women, quirky friends, yummy food and a dash of romance waiting for you.

And now, a recipe for Buxley Manor's special Railway Mutton Curry.

Recipe – Railway Mutton Curry

Created for the delicate palates of the ruling Englishmen, Railway Mutton Curry is a milder version of the food the natives in India could stomach. The Buxley Manor recipe has been honed over generations and has evolved into a warm, fragrant and comforting dish that still retains the nostalgia of the British Raj.

Ingredients

500g bone in mutton (goat or lamb), cut into chunks

1 cup onions, thinly sliced

2 medium potatoes

4 Tbsp vegetable oil

1 Tbsp mustard oil

2 Tbsp tamarind paste or vinegar

1 Tbsp coriander, ground

1 tsp Kashmiri red chili powder

¼ tsp garam masala

1 cup coconut milk

½ tsp sugar

Fresh coriander for garnish

For the marinade -

½ cup yogurt

1 Tbsp garlic, crushed

1 Tbsp ginger, grated

1 Tbsp Kashmiri red chili powder

1 Tbsp coriander, ground

1 tsp cumin, ground

½ tsp, turmeric, ground

Whole spices –

1 black cardamom pod

2-3 green cardamom pods

2-3 cloves

2 inch cinnamon bark

¼ tsp peppercorns

1 bay leaf

Method

Marinate the meat first. Add all the spices and yogurt to the mutton and mix well. Refrigerate for at least an hour or more, even overnight.

Heat the oil in a thick bottomed pot. Add the whole spices and stir for a few seconds until they sputter.

Add the sliced onions and fry until they turn a light golden brown.

Now add the marinated mutton. Stir well and fry until the yogurt cooks out and meat begins to glisten.

Add the ground coriander and red chili powder and fry for a minute or two. Season with salt, add the tamarind paste or vinegar and sugar, along with a cup or more of water.

Cover and cook until the meat begins to fall off the bone.

Add potatoes, add a little more water if needed. Cover and simmer until the potatoes are tender.

Now taste the curry and adjust seasonings. The sauce should be the desired consistency at this point, like a thick soup. Now add the coconut milk and mix well. Heat until it comes to a bubble.

Garnish with coriander and serve with steamed basmati rice.

Acknowledgements

Every author has a passion project. One they feel deeply about but are a bit hesitant to take up. Maybe even afraid to. This idea is like a niggle at the back of their mind, one that does not go away. The only solution then is to set everything else aside and tackle it and see it to completion.

The British Cozy Mystery series has been mine. Having read more Agatha Christie than school books in my teens, the historical mystery genre always held a certain allure. I conceived of this series almost three years ago, and thought on it even while I was raging with fever during the Covid-19 pandemic. The characters took shape and the plot unfolded, growing more complex by the day. I worked on the building blocks of this series while I was writing other books. And one day, finally, I took the plunge and began writing the first in the series, embarking on a journey that has been daunting and exhilarating at the same time. I do hope you have enjoyed being a part of it.

I would like to thank all readers who took a chance and chose to read my work. Some of your comments were very encouraging and kept me going through the toughest parts. Even after thirty plus books, it is hard to believe that thousands across the world enjoy my words and take pleasure and inspiration from them.

A big thank you to all advanced readers, reviewers and fans across social networks. They sing my praises and spread the word which allows new readers to discover my books.

As always, I am immensely grateful to my sibling who played a big part in conceiving the entire series, helping me navigate through every twist and turn. Mere words are not enough to convey my thanks and appreciation.

Join my Newsletter

Get access to exclusive bonus content, sneak peeks, giveaways and much more. Also get a chance to join my exclusive ARC group, the people who get first dibs on all my new books.

Sign up at the following link and join the fun.

Click here →
http://www.subscribepage.com/leenaclovernl

I love to hear from my readers, so please feel free to connect with me at any of the following places.

Website – http://leenaclover.com

Facebook – http://facebook.com/leenaclovercozymysterybooks

Instagram – http://instagram.com/leenaclover

Email – leenaclover@gmail.com

Other books by Leena Clover

Pelican Cove Cozy Mystery Series -

Strawberries and Strangers

Cupcakes and Celebrities

Berries and Birthdays

Sprinkles and Skeletons

Waffles and Weekends

Muffins and Mobsters

Truffles and Troubadours

Sundaes and Sinners

Croissants and Cruises

Pancakes and Parrots

Cookies and Christmas

Popsicles and Poisons

Biscuits and Butlers

Dolphin Bay Cozy Mystery Series

Raspberry Chocolate Murder

Orange Thyme Death

Apple Caramel Mayhem

Cranberry Sage Miracle

Blueberry Chai Frenzy

Mango Chili Cruiser

Strawberry Vanilla Peril

Cherry Lime Havoc

Pumpkin Ginger Bedlam

Meera Patel Cozy Mystery Series -

Gone with the Wings

A Pocket Full of Pie

For a Few Dumplings More

Back to the Fajitas

British Cozy Mystery Series

Murder at Buxley Manor

Murder at Castle Morse

Murder at Ridley Hall

Meg Butler Cruise Cozy Series

Sail Away Patsy

Bingo Bashed

Made in the USA
Middletown, DE
28 June 2025